Queen of Swords Press LLC

## Queen of Swords Press Titles by Catherine Lundoff

### WOLVES OF WOLF'S POINT SERIES
*Silver Moon*
*Blood Moon*

### COLLECTIONS
*Out of This World: Queer Speculative Fiction Stories*
*Unfinished Business: Tales of the Dark Fantastic*

### ANTHOLOGIES
*Scourge of the Seas of Time (and Space)*

# CATHERINE LUNDOFF

# BLOOD MOON

*A Wolves of Wolf's Point* Novel

*Blood Moon: A Wolves of Wolf's Point Novel*

Catherine Lundoff

Queen of Swords Press LLC

Minneapolis, MN USA

www.queenofswordpress.com

Published in the United States

Cover and Interior Design by Terry Roy

Cover Art by Terry Roy copyright © 2021

ISBN 978-1-7343603-0-1

Library of Congress Control Number: 2020952935

# CONTENTS

# Contents, *continued*

*To everyone who encouraged me to write more about my wolves and patiently waited for me to find them again and to everyone who asked questions that got me thinking.*

# INTRODUCTION

M Y ORIGINAL PLAN FOR *BLOOD MOON* was that it would
come out within a year or two of *Silver Moon's* original
publication date, but life intervened. A lot of life, as it happens,
and a lot of intervening. I ended up re-releasing an updated
version of *Silver Moon* from my new small press before I really
got a chance to get back to this sequel. But here we are, back in
Wolf's Point with the Pack. The town is fuller and clearer in my
head now, the characters like old friends who I haven't seen in
a while.

The Pack is growing and changing too, as time passes, so
there are some new faces and new challenges. But they're still
a community, a chosen family, fierce and magical. And in part
because I'm aging too, there are crone werewolves now, along
with the middle-aged ones. Once a Pack member, always a Pack
member, right?

There are some other changes too. Over the years since
*Silver Moon* first came out, readers have shared how much the
book meant to them. I've even had several people tell me that
it was their coming out novel, which is an honor that I cherish.
Readers have also told me about things they didn't like and I
tried to give that some thought too.

I hope you'll want to run with the Wolf's Point Pack again,
change with them, grow with them. A number of people have
been waiting for this book and I hope it's the book that they've
been looking forward to so very patiently. For everyone who
wants to return, come back with me to Wolf's Point and find out
what happens next.

WOLF'S POINT: *A TOWN IN a mountain valley where some women of a certain age go through more than a few physical metamorphoses. The local werewolves are the traditional defenders of the valley, their transformations shaped by the valley's magic.*

*Time: the present, variously defined. A few months ago, Becca Thornton, divorced and newly turned fifty, found herself changing more than she could have ever imagined when she joined the Pack. With her help, the werewolves survived their greatest threat to their existence when one of their former members returned to wreak vengeance on those she thought had destroyed her life. She offered them a choice between a dangerous cure and certain death. Becca was part of that victory but it cost her her home and things that she cherished from her past.*

*But now the werewolf hunters were gone, expelled from the valley by forces magical and mundane, so everyone's life could go back to normal. Whatever that was.*

# CHAPTER 1

E RIN ADAMS LOOKED OUT AT the mountains and tried not to think about what was in the trunk of her car. At least the mountains around Wolf's Point were still as beautiful as ever. She wondered if she'd ever get the chance to run through them again, feel the wind in her fur, the ground flying by under her paws. The Pack at her side.

That thought was enough to make her look back at her car. Erin rubbed her aching forehead with one hand and closed her eyes. This was, without question, the worst thing she'd ever done. Even if she couldn't remember doing it.

But maybe there was still time to call Shelly and get her help to figure a way out of this mess that she'd blundered into. That was what Pack Alphas did, or so Shelly kept reminding her. But that might make Shelly an accessory if they got caught. Or rather, when *she* got caught. Erin closed her eyes for an instant; lying was never a thing she'd been good at or wanted to get good at. Anyone she called would almost certainly go down with her.

That thought weighed her down like a rock. The Pack couldn't afford to be without its Alpha so soon after they got her back, not to mention what it would do to Pete and the kids. There was no way that she could drag Shelly into this.

Her thoughts turned to Becca, waded through a jumbled mess of emotions and came back with a single realization: they'd suspect her first. Becca was her friend, her housemate. Her...something they still hadn't defined, but which felt more like *girlfriend* every day. Her stomach did a slow, leisurely flip when she thought about that and she almost smiled. But this wasn't the time to think about Becca. She couldn't afford to be distracted, to be vulnerable. Not now.

Maybe there was another solution, a way to hide what had happened. But then what? She'd still know and she'd have to carry the burden of what she'd done, alone. And she knew where that road led. Falling off the wagon to cope with her guilt wasn't an option, either.

Besides, if she ditched the body out here and it was found, the regular wolves would certainly get blamed for it. The new governor was already pushing for a wolf hunting season and that would put things right over the edge. She didn't want that on her conscience either; the wild wolves were kin as much as they were cover for the Pack as well as being important to local ecology.

Erin ran her fingers through her short-cropped brown hair, wondering if there was anyone else she could turn to. But she couldn't think of any other Pack member who'd be able to do anything about this situation, not more than she could do herself, anyway. It certainly wasn't the sort of thing that her AA sponsor had signed up for, or any of her friends, for that matter.

So she was on her own. There was nothing for it but to lie in the bed she'd made for herself.

She pulled her cell phone out of her pocket and selected a contact. "Hi. It's Erin. I've done something...I need...can you come up to Spruce Point? Yes, it's important. I want you to see it before Sheriff Henderson does."

She clicked the phone off and glanced toward the road. Nothing to do now but wait.

BECCA THORNTON LOOKED AROUND PETERSON'S Hardware and sighed. Inventory was the worst. Better than unemployment, of course, but hands down her least favorite part of her job. How could she possibly have miscounted the ¾ inch screws twice? She stared at them ferociously in their little plastic case as if she could compel them to give up their exact numbers with her mind alone.

"Are you trying to levitate them or something?" Shelly Peterson appeared at Becca's side, her expression as baffled as her tone of voice.

"No." Becca put the screws down and stretched slowly, her muscles cramping a little from disuse. Not like they had before she started to change into a wolf once a month, but sore all the same. She twisted around, then back again, limited by the narrowness of the aisle. "I think I need a good run. How about you?"

Shelly grinned, her dark eyes lighting up for an instant, almost golden in the store lights, then shifting back to their usual black, the change too fast for a normal human to follow. But she shook her head. "And leave Pete to deal with this on his own? Not really fair, is it?" She picked up the box of screws.

"How about you work the counter for a little while and I'll count pointy bits of metal?"

Becca grimaced and shrugged. "That's why you're the boss. I'll take some stuff with me and work on inventory between customers." She got to her feet, thrilled once again at how effortless it was for her to stand up now, with hardly a creak or an ache. It was almost as if becoming a werewolf was its own weird little fountain of youth. She grabbed a couple of containers of loose nails and tried not to grin at them.

Shelly gave her a half-smile, responding as if Becca had spoken out loud, "I don't miss the classic middle-aged knee-pop, that's for sure. Or any of the other aches and pains. Pete even asked me to bite him last week to see if I could get his back to feel better. Like that would work around here." She rolled her eyes and sat down on the stool before picking up the container of screws.

Becca chuckled and hustled over to answer the phone. Wolf's Point's werewolves weren't like the ones in monster movies, at least not in most respects. You joined the Pack because the valley's magic called you, not because another werewolf bit you. She shivered at that thought: it would have been horrible to join the Pack by way of one of her friends or neighbors nearly mauling her to death.

Her thoughts rolled on from there at full speed, like they didn't have an off switch. Now she found herself wondering if getting bitten by one of her Pack and surviving it would make someone a kind of super wolf or something. A memory of the wall paintings in the Pack's cave made her wonder about that. There were more than a few unusual looking and quite possibly super-powered wolves depicted in that artwork. If she was being honest with herself, she found them kind of scary even when they weren't running around the cave chasing off werewolf hunters.

It had only been 2 months since she, Shelly and Erin had called upon the cave's magic to protect them from the werewolf hunters who had them trapped in the cave. The wolf in the back of her brain stirred sluggishly, sending a surge of adrenaline through her. Her thoughts might have gone next to the werewolf slayer leaders, Annie and Anderson, one transformed into a monster and living in hiding somewhere in the mountains, the other slain by the living paintings, but the store was suddenly full of customers.

It was several minutes later that she realized Shelly was taking a call of her own on her cell. "What?" Becca could hear the snarl in her Alpha's voice from several yards away. "You did...what? Why—no, no, never mind. Where is she? Explain it to me when I get there. Alright, I'm on my way." Shelly shoved her phone in her pocket as she lunged to her feet and surged toward the front of the store.

Her eyes were gleaming gold as she leaned across the counter, her body taut and tense. "Listen, Becca, I need you to stay here and keep an eye on things. Erin's been arrested and I need to go talk to Lizzie about it. I'll call you as soon as I know more about what's going on." She started for the door, pausing with a jerk when Becca leapt out from behind the counter and grabbed her arm.

"You can't just leave me with that! Dammit, Shelly, I thought we were past all of the 'Pack secrets, need to know' stuff. What's happened to Erin? Why would Lizzie do something like that?" Becca could feel her heart begin to race, the wolf running under the surface of her skin. *Control, control.* She chanted the thought to herself.

Shelly's lips tightened, and for a moment, Becca was afraid that she was just going to push past her and leave her to writhe in agonizing uncertainty. "I don't know more than this: she called Lizzie and turned herself in. She's confessed to murder and there was a body in the trunk of her car. Lizzie said that they hadn't identified it yet and Erin doesn't remember what happened. I'll call you as soon as I know more, I promise." Shelly squeezed Becca's shoulder before vanishing out the door.

Becca grabbed the edge of the counter to stop the store from whirling around her. Erin would never kill someone in cold blood, not as a human, anyway. She was too kind, too honest, too...but what if it had been Annie? The werewolf hunter leader was still free, running in the mountains in a monstrous half-wolf, half-human form and unable to change either way, as far as any of them knew. What if she had attacked Erin, and Erin fought back?

Or what if one of the others survived the explosion at their trailer and didn't get arrested afterwards and was back for revenge? Or maybe there was some new threat, something the rest of the Pack hadn't seen yet? Her brain spun with the possibilities.

Most important of all: how was she supposed to stay put at the store and act like nothing was wrong when everything in her screamed to go help Erin?

# CHAPTER 2

T HE WEEK HAD STARTED OUT in a very different place. Becca was sure of that much. She and Erin had been working on the yard and starting a garden just a few days ago. They even finished putting up a fence so that Clyde, their new puppy, couldn't get at the seedlings when they came up.

That was when it had really hit her: they had a new puppy. *They.* Granted, she had told Erin that he was going to be Erin's dog when they were picking him out at the animal shelter, but she knew better. Clyde was *their* dog. And they had started a garden. Together. There was a *they* now.

But was she ready for that? That was the question that had been weighing on her mind since she'd moved in with Erin after Ed sold their house out from under her. Before that, really.

It was all so new. She'd fallen into marrying Ed in her mid-thirties, long after the end of a short string of live-in boyfriends. When she thought about it at all after the divorce, she thought she'd wind up single for the rest of her life. Being with a woman or anybody else, really, hadn't seemed like a possibility back then.

But once she met Erin, her past felt like ancient history, like almost everything that came before she turned into a wolf. Her old life got packaged up neatly and put in an attic corner, or at least that's what it felt like most days. Everything glowed with new possibilities, new options, and Erin was a huge part of that.

As that thought crossed her mind, she found herself staring at her old house across the street. There it sat, with a 'For Sale' sign out front, and a pang shot through her just looking at it. Maybe it was too soon. Maybe she should move out before making any changes. That way, if she was wrong about her feelings, at least she wouldn't have to find a new place to live if everything went sideways. Maybe it wasn't too late to get her old place back.

Becca shook her head to clear her thoughts. So maybe not so neatly packaged after all. She sighed. It was hard not to miss having her own house, old life or not.

That was when the realtor's SUV had pulled up. He got out and put up a new sign, covering part of the old one. The word 'Sold' had gone through Becca like an arrow. She had felt herself start to tremble. Her life with Ed, the divorce, everything from back before she started to change, all of it was bound up in that house. It was the last reminder of her old life, when she was normal. Or at least, not a werewolf.

Now it was going to be someone else's, leaving her with nothing to go back to. Nowhere to go but forward. She choked a little as her throat closed.

"It's okay. I know how much you loved the place." As usual, Erin was paying attention and trying to be there for her. Her hand rested lightly on Becca's shoulder as she gave it a gentle squeeze. "Whatever you need, Becca. You know I'll try and make it happen for you."

Becca looked up at her through eyes gone misty with unshed tears. Erin's expression was serious, her attention completely focused. Becca reached up and squeezed her hand. Erin's skin felt warm and comforting against hers. *And wonderful.* The thought made her smile at the same time that it made her stomach do leisurely backflips.

Perhaps this was the time to let go of her doubts and fears. Becca had taken a deep, trembling breath, before she said, "Let's go inside. There's some things I'd like to say to you and I don't want to say them on the front lawn for the entertainment of our neighbors." Her voice was calm, at least to her own ears. But inside, *calm* was the very last word she'd have used to describe her feelings.

Erin's left eyebrow had quirked upward and the corner of her thin-lipped mouth joined it, giving her long face a quizzical expression. "I'm intrigued. Well, okay. That's if you don't want to watch what the realtor's doing, of course." She nodded across the street.

Becca had glanced back over and shrugged, trying to summon nonchalance. "I think I need to let it go. I made my decision a while ago. No going back on it now. Besides, I can see Gladys thinking about coming over here. It's like one of those cartoon thought bubbles over her head." She rolled her eyes and bit back another snarky comment. Just because someone was a Pack member and a neighbor didn't mean she had to like them. But she didn't have to be a huge jerk either, she reminded herself sternly.

She felt Erin laugh softly, her chuckle shaking her arm where it rested against Becca's back. Right where it should be. Maybe. Probably.

Once inside, Becca had closed the door behind them and looked up at Erin, trying to find the right words. She knew she really liked Erin, that she liked the way it felt when Erin touched her. Or when they kissed, the one time that had happened so far. So maybe that was enough. "I think I'm ready, Erin. I think I'd like to make things official."

"Official?" Erin had looked puzzled. "You're about to tell me that you're moving to New York to pursue your Broadway dreams?"

"What? No, I mean you and me. I think we should be... together. You know, girlfriends. I really like you and I'd like us to be closer." She had stared earnestly upward, looking for some kind of clue in the other woman's face. Was there some sort of rule, something she was supposed to say, that would convince her?

There was a short moment of silence as Erin's face had shut down, all expressions under wraps. Becca was horrified. She must have said the wrong thing. But the minute the thought crossed her mind, her inner wolf reached out, assessing the situation. Erin didn't smell angry or frightened, just confused. With that knowledge, Becca had forced herself still, waiting for an answer, not pulling away.

Erin had glanced away first, running her hand through her hair. "Look, Becca, forgive me for asking this, but the timing of this doesn't have anything to do with your house selling, does it? Please, please don't think that we have to be romantically involved for you to go on living here. I have some idea of how hard all this must be for you."

Becca opened her mouth to deny it, to tell Erin that she'd been thinking about this for ages now, that she was totally sure, but the chime of the doorbell had cut her off. Erin cursed as whoever it was pressed again, the sound echoing through the hall around them.

"We could just ignore it." But as soon as the words were out of Becca's mouth, Clyde galloped around the corner and started barking at the door. Whoever it was leaned on the doorbell one more time, with increased enthusiasm. The puppy barked louder.

Erin had looked at Becca and sighed. "I do want to continue this conversation. I like you a lot, too, Becca." She rubbed her hand on her forehead and frowned at the door. "But I also don't want to rush into things. I've done that before and it didn't work out. What we've got is, or at least could be, really special. If we don't screw it up. Let's talk after we get rid of whoever this is." She had stepped back, holding Becca's eyes with her own for a long moment before she opened the door.

Ed was standing on the doorstep and frowning at them. Erin frowned back until he cleared his throat and said, "Hi," in a very cautious voice.

Becca wanted to reach out and slam the door in his face. Of all the times and all the people to decide to drop by, he had to pick now. But then, timing was never his strong point. She reminded herself that it was probably about the house and swallowed her frustration with a visible effort. She deliberately looked at his growing bald spot before letting her gaze wander over his middle-aged body and slightly rumpled clothes with the blankest expression she could muster. He'd tried to make her feel old and worthless the last time they saw each other; now, she'd try and return the favor, at least a little bit. She could always berate herself for pettiness later and enjoy it now.

"Sorry to drop by without warning like this, but the buyers wanted to close as soon as possible. I told them that today was just fine, didn't want to lose a sure thing. And they paid cash for the place, Becca!" He grabbed Erin's hand with an unexpected handshake, then dropped it like it was on fire before holding out an envelope to Becca with his other hand. His face lit up with a huge grin. He looked like a man who couldn't believe his good fortune and it gave him laugh lines and a cheerful glow.

Becca could feel the wolf stir inside her again. Something felt wrong, out of place, but she reached for the envelope automatically. She wondered who the buyers were, wondered if Ed had even bothered to check that part out. It wasn't his neighborhood anymore, after all. Or even his town, for that matter, so why would he care?

But it was her town, her neighborhood. And it was the Pack's job to protect this town and this valley. Though hopefully, not before they had recovered from the last time. She thought about recent events: werewolf hunters, shootings, murder, drugs and magic was more than enough for one year. She shuddered as she considered the possibilities for a long moment.

When she tuned back in, Erin and Ed were studying each other like wary dogs. "Do you want to come in?" Erin asked, her tone polite, if not precisely welcoming.

"No, that's okay. Christy's waiting for me back home. We've got a celebration planned." He grinned at the two of them like they were all pals. "Howard, that's the realtor, said he'd call if he needs you to sign anything else, Becca. Looks like we're all set now, though. Can't believe how fast the old place went!"

"Me, either," Becca muttered, frowning at the realtor's SUV. Her sense of foreboding wasn't getting any better. She might feel sentimental about the old place, but that didn't mean that it was without its flaws. Wolf's Point wasn't like some of the surrounding towns, where it looked like most of the houses were for sale, but the kind of person who could pay cash for a house, even in this market, had other options, bigger towns, fancier places. Why pick this one?

Ed was shaking Erin's hand again when she had looked back at them. He glanced Becca's way and stepped forward, reaching out like he was going to hug her. Becca could feel imaginary fur rise on her human neck and tried to clamp down on her reactions before Ed found himself hugging a wolf. Whatever he did notice was enough to stop him mid-reach and drop his hands to his sides. She stuck out her hand and he shook it quickly.

"Well, Becca, I just wanted to say that I'm glad things worked out. You should be fixed up for good now. Heck, maybe you could quit that hardware store job, do something else. Maybe even retire and travel." He gestured to the envelope in her hand.

As if he hadn't said enough about that back before the divorce. Suddenly, even the upcoming inventory at the store sounded great. Better than great, even. "Indeed. I think I'll be keeping my job for a while longer. Good luck with...the baby." Becca felt her lips twist into something that wasn't a smile. Apparently, there were still some things she wasn't ready to forgive. With an effort she suspected was clearly visible, she tried to make her smile more genuine. "Before you take off, do you know who bought it?" She hadn't been able to bring herself to say *our house*, not to him.

Ed had looked away quickly, guiltily, and shook his head. "Nope, sorry. Howard said that they seemed like nice upstanding folks, just the kind you'd want as neighbors. Well, time for me to get going. See you gals around." He didn't actually break into a run as he headed for his car, but it was a definite trot. He didn't look back.

Erin cleared her throat. "I really see what you saw in him. The chemistry is palpable."

Becca had snorted and shoved her arm against Erin's shoulder, herding her back so that she could shut the front door. "Petty much? He was a different guy when I met him. Now, he's Christy's problem. How about I take you out to dinner?" She shook the envelope, then opened it and blinked slowly. "Damn, that's a lot of money."

"I recommend that you let your accountant point you toward some sound investment options." Erin gave a low whistle as she glanced over Becca's shoulder.

"Good thing I have one, then, isn't it? Even though I had to move in with her to afford her services?" Becca tilted her face and grinned impishly at Erin. The look she got made her stomach a dance floor for butterflies.

"I would have cut you a deal, you know. Cute Pack members get a discount. But I think I'll take you up on that dinner offer. I know I don't feel like cooking tonight."

They had cleaned up and changed, then settled Clyde into his fenced-in corner of the kitchen. Becca almost forgot her misgivings about their new neighbors until they walked outside, and the feelings came galloping back, stopping her in her stride. "Who pays cash for an old rundown house, Erin? Especially this much cash?" She frowned across the street.

"You want the good options or the bad ones?" Erin looked at it with her. "Drug dealers and criminals, of course. Apart from that, I dunno, someone who doesn't like going into debt? A lottery winner?"

"It seems to me that all of those kinds of people have more choices than this. What if they're more of Anderson and Annie's people, and they're here to try and hurt us?" Becca let Erin nudge her down the driveway and into her car.

"Well, we'll find out soon enough. How about we don't borrow trouble until we've got more information?" Erin waved at Gladys, who was out trimming her bushes, and pulled into the street, heading for downtown Wolf's Point.

"So where am I taking you?" Becca gave her old house one last look in the side mirror before turning resolutely to stare at the road ahead of them.

"How about El Rincon? I haven't been there in ages." Erin glanced at her sidelong. "And we've never been there together."

Something in her tone made Becca whip around and stare at her wide-eyed. "Why, Ms. Adams, are we going on a date? Like a real live date? Do you think you might ask me to the prom later?"

"That seems a little sudden, Ms. Thornton. Though perhaps you could start wearing my letterman's jacket around school now." Becca started to giggle and Erin picked it up like it was contagious and they laughed all the way out to the restaurant.

Dinner was pure joy, or at least that's how Becca remembered it now. She drank ice tea instead of her usual beer to support Erin, not because the other woman had insisted on it. Not that Erin would ever insist on it, but she could see how much Erin appreciated the gesture and promised herself that she'd stick with tea or water for future dinners. They'd talked enough that she knew that Erin's recovery hadn't been easy. Any little thing she could do to be supportive made it all worthwhile.

They talked about the Pack and the plan to rebuild the Women's Club, still in ashes after the slayers attacked it. What they didn't talk about was what would happen next, or at least not beyond the rafting trip they had planned in a couple of weeks. Becca thought about bringing up the subject, but it was as if the conversation always turned down a different path, running on flying paws toward some new destination.

Maybe it was better to just let things happen on their own, without pushing, she thought. It wasn't as if she was completely sure that she wanted to continue that conversation, not yet anyway. It was risky. What if it went wrong, like her and Ed? Where would she go, what would she do? Could she stay in the Pack or even in town if that happened? It was easier to talk about other things, particularly when she remembered how hesitant Erin seemed earlier.

So she didn't push it. Now she stared at the box of nails in front of her without seeing it, trying and failing not to regret everything she hadn't already said to Erin. There might not be another opportunity to try and ask again.

# CHAPTER 3

B ECCA WAS STILL STANDING AT the counter staring blankly at a container of screws for minutes after Shelly left. Erin's remembered laughter rang in her ears until a car drove by on the street outside and the sound brought her back to the present. She shook her head to clear it. Did she really know Erin well enough to know that she wouldn't kill someone if she thought she had to, maybe to defend herself or someone else?

It wasn't as if Becca could throw stones on that score. But she'd killed as a wolf, not as a human, and it felt like different rules applied to that. Especially since he'd been trying to kill her at the time.

So was Erin's situation different? Why would she confess to killing someone as a wolf, knowing it might expose the Pack?

Becca rubbed the goose bumps from her arms and tried to organize her thoughts. She would have been willing to kill as a human to save that little boy. Or at least that's what she thought today, here in the safety of the store in broad daylight, with that original decision far behind her. So maybe it was okay with her if Erin had killed someone for a really good reason?

After a moment, she realized she was still rubbing her cold arms, and had been doing it hard enough that it felt like she was having a hot flash. She made herself put her hands on the counter, but her fingers began drumming out a steady rhythm of their own invention as if they belonged to someone else. Images of running through the woods on all four paws filled her brain until she felt like she could change right then and there at the register.

But even if that were possible, then what? It was midafternoon and the streets were filled with people. A wolf in downtown Wolf's Point would be a disaster on so many levels and that wouldn't help Erin any.

Instead, she reached out and picked up the box of screws and started counting, over and over again, until the numbers matched the printout. Then she walked to the shelves and grabbed another container. Then another, repeating the process each time. By her fifth trip, she was almost ready for the customers as they trickled in.

Not that they made the time go any faster. It still felt like years before Shelly called. Becca could tell that the news wasn't good, just from the way her Alpha said, "Hello." She closed her eyes and clutched at the worn wooden counter, praying no one would ask for her help just then.

"Oh no. She did it, didn't she? She actually killed someone. Who was it?" Becca's voice quavered with the words and she tried to swallow the flood of tears that threatened to pour down her cheeks.

"Lizzie and I told Erin not to say anything more. They're still identifying the body. The remains are pretty messed up. I've called Milchester and Jones." Shelly's voice went up a little on the last part, as if calling on the most expensive lawyers in the valley was something to get excited about. Becca supposed it was, especially if the emergency fund didn't have much in it and the Pack needed to raise funds to pay them. A vision of werewolf bake sales by the light of the full moon waltzed unbidden into her mind and she bit back a hysterical giggle.

"What can I do?" And that, really, was the most important thing she could be asking right now. There had to be something: phone calls, emails, baking, giving Shelly all the house sale money from Ed, something. She didn't ask the question she really wanted an answer to: did Erin want to see her? She hoped so. But what if the answer was "no"?

Or, what if the answer was "yes," and she made a fool out of herself and somehow managed to make things worse? Could they actually be worse? Her imagination ran wild for a few long seconds until Shelly spoke again.

"I need you to let the Pack know and to keep the store going until Pete gets over there in a little bit. You can take off as soon as he gets there. I know you need to check on Clyde this afternoon so I'll tell Erin that you'll stop by the jail later, okay?" Shelly's voice had taken on more of an Alpha edge. "Okay" was not a request.

Becca felt her shoulders straighten and she stood up taller in response, letting out a small sigh of relief. Little things counted too, right? Erin would be horrified if she forgot about Clyde or ran out of the store during her shift like a crazy person. She had responsibilities, and with any luck, while she was fulfilling those responsibilities, Shelly would work with Lizzie to figure out what they needed to do next. Then she could step up and help them carry out the plan, whatever it was.

The feeling evaporated the second she hung up the phone. This was what Erin sometimes called Shelly's "Alpha whammy." Since when did she wait around for her answers? If she was brave enough to go into a werewolf slayer's camp and get injected with their lycanthropy cure, she was brave enough to figure out something more that she could do beyond tending the store and walking the puppy. Not that she wouldn't have to do those things too, of course.

She logged into her email and sent out an alert to the entire Pack. Shelly had said she'd let them know when they would be meeting so she'd have to contact them all again later, but at least this way no one would be horribly surprised.

In the meantime, she needed to think. She let herself sink into the repetitive tasks of the inventory while her brain worked its way through the situation and what she needed to do next. First and foremost, she needed to find out what the lawyers could do and how much that would cost. She had her half of the house money and a small retirement fund so those would be enough for a start.

Then there was the matter of the body. What had Shelly said? "It was pretty messed up."

Well, that sounded unappetizing, especially since it sounded like it wasn't easy to identify whoever it was. She cringed at the thought. How messed up did a corpse have to be before the only word that immediately fit was "it"? Becca felt queasy just thinking about it.

She took a deep breath, counted a few more screws, and moved her thoughts onto the next problem. What around here could do that kind of damage? Her brain cheerfully offered up: drug addicts, serial killers, wild animals and werewolves, both local and imported. But if it was the latter and assuming the remains were quite...fresh, Erin had to have changed or started to change before she did it. And the moon wouldn't be full for another four days.

Erin had never said that she could change without the full moon's call, not the way that Becca had. In fact, she'd pretty much said that she couldn't. But maybe extreme duress changed that? After all, Becca hadn't known she could do it until she had to. But what if there was something out there that worked like the "cure" that Annie and her pals had used? Becca had been stuck between forms for over twenty-four hours after they dosed her with it. It had been like turning into something out of a monster movie.

But how could that have happened to Erin? Her imagination ran wild with other possibilities: Annie returning from the mountains, vials of the cure in her claws. Of course, it didn't have to be her. It could be one of the others that they hadn't accounted for, like their medic, Leroy. He had a whole fridge full of their cure back in the trailer where she had been held captive. Becca didn't know if any of the Pack had made sure that it had been destroyed when the slayer's trailer blew up.

And truthfully, she didn't have any idea if Leroy had created it himself, or had gotten it from someone else with a lab in another location. Adding all that up, there was a possibility that someone could have given Erin the slayer's "cure," or something like it. That might have been enough to make her lose control and hurt someone.

Becca had to admit, though, that the more she thought about that particular possibility, the more improbable it seemed. Erin had only been gone a couple of hours and that wasn't long have enough for her to be dosed, change and change back. Or at least not the same way that Becca had experienced. Another possibility occurred to her and she added it to her growing list. She was assuming that Erin was in human form when Lizzie took her in, but what if she was wrong?

The cure, such as it was, made her unstable but not homicidal. Becca made herself remember how slow and foggy her thoughts had been, how it had made it harder to smell and to hear with her wolf senses. Then she'd shifted anyway, even though Annie had said that any change was impossible. But once she was scared and angry enough to shift, she'd been stuck halfway until she got to the Pack's cave and its magic cured her.

That part alone had taken her most of a night, so if someone had somehow given Erin the cure, she probably would have been half-wolf when she killed whoever she killed. Lizzie wouldn't have taken her in to the Sheriff's Department that way, she would have called the Pack for help. She'd never let the Pack get targeted like that. So Erin had to be human now, at least.

Her brain was helpfully conjuring up possibilities like werewolves from outside the valley when Pete Peterson swung open the store door, interrupting her thoughts with a jangle of the bell. His massive frame and shoulder length blonde pony-tail triggered a version of the Viking fantasy that sometimes popped into Becca's head when she saw him and she shook her head to clear it of ships and axes and berserkers. He looked worried as he shut door behind him. "Hey, Becca. Sorry it's taken me so long to get back. How are you holding up?"

And that was that. It was as if all her resistance, all of the walls she'd spent the afternoon building up were washed away with those words. Becca stared back at him, lower lip trembling as her eyes filled. Pete locked the front door and led her toward the back room as the tears poured down her cheeks.

Then he sat with her while she tried to let go of all of her fears and anger. How could Erin do this, whatever it was? Why hadn't Shelly taken her along to meet with Lizzie? How was she going to face Erin after this? What were they doing to do? Becca's thoughts swirled between sniffles as she cried herself out.

# CHAPTER 4

I T WASN'T UNTIL AFTER SHE'D gone home and fed Clyde that Becca remembered that they were getting new neighbors sometime soon. She stared across the street at her old house and wondered what kind of a housewarming gift they'd like to receive from the neighborhood jailbirds. A vision of bad television comedies danced in her head until Clyde jumped up and reminded her that she had other things to think about now.

There would be time to worry about the neighbors...or to just plain meet them and welcome them to the street, once she knew what was going to happen next with Erin. She gave Clyde a brisk and determined walk around the block until he did his business and cleaned up after him before heading back to the house. She'd have to think about where he could stay during the day when she was at work; Erin usually worked from home and could let him out.

A tear rolled down her cheek and she brushed it angrily away. How dare Erin leave her to be a single puppy parent? She hadn't signed on for that. Clyde, despite his playfulness, realized that something was wrong and whined wistfully at her. She stopped to pet him until she got herself back under control and headed back home to turn the puppy loose in the backyard.

Walking in the back door sent her thoughts back to the hardware store and her conversation with Pete. He kept saying that it had to have been an accident or self-defense, anything that would help shed some light on why Erin had done this. She knew he was trying to help, but since he didn't have any better idea than Becca did of who the victim was or why this had happened, it just made her more anxious. So many questions and not an answer in sight.

She had to be honest with herself: even if those questions were answered, then what? Becca wasn't sure what she would do next if Erin were charged with murder. Maybe it would depend on the answer to why this had happened. Once she knew that, maybe she could break Erin out of jail and they could go on the run, just a couple of middle-aged female werewolves and their half-grown puppy hiding from the police.

She snorted at her fantasy, then clutched it like a lifeline a moment later. Here was something new to think about, even if only for a little while. They'd still be werewolves if they left the valley; she'd established that much herself when she tried to run away to Mountainview. Even two hundred miles away wasn't enough to stop the change. But she also had a sneaking suspicion that the valley's magic could call them back to Wolf's Point if it wanted them, holding them there until they were too old to be useful to it and then releasing them to the Circle, the Pack's elder ex-wolves. If they made it that long.

Ever since the fight at the cave when the slayer leader Annie got changed, Becca had been wondering if Wolf's Point had called the other woman back to the town for some reason of its own. Sure, Annie thought she was coming back to revenge herself on her old Pack, but what if she was wrong? What if the magic was trying to change her or change the Pack or something like that?

Becca grimaced. If only the Pack Archives hadn't burned up when Annie and her men torched the Wolf's Point Women's Club, she could do some research on this. It would help to know if any of the wolves had ever succeeded in leaving the valley, never to return.

Without knowing that, she had to assume that she and Erin couldn't run away, or at least not very far. She shook her head impatiently at her whirling thoughts. Here she was wasting time, time that could be better spent checking on Erin. Becca wandered through the kitchen and looked around the tiny laundry room, empty of everything except the washer and dryer and utility sink. She wished that she'd thought to ask what she could bring to the jail for Erin that wouldn't get confiscated.

But maybe it wasn't too late for that, at least. She called Lizzie Blackhawk's cell and let it ring until it switched to voicemail. "Hi. It's Becca. Sorry to bug you, but I was wondering if I could bring Erin something when I go over there. Not like a cake with a file in it or something, but stuff like towels and a toothbrush, that kind of thing. Thanks." She clicked off, wishing she felt less useless.

Then she went upstairs to Erin's room, stopping in the doorway before she went in. She would have laughed out loud at her hesitation at any other time. One minute she was propositioning Erin, the next she was worried about going into her room without an invitation. It wasn't like she hadn't been in here before, but that had been when Erin's shoulder was still healing. And she'd been invited.

This felt like an intrusion, as if they had so much unfinished business she shouldn't be crossing the threshold without express permission. She leaned against the doorjamb and closed her eyes, letting her wolf senses tell her about the room, or perhaps more about the woman who occupied it.

It smelled like Erin, wolf and human, which was no surprise. There were scents of Clyde, and even her. But when she concentrated, there were other smells as well: the organic products Erin put on her body, a tang of sweat from her running clothes, earth and plants from the woods outside.

There was something else, too, a strange musty smell that Becca didn't recognize. She opened her eyes and walked in, looking carefully around her. It felt different and it wasn't just Erin's absence that made it that way. It was neater than usual, almost as if Erin suspected she wouldn't be able to tidy up any time soon. The bed's patchwork quilt still covered up the wrinkles in the sheets underneath, though. Becca reached out and pulled the sheets taut under it, tucking them in and smoothing them out almost automatically.

Then she lifted the coverlet to see if she could find the source of the smell, but the only thing that she picked up was Erin's scent, clean and dry. Becca dropped the coverlet back in place and bit her lip, sniffing the air again. She could still smell it, whatever it was. She checked the pillows, then under the bed, but found nothing under the latter but a couple of dust bunnies and an old sock. She stayed where she was kneeling beside the bed and looked around the room again, trying to see it with new eyes.

The nightstand held a lamp, a black stone bowl with some rocks in it, an alarm clock and a couple of paperbacks, one left open and upside down to hold Erin's place. She opened the drawer to find a little carved box inside. With a certain amount of trepidation, she opened it up. It took a minute for her to recognize Erin's sobriety tokens and the sight of them made her snap the box's lid closed in a hurry. She put the box back after checking the rest of the drawer and closing it slowly.

Did she want to hope that Erin had fallen off the wagon? Or that she was a cold-blooded murderer? It was one hell of a choice. She drew in a trembling breath and made herself keep looking around.

The walls and most of the furnishings were different shades of brown and beige, soothing and a bit dull. Only the quilt lent the room a lot of color. That and the photos and artwork on the walls. There was a picture of Erin's old dog, the black Lab who had died around the time that Becca had moved to Wolf's Point, and a few photos of friends and family, including Becca herself, smiling back from the rocks bordering a swift-running creek. That one made her bite her lip, wishing she could turn back time.

She looked at the other wall. There was a painting of some wolves on the wall above the lamp, alongside a framed photo of Erin and Shelly and their state high school championship basketball team. Becca got up and walked over for a closer look. Erin towered over Shelly, all teenage arms and legs and long torso. But she still had the same grin, and Becca found herself reaching out to touch that smile.

Shelly looked fierce and angry, her scowl radiating out of the photo. Becca wondered what she had to be so annoyed about. Maybe the practice hadn't gone well; they'd won most of the games, after all, but not all of them. But whatever it was, it didn't have anything to do with the weird smell, so it would keep until she could ask Shelly herself.

Becca sniffed harder. The scent was stronger as she bent down closer to the floor and she looked down at the throw rug under her feet. It was a sedate mix of blacks and browns and it didn't look like anything had ever been spilled on it. Ever, which was surprising since she knew Erin liked to curl up in bed with a cup of tea, a few cookies and her novels. Perhaps she'd just washed it or had it cleaned.

Becca crouched down and touched its nap, trying to feel anything sticky or odd about it. Her fingers explored the surface, trying to find something more than her eyes told her about its black-on-brown pattern and short, slightly bristly self. Nothing felt out of the ordinary to her touch, but the smell still lingered around it.

It made her think of dust and decay. An image of old bones popped into her head. Her wolf self gave a distant snarl.

When she couldn't stand it anymore, she yanked the rug away from the floor to see what was underneath. The floor-boards of Erin's room spread out before her, slightly golden in the afternoon sunlight that streamed through the blinds. If it was possible for oak flooring to look innocent, these boards were doing the best job ever.

Becca sighed and rubbed her face. She was imagining things, or maybe she just needed to take a mop to the room. She and Erin had different takes on what it meant for a room to be really clean.

She put the rug back and began to tidy things, straightening up the way she did when she was still with Ed. She picked up a pair of boots that were lying on their sides on the floor and put them in the closet, then tossed the pair of socks that were tucked inside them into the hamper. She found a bookmark in the nightstand drawer and put it in the book that Erin had left upside down on the nightstand, glancing at the mystery's title without really reading it as she turned it over and closed the cover.

It was only then that she considered that she might really be intruding now, imposing her order on Erin's world in a way that the other woman wouldn't welcome. But it seemed just plain silly to put it all back the way she had found it now that she'd changed it. She sighed again. There would be time to ask for forgiveness later. She hoped.

Becca checked her phone but there was still no response from Lizzie. She pulled an overnight bag out of the closet and packed it with clean underwear and some toiletries, a few other things that she hoped they'd let Erin have. Glancing at the clock, she realized that she'd have to leave now or she wouldn't have the chance to see Erin today. She dashed downstairs and let Clyde in, and urged on by Clyde's excited barking from the other side of the kitchen's robust puppy gate, she grabbed her purse on her way to the front door.

It swung open as she yanked on the handle and she and the people on the porch stared silently at each other for a long couple of seconds. A part of her mind registered that the man had been reaching for the bell and was just drawing back.

Now what? Missionaries of some kind? She squinted a bit against the sunshine to see the couple better, not that it helped. They were both so blonde, it looked like they had halos. And their smiles had a radioactive glow in the sunlight. "Yes? Can I help you?" Becca could hear how peevish her tone sounded, even in her own ears, but she really didn't have time to be polite. If it made them feel less like hanging around, all to the good.

"Hi!" The couple on the doorstep were still a vision, even without the halos, which disappeared as Becca's eyes adjusted. They both were taller than her and fit in a way that only came from lots of workouts. *They're Ken and Barbie*, Becca thought before she could stop herself. Her wolf senses told her that there was something else that was odd about them, but she shut them down as well as she could and tried to look polite, if not enthusiastic.

"We just bought the house across the street and the realtor mentioned that it used to be yours. So Kari thought it would be nice if we dropped by and introduced ourselves. I'm Jim." He reached out his hand expectantly.

Becca shook it with an automatic smile at both of them before her sense of urgency overrode her manners. "Lovely to meet you. I'm so sorry to be rude about this but I'm on my way out to…an appointment. Can I stop by later and see how you're doing?" She found herself rubbing her hand against her jeans as if to clean Jim's touch off her skin and forced it still.

"Of course!" Kari's voice didn't so much emerge from her lips as it burbled up her throat and spilled out in a flow of trills and ripples, like a brook. "Sorry to have caught you at a bad time. We'll see you later!" With that, they swept off the porch, heading for a moving van that seemed to have appeared out of nowhere on the street in front of Becca's old house.

Becca caught herself staring after them for a minute before she dragged her attention away and locked the door behind her. It wasn't until she was in her car and driving downtown toward the jail that she realized that something hadn't felt right. Kari and Jim felt unreal, like one-dimensional cardboard cutouts of supposedly ideal neighbors. Her fingers still tingled where they had touched Jim's, which didn't help calm her thoughts any.

And there had been something else, that extra odd thing that she just couldn't put her finger on yet.

Unless all of those things were another manifestation of "menopause brain," as she'd started to call it? Sometimes it felt like her reactions to scents, smells and touch were all out of whack, coming across much stronger and more intense than they had been before she started her changes, either of them. It hadn't been the best day, after all. Maybe she was just imagining things about weird smells and odd neighbors.

A hot flash shot through her at the thought, and she almost missed a stop sign and skidded slightly when she braked. Then she had to spend a few precious moments cooling herself off on her car's ailing air conditioning system. Fretting about how she was going to get it fixed if the house sale money had to go toward Erin's legal fees was enough to wipe Jim and Kari out of her head for the rest of her drive.

# CHAPTER 5

D EPUTY LIZZIE BLACKHAWK WAS OUTSIDE smoking a cigarette when Becca got out of her car and headed up the steps to the county jail. She threw the butt down and stomped it out quickly when Becca walked up, then scooped it up and tossed it in the outdoor ashtray. When she looked back up to face Becca, her sunglasses concealed her eyes, though the set of her shoulders looked tense and wary.

Becca nodded at her. "You'll have to give that up when you start to change." Her nose wrinkled instinctively and she snorted, the wolf in her responding to the burning, acrid odor. That was the thing about changing: she might only be a wolf once a month, but the side effects spilled over into daily life more than she could have ever expected.

Lizzie's full lips twisted in a wry smile. "Hell, I'll have to give it up to get my kid off my back long before then. He wants me to quit now, and he's got a point. But we've got other things to worry about right now." But she gave a wistful glance out at the mountains, in the general direction of the Pack's cave, rather than at the building behind her.

Without following her gaze, Becca knew where she was looking and at least some of what she was thinking. Lizzie was too young for changing yet and even when menopause did kick in, there was no guarantee that the valley's magic would call her to join the Pack. Just wanting it more than anything wasn't enough.

It was a shame there wasn't a way any of them knew of to influence that choice. Becca had a suspicion that Lizzie would make a better Pack member than she had, so far anyway. Certainly a better one than Annie had, though that was a low bar. She held back a twitch at those memories. Hard to believe that one werewolf would deliberately inflict that kind of damage on another, but then there were werewolves and there were werewolves. She'd certainly learned that much the hard way in the last couple of months.

"Sorry I didn't call back." Lizzie nodded at the bag and yanked her back to the present. "I was in a staff meeting until a few minutes ago and my boss doesn't take kindly to texting or phone calls during those."

Becca nodded back, despite how numb she felt. "I took a guess on what I could bring in." She opened the bag and held it out so that Lizzie could see what was inside.

"Just the underwear. Everything else has to come through us, unfortunately. That way we know none of it has a file in it." Lizzie shoved her shades up onto her head. Now that Becca could see her expression, she wished that she couldn't. Whatever was coming next wasn't good. "I'm not going to sugarcoat this, Becca.

It looks really bad for Erin, and unless the Pack lawyer can get a judge to rule on bail so she can stay here, she'll get transferred to a higher security facility outside the valley soon."

"Outside the...and what happens when the full moon rises?" Becca stared back at her in horror. Visions of Erin tearing her way through guards and prisoners ran through her head, followed immediately thereafter by a picture of Erin shot and dying on a cold cement floor once someone got their hands on silver bullets. Her brain shut down, despite an instant of speculation on how hard it was to make bullets from silver.

That thought was followed by a second: *This really isn't helping.* Becca shook her head, trying to get her thoughts in order.

A grimace crossed Lizzie's face and Becca wondered if she was thinking about what could happen if Erin changed right here in the local jail. Then the deputy rubbed her eyes for a moment and looked at the ground. "Let's get you through this visit first. Then we can talk about the options with Shelly and whoever else she wants to bring from the Pack. Tonight, since we're going to need a solution yesterday, if not sooner."

She gently herded Becca into the building and Becca went with her like she was sleepwalking. She hadn't even begun to really think about the implications of what a murder charge would mean. What Lizzie was telling her came as a complete shock, hitting her like a punch to the gut. Even if she stayed here and they could somehow cover up her change this month, the wait for the trial could take a lot longer than that. Sooner or later, she'd change and law enforcement was not going to handle it well.

And yet, somehow, this wasn't the time to think about any of that, not now when she was actually going to see Erin.

She could break down later if she had to. But now she had to be strong, encouraging, present. Optimistic. It was what Erin would do for her.

With that thought, she took a deep breath and let the wolf rise, just a little, inside her. The wolf would be strong enough for both of them. She had to be. And Becca had to be strong enough to control it: a quick glance down told her that her hands looked normal, no major hair growth or claws showing. She was ready to go in.

After she checked her hands, she forced her feet, one after the other, through the metal detector, past another deputy and into the jail's tiny visiting area. She sat down in one of the hard plastic chairs. Erin wasn't on the other side of the bulletproof glass, not yet, so she had another minute to compose herself.

She closed her eyes and took a couple of deep breaths, then coughed as whatever they cleaned the place with burned the inside of her nose. Switching to shallow breaths, she tried to still her racing heart, letting her wolf run through remembered forests for a few seconds.

The door opened just as she realized that she was rubbing her hand against her jeans again. Her fingers still felt odd and tingly. It wasn't as if Jim had gripped them too tightly or anything, at least not that she could remember. His hand had been perfectly dry, his grip just tight enough to inspire confidence that he was a regular guy. Perfectly normal. Maybe too normal. There was nothing obvious about their encounter to make her feel the way she did. Maybe she was allergic to their new neighbors.

Erin walked through the door at last, ushered inside by one of the two other deputies. She was wearing an orange jumpsuit that sagged on her like it was a couple of sizes too large. It was a man's prison jumpsuit, Becca realized a minute later. Their county jail was so small that they probably didn't have jumpsuits in a full range of women's sizes.

Erin sat down in the chair on the opposite side of the table and gave Becca a long unreadable look before she said anything. Then she put her handcuffed hands on her side of the table, gave the deputy by the door a quick glance and cleared her throat. "Hi. How's Clyde holding up?"

"You're worried about the puppy?" Becca stared at her in disbelief. Erin's lips quirked in a small grin, but it didn't look like she meant it. She looked exhausted and distant, her eyes flat, as if she was still up in the mountains somewhere. Like maybe she needed to stay there so she could get through this.

Once that realization sank in, Becca sat up straight and said, very carefully, "The puppy is doing okay for now. But he'd like both his people around. Any light you can shed on why that won't be happening soon? Apart from the obvious?" She gestured at the jail around them with her right hand. Her fingers tingled with the gesture.

Erin shook her head, her mouth tight and grim. Becca could feel herself getting shut out and pushed away. It made her want to scream and curse, throw chairs at the plastic that separated them. Break it down and shake it out of Erin to find out what she'd done and why she'd done it. How could she do this to her friend…her…whatever they were to each other?

Her wolf howled inside her, rage and grief for her Beta welling up inside her as it fought to break free. She would break down the walls and free her. They would run away to the mountains, wolves forever. *No.*

Becca fought for control, digging her fingers into her palms, letting the nails dent her skin. She would find the strength to get through this, no matter what it took. Calm, strong, human. She took in a trembling breath and made herself focus on the pain in her hands. It would only make things worse if she couldn't get a handle on herself.

At least the odd feelings in her hand made her think of something else to say. "Okay, different topic. We have new neighbors, the ones who bought my old place. I met them just before I left to come over here. They look like Ken and Barbie brought to life, but their names are Jim and Kari." She was babbling now, her words rushing out to cover how she felt. "Jim shook my hand and I seem to be having an allergic reaction to him or something. My hand feels really weird now." She laughed, the sound flat and fake even in her own ears.

Erin frowned, her face coming back to life for an instant. "That's strange. Maybe you should check with Dr. Green, make sure that there isn't something else wrong."

Becca laughed again. "I'm sure it's just some silly stress-related thing." She shrugged as if to get rid of the subject with the gesture, but Erin was still frowning. This seemed to be making her more anxious, and that wasn't what Becca had come here to do. She held up her hands in a conciliatory gesture. "Okay, okay. I'll check with the clinic and see what's going on. I promise. Now, it's your turn: have you talked to the Pack's legal team yet?"

Erin's face closed up and shut down again, and Becca cursed inside. They only had a few minutes left. This was no time for the other woman to close her out like this. But she couldn't think of what to do to break through.

After a moment of silence, Erin spoke up again, "How's inventory?" Erin's tone made it clear that she was done talking about anything important.

*Not that we have so far, anyway,* Becca thought impatiently. "I need to you to talk to them." Becca put everything she had into that statement: pleading, longing, anger, frustration. "For the rest of us, if you won't do it for yourself."

"There's nothing to be said that'll fix this, Becca." The deputy walked over and opened the door behind her. When he turned around, he held a bag out to Erin and Becca almost didn't recognize it as the one she had brought to the jail, battered as it was. Erin got up and glanced into the raggedy cloth bag as she accepted it. "Take care of yourself. And Clyde. Thanks for the underwear." She looked back and gave Becca an unreadable look before she shuffled away and the door closed behind her.

Becca smacked the countertop in front of her and swore. What was wrong with the woman anyway? Hadn't she ever heard of those plea deals they were always showing on TV? There had to be something they could do, some extenuating circumstance or whatever they called those things. She got up. Well, if Erin wouldn't help herself, they'd just have to find a way to help her without her assistance.

She stormed out of the visiting area looking for Lizzie. The deputy was nowhere in sight and neither was the rest of the department's small staff. Glancing across the office, she could see them all in a meeting room, looking at something. For a wild instant, she thought about storming in and demanding that Lizzie talk to her right away. *Okay, that was definitely menopause brain.*

Instead, she looked away, intending to walk out the door and call Shelly. Her glance fell on a photo on Lizzie's desk: a handsome teenage boy with a beautiful smile looked back at her from a photo that was nearly hidden behind the computer. He looked like a masculine teenaged version of Lizzie, at least from here, only with light brown eyes instead of nearly black ones, like his mother's.

Becca couldn't see anything else, though she thought about having a look around the empty desks. What she'd be looking for if she did that, she couldn't say. But maybe she could find something that would help Erin, or at least find out whose body was in the trunk.

Or maybe she'd end up joining Erin in a cell. This was nuts. She risked a surreptitious look around, craning her neck to look at the papers in the reception desk inbox. Nothing jumped out at her. There were forms and files aplenty, but she would have had to pick them up and look at them more closely to read what they said.

The sound of chairs scraping on linoleum told her that Sheriff Henderson's meeting was nearly done. He and his deputies would come out and find her standing here. They couldn't help but wonder what she was up to, now could they? And that much wondering might reflect badly on Erin, somehow. Her mood sank even lower and she walked outside, yanking her cell from her bag as she went.

She wanted to talk to Shelly now, before the Pack gathered. There was no point in being blindsided by whatever her Alpha's plan was. If she had a plan, which Becca devoutly hoped that she did.

# CHAPTER 6

IT WAS A LONG, LONELY drive out to Shelly and Pete's place by herself. Even having the puppy along didn't make up for Erin's absence. Feeling bad about abandoning him temporarily, Becca had swung by the house and picked up Clyde first. He could spend time with the other dogs in Pete and Shelly's barn while she met with the Pack in the house.

The thought sent her gaze up towards the moon, inching its way toward full as it hung over the mountains. The silver light sent tendrils through her blood, calling the wolf until it ran just under her skin, its wildness howling to possess her.

Clyde whimpered, bringing her back to herself. He was sitting in the back seat, big eyes stretched wide at whatever he smelled in the car. Probably her going slightly wolfy. "It's okay, baby. We've got a long way to go before I'd eat you." *I hope.*

Now there was another happy thought. They just popped up one after another, almost as if the situation was...hopeless. But it wasn't! She almost screamed the thought out loud. They would come up with something to save their Erin. It was what the Pack did, right?

She pulled into the turnoff for the Peterson's drive and found a space near the corral between two other cars. Clyde would have bolted if she hadn't caught his collar as she opened the door. "Stay." He did, though she could feel his reluctance and fear beat against her wolf senses like a drum.

Erin said he'd get used to it. She would have to remember to ask Shelly what she did with their dogs on full moon nights. Could you train them to adapt to their human's complete transformation into something that could eat them? She hoped they... she could and that it wouldn't take too long.

The moon called to her, stirring its fingers in her blood, but sluggishly, as if she were a pot not yet ready to boil. She forced herself to look away, to take Clyde to the barn and let him sniff and be sniffed by Shelly and Pete's dogs. Watching them, she wondered if she did the same thing when she was a wolf. An image of her sniffing her neighbors' butts almost made her laugh out loud.

It was also enough to remind her that it was time to go inside, and she left Clyde to make new friends as she closed the barn door behind her. The ground crunched a little underfoot as she walked to the house, underbrush and a light frost crackling beneath her soles. It was getting colder now and soon the Pack would be patrolling the mountains in the snow.

Without a Beta, unless they figured something out. She shivered at the idea and gave the front door a preemptory knock. Shelly and Pete's daughter, Kira, opened it and stepped aside. "Mom and the others are in the living room." She hesitated a moment, then tugged her ear buds from her ears and tilted her head up to look at Becca. "I'm so sorry about Erin. I don't think she did it. She's been, like, Mom's best friend forever. There's no way Mom's wrong about her, not after this long." She shook her head and vanished back into the kitchen before Becca could say a word.

Not that she had one to hand, seeing as she choked up about halfway through Kira's speech. Becca blinked back tears as she stepped inside and hung her coat up in the hall closet. The Pack was waiting for her, she could feel them, smell them even, though she preferred not to think about that part too much.

There was something a little weird about consciously categorizing her neighbors' specific scents. But it was handy. Even before she entered the room, she knew which Pack members she would find waiting for her: Shelly, Molly, Mrs. Hui, Gladys, Adelía. She wondered where the others were, but maybe they weren't needed for this part.

She walked into the living room and froze in her tracks. There was someone new sitting between Shelly and Molly, someone who she hadn't been able to smell from the hallway. *How was that even possible?* The man watched her for an instant before nodding politely, as if he was used to having unusual effects on Pack members, and turned back to Shelly.

Becca studied him a minute longer than he had her; whoever he was, he was middle-aged, and pale-skinned with graying hair and a pronounced widow's peak. He gave the impression of immense size without taking up more room than he needed. There was something about him that suggested a predator of some kind, but he wasn't anything that Becca had seen before. Erin told her that there were only two kinds of wolves and she'd met both of them. Ergo, not wolf, but something else. But what? How many other werecritters were out there anyway?

Shelly cleared her throat in a way that suggested that she'd done it more than once in the last few minutes. Almost as if everyone else had been focused on trying to catch the man's scent and failing and not paying full attention to their Alpha as a result. "Come and sit down, Becca. This is Larry Milchester, one of the Pack's lawyers. He's explaining the legal precedent for keeping Erin in the local jail and hopefully getting her bailed out as well."

Becca dashed into the room as if her feet had wings and hurled herself into the one of the remaining unoccupied chairs. "Sorry to interrupt. Nice to meet you. Please continue." Her heart was pounding so much she wondered if the others could hear it.

Larry glanced her way and paused, gray eyes suggesting that he, at least, could hear every beat. He looked away and her wolf growled softly in the back of her head. *What the*...she gripped her fears with both hands to rein them in. Where had that come from? Shelly wouldn't have him here if he were dangerous. She was sure of that much. Almost, anyway.

"As I was saying," Larry's voice was low, his tone utterly neutral, "we don't have the most solid and clear case for keeping her here in the valley. But I think I've found a case from 1962 that does give us a toehold on precedent."

"What is it?" The minute she blurted out the question, Becca cringed. She couldn't bring herself to meet Shelly or Mrs. Hui's or even Larry's gaze and stared at the carpet instead. This was the same lack of control that had gotten her into trouble the last time. Of course he was going to tell them if she just gave him a minute. He knew they were all waiting.

"Well, the gist of the case was that the local court ruled that an accused murderer had to stand trial in the valley if a fair trial was assured. We don't get a huge number of murders around here, not surprisingly." His faint smile took in everyone in the room, "so even though it's an old case, I think we can use it to get a stay on her transfer. Once we do that, we can use it to request that the trial take place here, maybe in Wolf's Point itself."

"How long do you think that will take, Larry?" Shelly's voice sounded weary and a little hoarse, as if she'd been talking for hours already.

Becca tried not to hold her breath as Larry looked at the paperwork in front of him. She couldn't help studying him, trying to figure him out. He didn't fidget the way most people did, no useless movements with his hands or feet, even though she knew she wasn't the only one watching him. She'd be climbing the walls with that much tension in the air, that many eyes watching every blink, every gesture.

But Larry's voice was unearthly calm and neutral as he continued, "I've already got the request filed with the judge, but it may take three more days for processing."

This time Molly spoke before Becca could choke out the words. "That's after the next full moon!" Her frantic tone mirrored Becca's thoughts. *They had to get her out before then!*

"What about bail?" She and Gladys asked the question in stereo, their words landing sharply into the crackling tension of the room.

"That's a possibility and we'll be pursuing that too. I understand the...time crunch that we are under. I will make sure that we pursue every option available to us." Larry glanced at her and the others briefly, then refocused on Shelly. She nodded, her expression worn and pale.

The lawyer seemed to take that as dismissal and put his papers away in his briefcase before standing. Something in his motions brought Becca's wolf back straining toward the surface. He felt…weird. He was also far faster than any human should have been, moving to the door in the blink of an eye.

She had to dig her fingers into the chair to keep from going after him, to stop him and sniff him and taste him to see what he was. *What the*…Becca dragged herself out of her wolfish thoughts and blinked at the others.

"What is he?" The words were out of her mouth as the door clicked shut behind him.

Gladys and Molly looked at her blankly, as if they weren't sure what she was asking. Mrs. Hui raised her eyebrow and cocked her head to one side. Maybe it was just her imagination, if the others hadn't noticed anything unusual. Or maybe they just took it for granted.

Only Shelly smiled slightly as if Becca had passed a test of some sort. "You're right. He's not human or wolf and he is a supernatural creature, but he's cloaking it. We've chosen to let him tell us what he is when he's ready. I think you're reacting to the combination of his inner self and the magic he's using to conceal it. I've worked with his partner before, but I haven't met him in person until tonight. Honestly, right now, I don't care. If he can get Erin out before she changes, he can be a sparkly vampire and I'd be okay with that."

Becca hesitated, then nodded reluctantly. It still seemed important to know what the lawyer was, though. At least in her own head. But this was a puzzle she could try to solve later. Shelly was right: worrying about it now was just a distraction.

Molly's voice interrupted her thoughts, "What do you mean, you don't know what he is? I know he's a lawyer and all, but it's not like they're a separate species!" She laughed, the sound filling the room.

For a moment, Becca felt silly, as if she had imagined it all. Then she straightened in her chair, "Couldn't you...not smell him?"

"Oh, I could smell him alright. He was wearing a bit too much cologne." Molly snorted, then paused. "Okay, admittedly, I used to smoke, so I might be missing whatever it is that you're picking up on."

Becca frowned. She had smelt the cologne too, but it was what was or was not underneath that more obvious scent that had her worried. Was Larry able to hide himself from their senses? Shelly said something about "cloaking," which sounded scary in its own right. It was hard to like the idea that there were things that could hide from her wolf senses. And she could see that the other Pack members, with the exception of Shelly and perhaps Mrs. Hui, didn't indicate that they noticed anything odd about him.

Before she could say anything more, Mrs. Hui stood up with a nod to Shelly. "If we're done here, it's time to go over to Circle House. Shall we leave now?"

"Can I come with you? I've never been over there." Becca realized the instant after she asked that perhaps they had business with the Pack elders, business that might not concern her. She blushed hotly. But Circle House was where the older Pack members went to live when they got too old to change and needed help at home, and she'd never met the elder wolves.

And, after the Women's Club got burned down with the Pack archives in it, they were the best remaining source of information about the Pack's history and traditions. She might be able to find out something about the questions that had been galloping through her head since Erin got arrested. If she had to go rogue and break Erin out of jail, it would be good to know if they had options. Not that she would need to do that, of course. Becca tried to shove the thought away.

But thinking about the archives gave her an idea. Wasn't it time that one of them started interviewing the elders and writing down what they had to say? The thought was no sooner in her head than it was out of her mouth. "I'd love to start writing up the Circle's memories and what they can recall about our history. We've got to try and replace the Pack archive as soon as possible, and that would be a great place to start." At least it would be better than sitting around waiting for the worst possible news about Erin. She'd feel a bit more useful.

Shelly nodded. "That makes sense. Yes, please do come with us. Clyde can stay here and play with our pups and we'll drop him off at your place tomorrow." Everyone else got up and prepared to leave as Becca trailed after Shelly and Mrs. Hui. She found herself wondering what business the restaurant owner had at Circle House tonight and that, in turn, made her wonder what she might be able to find out there herself. The mystery that was Larry Milchester slipped clean out of her head for the moment.

# CHAPTER 7

CIRCLE HOUSE WASN'T IN A separate building from the larger assisted living place, or at least not in the way that Becca had pictured it. She realized that she'd been expecting a small compound or something like that, maybe a structure that would remind her of the cave…or a wolf's den. *Maybe with a "Beware! Old Wolves!" sign out front.* She snorted very quietly at the picture forming in her head.

Shelly parked in front of the Greenleaf Assisted Living Facility in Wolf's Point while Becca studied the thoroughly ordinary building in a way she never had before. It looked like any other building of its kind: institutional red brick, white trim, wheelchair ramps and big windows. There was a garden on one side of the building with trees and a gazebo, and concrete paths with benches wound around the front.

But if Circle House was here, it couldn't be that ordinary. What other secrets was her town concealing behind a veneer of normalcy? Some days, her brain just whirled trying to keep up with it all.

There were three elderly women sitting on the patio near one of the side doors enjoying the last of the afternoon sun before the gentle chill drove them back inside. One of them was sitting in a wheelchair and looked like she might be of Asian descent. She was parked across from the other women who sat on one of the benches. One of the other women reminded Becca strongly of Shelly and Lizzie due to her brown complexion, high cheekbones and black hair fading into gray, while the third had pale skin, gray-blue eyes like a huskie and hair so short, it looked like a military buzz cut.

They were having an animated conversation with lots of gesturing and the occasional guffaw, audible from the street. Becca smiled as they walked toward them, reassured by how cheerful they seemed to be. Maybe being a retired werewolf wouldn't be such a bad thing. Some day though, not just yet. She wasn't ready to give up running through the woods under the moonlight, not now that she'd discovered it.

Belatedly, she realized that she'd forgotten to bring a pen and paper and her phone didn't have a recording app. Some archivist she was turning out to be. Well, she'd just have to pay lots of attention and make plans to come back later. Her thoughts spun back to Erin, hoping that she'd have other plans "later," whenever that was, and she dragged them away. Obsessing wouldn't help right now, but info gathering might. She fixed her best social smile on like it was an accessory and followed the others.

"Hi!" Shelly greeted the women as they got closer. The three looked up, eyes bright and sharp as they studied the younger women approaching them. It was almost as if their ears perked up as well and Becca hid a smile. Once a wolf, always a wolf?

"This is Becca. She was called to join us a couple of months ago. Becca, this is Mei Lin, Sharon and Robin." Shelly gestured from the woman in the wheelchair toward each of the others with each name. Becca nodded shyly as the women turned to look at her, with a brief flare of nostrils. She wondered what they could smell from her, if anything. Bewilderment and stress, probably. Only Sharon smiled at her.

An aide bustled out and hovered nearby, clearly waiting to shoo them all inside from the expression on his face. After they had shaken hands, they all followed him in. "Afternoon med time." Mei Lin grimaced at Becca right before she rolled up the ramp.

Becca wrinkled her nose back and followed them all into an institutional hallway full of doorways, noise and gray carpet. Shelly walked into a large conference room and she followed, wondering what she was supposed to do next. Shelly grabbed a few chairs and began rearranging them around the biggest table and she went over to help out.

When Mei Lin came back in with a small container of pills, Becca realized that they'd been making space for wheelchairs and scooters. Everyone trailed in a few minutes later and they all settled in around the biggest table. The room opened into a big lounge area with a couple of couches, some chairs and three tables. One of the smaller tables was occupied by four other women, all of whom smelled like wolves, playing cards. As they got settled in, the other women broke up their game and moved over to join them. A few more trickled in and someone closed the doors to the meeting room and the lounge.

Becca wondered how to broach the subject of interviews when Shelly did it for her, along with revealing the other reason they were there. "This isn't a purely social visit, unfortunately. Erin Adams was found with a body in the trunk of her car.

She's confessed to murder, even though she says she doesn't remember doing it, and she will be charged, barring a miracle. The Pack lawyers are working on it, but we're hoping to get more context from you."

The other women made small noises of distress and anger. Robin looked particularly shocked and fired questions in a torrent of words, "Was she on Pack business? How did she get picked up? Who was it?"

Shelly glanced sidelong at Becca, then continued at her slight nod. "Erin is a recovering alcoholic and there weren't any witnesses, as far as we know. We don't know what she was doing up in the mountains when it happened. She turned herself in before she called me because she thought she had fallen off the wagon and had a blackout. And she isn't talking yet, beyond telling Lizzie Blackhawk that she isn't sure what happened." Shelly paused, closing her eyes for a moment. "We're all waiting on the lab tests on the body. His face was too damaged to recognize and his fingerprints weren't in the system."

Shelly opened her eyes and Becca could see tears gathering on her lashes. She choked back a sob of her own and placed a comforting hand on her Alpha's shoulder, squeezing lightly before turning away to blow her nose in her handkerchief.

"Well, crap," Robin muttered, her wrinkled face crestfallen as she studied the industrial gray carpet under her feet. Then she leaned forward, elbows on the table, and rubbed her face with both hands. She seemed to speak for all of them, and there was silence for a long couple of minutes. Robin rubbed her short hair the wrong way, like she wasn't paying attention to what her hands were doing.

After a few minutes, she looked up. "So, you want us to engineer a jail break? I know Erin. She wouldn't have done something like this without a damn good reason. If she did it at all. Maybe she was framed." Becca flashed her a grateful look.

Shelly's lips twisted slightly and she glanced at the doorway that the aide had just exited through. "If that's what I wanted right now, Grandmother Wolf, I wouldn't have picked here and now to talk about it." She paused a moment until Robin looked sufficiently chastened and Mrs. Hui got up and locked the doors.

She continued once Mrs. Hui sat back down next to Mei Lin, "Right now, what I need from all of you is ideas and Pack history, our history. Becca here is going to start documenting everything you can remember. We'll take a good look at other options before trying anything...more unusual."

"Ideas about what?" a very old woman asked. "I got plenty. Where do you want me to start?"

A quiet chuckle went around the circle of chairs. Mrs. Hui placed a hand on the other woman's arm and Becca could see a family resemblance between her, this woman and Mei Lin. Mother and aunt, maybe? Once she started paying attention, she could see that Sharon and Shelly were clearly related. She was going to have to ask about Pack genealogy too. Maybe the valley's magic sometimes went along family lines.

Shelly grimaced. "I'm sure you do, Amy. For right now, I'd like to focus on the current problem. Has anyone else had experience with blackouts or known another wolf who did?"

"Honestly, not really. Not with a senior wolf who's used to changing." Robin shrugged. "Most of us left any addictions we had behind when we accepted what we were. And I can't think of anything besides a head injury or some weird illness that would make any of us black out that badly. Of course, there have been...accidents with new wolves." She glanced quickly at the other women from the Circle, as if she was asking permission to speak.

The air nearly rippled with expectation, at least to Becca. Whatever they were about to be told didn't get spoken of often. "Please continue, Robin," Shelly's tone took on an Alpha edge, not quite compelling the other woman to speak, but making it hard to deny her.

Robin nodded and looked at her hands, fingers twisting in her lap. "Back when I first joined the Pack, there was another wolf called at nearly the same time I was. Sharon was our Alpha back then, back before Margaret and all that other stuff that happened." She paused to take a deep breath, as if those memories were too distant or painful to call up easily.

Becca watched everything she did, filing it away for when she did have a notepad handy. Annie had killed Margaret, or so she'd been told. But somehow, Shelly got to be Alpha instead of Annie. Maybe she was finally going to get the whole story about that now.

Robin looked around, letting Sharon catch her eye. They stared at each other as Robin continued. "So this other wolf, Paula, her name was, she was having a tough time even before the magic called her. There was a divorce and her ex was an abusive bastard. He came back and tried to hurt her again after she started changing. That was how the Pack got involved. Sharon took a few of us over to their place and ran him out of the valley, considerably the worse for the wear." She looked away from Sharon to glance at Shelly, who nodded in acknowledgement.

"Anyway, so Paula had a problem with booze and drugs and couldn't let go of it, even after she started changing. Maybe it was because of the ex, maybe something else. Whatever it was, she was a broken woman in a lot of ways. So we were all pretty surprised when the magic called her to join us. I think up until then, most of us thought there was some kind of logic at work and that it was all about the land protecting itself. We figured the land would pick the strongest and most capable of the older women that it had to choose from. But once Paula changed, we started to wonder if maybe it wasn't something inside us that called us to change rather than the other way around."

Becca sat up straighter, her thoughts immediately turning to what she'd been feeling before the first time that she changed. She remembered feeling empty and lost after the divorce, sure, but she'd worked through that. She hadn't needed the magic or the change or the Pack to fix that. Had she?

"What was clear was that Paula was a mess. We all did the best we could. Sharon practically moved in with her and her kids to try and get her clean and sober and dealing with changing. But Paula, she just got wilder and wilder. You could see the wolf looking out of her eyes any time of the day or night, moon or no moon. And with the booze and all eating away at her self-control, she started to change little by little until she hardly seemed human sometimes." Robin took a sip from a cup of water that Shelly handed her. Around them, the other Pack members sat silent, heads bowed as if in prayer.

"Then the ex came back. We couldn't stop him, short of killing him on the threshold. And we wanted to, but Sharon said that was Paula's right to do that if she wanted to do it. None of us was sure that Paula didn't want that, but she wanted him, too. It just kept getting worse from there." Robin paused for another gulp from the cup and rubbed her hand across her forehead.

Becca could feel them all brace themselves, at least those of the group who knew how the story ended. Sharon rubbed her eye with one trembling hand. Then Robin started speaking again and Becca stopped paying attention to the others.

"Finally, it was a full moon and he locked her in the house with him and the kids and set the place on fire. We broke in and got two of the kids out. But we were too late for the third one. And for her ex. He was no great loss, so I won't say we tried very hard." Robin's eyes looked tortured now, as if she could see the past clearer than the lounge around them. Her voice trailed off.

She closed her eyes and sighed before she continued. "Paula got out of the fire on her own and she was human again for awhile, or almost human. Always said she couldn't remember a thing that happened that night. I wondered how true that was, right up until she disappeared one night a few months later. We looked for her, all of us. The old sheriff, the one before Henderson, was looking too since she was his main suspect for the fire. But we never found her and neither did he. Your cousins, Paula's cousins, too," here she paused to look at Shelly, "they took the two surviving kids in."

Becca's eyes widened. Annie had told her, "The wolves killed my parents." There couldn't be multiple stories like this in the valley, could there? That thought was pretty horrifying.

But her brain was full of memories of Annie running around the mountains after the magic changed her at the cave. Packless, just like her mother before her. She stared at Shelly as if she could get her Alpha to say her cousin's name by sheer force of will. But Shelly was looking into space with a sad expression on her face as if she, too, was remembering some things she didn't want to recall.

She would have been way too young to understand much about the wolves back then, but she must have heard the stories. Becca wondered if Wolf's Point families ever scared their children and grandchildren by telling that a big bad wolf was going to get them. That could explain a lot about Annie and her quest to wipe the wolves out. Who doesn't want to destroy the monster under the bed, once they get old enough?

Robin took a deep, shuddering breath and concluded, "We never found Paula again, as I said. The kids, well, you know what happened to the girl. The boy left the valley and moved out East. I think he sends a card to your cousins once a year and calls sometimes. Anyone else know of another wolf going through anything like that?" She swept the circle with her gaze, stopping when she got to Amy and Mei Lin, the oldest women in the room.

Becca couldn't hold her question back. She had to know, to be sure which story was who's in the sea of partial truths she'd absorbed in the last couple of months. "So the daughter was Annie?"

Shelly turned slowly toward her and nodded. Her face was pale and her lips were set, making her look angry. For an instant, Becca thought she had upset her Alpha, but just as quickly as the look crossed her face, it vanished. Her expression when she met Becca's eyes was solemn, but nothing more than that.

Becca desperately wanted to ask the most obvious question: *How does this help Erin?* It was hard to know whether or not to hope that Erin had been drinking again; at least then there would be some context. But she ached at how devastated Erin must be, thinking that she had relapsed and done something awful.

Mei Lin's voice broke into Becca's thoughts as she started telling another story, one that she had heard years ago when she first turned. A member of the Pack had a series of blackouts or seizures, forgetting everything that they had done either as wolf or as human from time to time. One night, she forgot that she had ever been human and disappeared from the valley, at least according to what Mei Lin had heard.

Now they all looked solemn and quiet. It was Shelly who broke the silence this time. "All right. So some things like this have happened before. I had wondered if Paula had blackouts after she turned; thank you for telling that bit of the history, Robin. I know this hasn't been easy. When we are wolves, we want to be wolves, and when we are human, we want to be in control. The thought of losing either part of ourselves, once we've adjusted, is difficult to say the least. I need to give Lizzie a call, but I'll take you back to our place for dinner, Becca, if you're ready. Lin is planning on walking home so we don't need to wait for her."

Becca started to say that she wanted to stay, wanted to start writing down stories and history this very minute. But she could see the women of the Circle were tired, some more than others. Robin looked as though she had turned inward, entirely lost in her memories.

Mrs. Hui stood up and unlocked the door as if the decision was already made, then came back and started wheeling Mei Lin away. So Becca nodded and gathered her bag as they bid their farewells. It felt like a spell had been broken, and Erin was once again the only thing on her mind now. Was Shelly going to find something to get Erin out, just in case the lawyer didn't succeed? There was only one way to find out and that meant leaving now so she could ask. She told the Circle she'd be back in a day or two and followed Shelly outside.

# CHAPTER 8

T HIRTY-SIX HOURS UNTIL THE FULL moon and Erin Adams was climbing the walls of her cell. She paced back and forth and around in as much of a circle as she could create while dodging the bunk bed, the toilet bowl and the tiny sink. The woods and the mountains were boiling in her blood, sending the moon's song through her until she felt like she'd be changing any moment.

But then what? Good thing she didn't have a cellmate or she'd be tempted to eat them. She snorted at the thought and switched from pacing to doing lunges and stretches. Anything to work off these feelings that were driving her, well, "wolfy." "Batty" wasn't going to cut it tonight.

Shelly and Becca had stopped by during visiting hours that afternoon, all excited because the lawyer from the Pack firm thought he might have found something that might get her out of here. She wanted to share their enthusiasm, she really did, but the more time she spent looking at concrete walls and iron bars, the less optimistic she felt. And she'd let that show and had shut Becca out. She didn't feel very good about that right now either, and she gave the wall next to her an open-handed smack to let off some steam

Wolf's Point had an old jail, cold and slightly damp, but that wasn't the real problem. Erin felt as if she could touch all the occupants the cell had ever had when her hand hit the wall. Despair, cunning, rage, depression: it was washing over her in waves the longer she stayed in here. True, the full moon was close, but she wasn't a new wolf anymore. This shouldn't be hitting her as hard as it was.

Thinking about the moon got her thinking about how long it might take before the lawyer got a judge to post bail or bond or whatever it was. If he could find one who would. She looked up at the security cameras and down the echoing hallway where she could hear the guards from the jail's small staff taking their break. If he took more than thirty-five hours, it wasn't going to matter anymore. The best she could hope for was getting sent to a lab somewhere for study.

The alternative was even less pleasant.

Part of her wanted to smack her head against the concrete walls instead of her hand. She shouldn't have turned herself in, she should have run and kept running. But then what? Everyone she cared about, with very few exceptions, was here in Wolf's Point. This was where she belonged, not on the run without a Pack.

But wasn't this making it harder on everyone? She could see it in her friends' eyes when they came to visit. Shelly, Becca, Molly, they all looked strained and exhausted. Yet they came anyway and tried to cheer her up even after what she'd done. She really didn't deserve them.

Erin stopped pacing and dropped onto the lower bunk. She buried her head in her hands for a few minutes. Then jerked her head away from her fingers. She could smell the blood on them, she was sure of it. If only she could remember whose blood...and why. That was the worst of it: the not remembering.

Why had she been drinking that day? She couldn't remember that part either, but that had to have been what happened. Why else would she have lost control like that? Five years of sobriety down the tubes and she couldn't even bring herself to let Shelly call her sponsor. She'd never been so ashamed of herself before.

No, that wasn't strong enough. This was more than shame; in fact, it was something that she didn't think she even had a word for yet. She'd let down the Pack and Becca and Shelly and she'd let herself down too. Not to mention the poor sod, whoever they were, who she'd killed.

Becca was better off without her. They all were. She collapsed onto the rock-hard mattress, closed her eyes and tried not to sob too loudly.

It took awhile for her to notice the smell. There was something familiar about it, a quality that made her think about pine floors and mild perfume, but with an undercurrent of the full moon, blood and change. She'd smelled it before and recently. Erin opened her eyes and sat up slowly.

The couple in the corridor outside her cell looking in at her certainly weren't guards. And neither one of them looked like Al in the cell across from her, brought in for petty theft just yesterday. In fact, they looked like the people that Becca had been talking about. There had been a comment that she'd made about some people she met looking like "Ken and Barbie." Well, these two certainly fit the bill.

"Hi!" The young blonde woman with the perfectly coiffed hair flashed a smile at her, white teeth brilliant in the gloom. She and the man with her moved like runners, maybe with some Pilates workouts thrown in for additional grace and flexibility. She gestured toward the bars and he stepped sideways, making himself a smaller target with a movement that looked choreographed.

There was a clicking noise, but nothing else happened as far as Erin could tell. They all stared at each other through the cell bars.

Erin got up and backed away from the bars and the door. Whoever they were, they'd snuck in here somehow, and for the life of her, she couldn't figure out how or why. She risked a glance up at the camera; the red light was on. Did the guards know these two were here? Had they been paid off to ignore what was going on in the cellblock? She strained her hearing, pricking up her phantom wolf ears to listen to the break room as she managed a croak that might have been, "Hi."

"I'm Kari and this is Jim." The woman gestured at her companion. He wrinkled his otherwise flawlessly high forehead with a quick frown, then switched to a tentative smile, as if he wasn't sure he wanted her to know their names.

Erin frowned back. There was a stretcher on the floor behind them, tucked away so she hadn't noticed it before. She wondered why they had that with them. "Our new neighbors? What are you doing here?"

"Oh, Becca must have told you that she met us. She's just the sweetest thing, and worried sick about you. I can see it in her eyes. Jim was telling me how bad he felt for you two and

I knew that we just had to help out." Kari flashed that smile again, her blue eyes shining with enthusiasm as she moved closer to the bars.

"Help?" Erin asked nervously. There was no way that Becca would have turned to these strangers, not when she had the Pack. Who were they? What was that sound, like something being sprayed? The smell was much heavier now, and the stronger it got, the more tired she felt. If these two would just leave, she could get in a good nap before...before...

The cell door opened and Erin realized that she was lying on the floor for some reason. What was she doing down here? There were feet getting closer and closer to her, and from far away, she heard a woman's voice say, "See, Jim, I told you it would work. Get her head and I'll take her feet."

Erin disappeared into the dark, running and running through the trees under the brilliant light of the full moon.

# CHAPTER 9

**"W**HERE IS SHE?" HER TONE was as close as Becca had ever heard to a shout coming from Lizzie Blackhawk. The deputy was inside the hardware store the moment that Becca unlocked the door and turned the lights on.

Becca wondered who she was talking about and why she hadn't just called. But only for an instant. "What are you talking about?" Becca asked, the question automatic. It had to be Erin. Something had happened to Erin. Her stomach plummeted through the floor. They were so close to the full moon as it was. Had she changed early and escaped or something?

Becca tried to brace herself for the worst. She hadn't slept a wink all night as it was, tossing and turning and obsessing over all the things that could go wrong, had gone wrong. An angry deputy hadn't been among them, though certainly werewolves had.

Lizzie's eyes narrowed as she stared at Becca, her expression suggesting that she was a woman pushed to the brink and beyond. Her lips parted to let what looked liked they'd be some choice words out.

Shelly and Pete walked through the open door behind her at exactly the right moment to interrupt whatever the deputy had been about to say. "Hi. What's up, Lizzie?" The confusion on Pete's face was echoed in his voice.

Lizzie whipped around and stalked up to Shelly. From where Becca stood, it looked like her hackles were up. Or would have been, if she'd had any. "What have you done with her? I was going to handle it. Do you have any idea how much trouble you're about to get us into?"

Shelly's face mirrored Becca's own puzzlement for an instant. Then, Becca could see the Alpha rise to the challenge. She darted over to the door and very gently closed it behind all of them, flipping the sign to "Closed."

When she turned around, Lizzie and Shelly were glaring at each other. Becca stepped cautiously to Shelly's side. "Maybe we should go in the back and you can tell us what's happened, Lizzie. I know I don't know what you're so upset about and I'm guessing they don't either."

The deputy glared at her again, shoulders rigid, then back at her cousin. For a wild instant, Becca feared that both of them were going to turn and fight it out in Peterson's Hardware. Lizzie looked like she was going to manage to change on sheer willpower alone right now, magic or no magic.

Something in Becca's tone must have convinced her though, because after what felt like an hour, she stepped back and jerked her head toward the back room. Shelly led the way, Becca trailed after her and the deputy stalked after them.

"Right. I'll just open up the store." Pete's mutter would have been inaudible to human ears. Becca was torn between giggling and going back to help him. But if she did that, there'd be no one to mediate between Shelly and Lizzie. And that didn't seem like a good idea.

She squared her shoulders and followed them into the room. Lizzie closed the door behind her, stopping it just short of a slam. "Erin's gone. There's nothing on our security cameras, so wherever she went, I'm guessing it wasn't down to the corner for coffee. I can't think of anyone else who would have stopped by just to let her out, can you?"

Shelly stepped forward as Becca gasped. "What the hell do you mean 'she's gone'? It's a prison. You've got cameras. You've got guards. How do you lose a full-grown woman?" She whipped around to Becca. "Tell her what we were doing last night."

Becca could feel her mouth open and shut like a fish gasping for air. What did Lizzie mean? She couldn't be gone. Where would she go? "We were at Circle House for the afternoon, then at Shelly and Pete's for dinner. Ask him or the kids. I left late and we sure weren't planning a jailbreak then." Her voice sounded like it belonged to someone else, someone who spoke with a tinny, hoarse whisper.

Lizzie smacked the wall behind her with her open palm, the sound echoing through the little room and making Becca jump. "Then who helped her? Yeah, we've got guards and cameras. You know what they saw last night? Nothing. Not a damn thing. Someone or something put the camera on a loop. All it showed was Erin sleeping. And why they didn't see anyone go past is anyone's guess. Who else can do that besides the Pack?" Lizzie raised her hand and ran her fingers through her hair with a quick jerky movement.

Becca's jaw dropped and her brain spun. *Someone had...taken Erin?* The thought was more than she could process.

Shelly dropped with a thump into the tired armchair next to the desk. It looked like every emotion in the book galloped across her face, sometimes two at a time. Finally she gave a tiny cough, almost a growl. "I won't deny that I was thinking about it, planning it, if we couldn't get her bailed out before the full moon. But I was going to give the lawyer another twelve hours before we did anything drastic."

The lawyer? Becca could feel her eyebrows rise like they were on cords. What if he had something to do with this? Though as she thought about it, she was hard-pressed to find a reason for what she was thinking, apart from thinking that he wasn't what he seemed to be. Not unless Shelly had only promised to pay his firm for successful results or something, and that seemed unlikely. Maybe Erin had gotten freaked out about the full moon and their lack of progress and escaped on her own. Now *that* seemed a possibility she should keep to herself, once she'd thought of it.

When she started paying attention to the other two women again, Lizzie was giving her a considering look. "Got an alibi for last night after you left Shelly and Pete's?"

"Uh..." She looked at Shelly for help. Unless Clyde counted as an alibi, she had nothing. "I didn't do it. I wanted to. But I didn't."

There was nothing but silence and tension for a really long couple of minutes. Then Lizzie sighed with frustration. "Do either of you know anyone else who could have done this? I'm not ruling out Erin herself, mind you. It just seems weird to me that she'd turn herself in only to turn around and escape. But I can believe that she could have been talked into it."

Shelly shrugged, the gesture acknowledging Lizzie's comment without admitting anything. "I'd like to know the answer to that myself. But I'm more concerned about whether or not Erin is safe. That's my priority." She stood, meeting her cousin's eyes.

Lizzie's walkie-talkie beeped from her belt. She pulled it out and frowned at them. "I need to answer this. Can I get a minute alone? Police business."

Dismissed, Becca and Shelly went back into the store. Pete was waiting on a customer and smiling like nothing was wrong. Shelly reached out and touched Becca's shoulder lightly. "We'll get her back and we'll figure this out." She hesitated, then asked, "It wasn't you, was it? I won't tell her until I have to."

Becca snorted. As if she was ever that good of an actress. "Nothing to tell. I wish I had! Then I'd know where she was and that she was safe." Becca struggled against the tears that were threatening to pour down her face.

Lizzie walked out of the room behind them. "We got an ID on the body that was in Erin's trunk." Her tone was grim and Becca flinched away, not ready to hear more bad news. "It was a guy from the group Annie brought in, one Leroy Callan."

"Leroy?" Becca gasped. When last she'd seen the medic, he'd been in the midst of a gun battle at the trailer where they'd been holding her captive. She assumed he'd been killed when it blew up or arrested later when the Pack rescued Shelly or run off or something. He hadn't been with Anderson and Annie at the cave.

But there was no need to ask why Erin would have wanted to kill him herself if she'd run across him: he'd given Becca and Shelly the slayer's "cure." Becca was still having nightmares and some aftereffects, and Shelly wasn't talking it about it much, a bad sign in itself. Somehow, it was easier to imagine Erin killing somebody like him than almost anyone else.

Becca rubbed her forehead and wondered whether she should look relieved or upset. Something that combined her knowledge of her own innocence and the suggestion that Erin might have done this in self-defense was clearly the way to go. "Maybe he tried to cure her," she mumbled finally.

Shelly twitched, but it was Lizzie who spoke, her expression impassive. "I'd like to have you come by the morgue to confirm the ID, Becca, since you're one of the few people around here who dealt with him when he was still alive. Can you spare her for an hour?"

This second question was to Shelly, not her. Becca sent out a deep and fervent hope that her boss would say that she couldn't be spared, but Shelly disappointed her by nodding in agreement instead.

Shelly and Lizzie exchanged a few words that Becca didn't quite catch before Lizzie left the store. Becca trailed reluctantly after her like she was on an invisible leash. "How bad is he messed up?" Her brain was full of all kinds of gory images from TV and movies. It would be like one of those forensic lab shows, she just knew it. The kind where the bodies looked like bony hamburger. Breakfast roiled in her stomach.

"You're a werewolf and you're this big of a wimp?" Lizzie's sunglasses were back down over her eyes as they climbed into her car. "I won't deny that it's pretty bad and that you're likely to be able to confirm that it's him based on your sense of smell and not by the way he looks. But it's not like he had a bunch of other 'acquaintances' in these parts so I don't have too many other people to ask."

*And it gives you a chance to cross-examine me again to see if I'm holding out on you.* Becca bit back that thought, as well as the second one: *Shelly would recognize his smell, too.* The deputy was doing her job and it wasn't as if Becca knew anything about what Erin had done or why. She had no secrets to betray. Somehow, that hurt the most, if she stopped to think about it.

But this wasn't the time to wallow. Instead, she asked another question that had been on her mind. "You spend any time at Circle House?" There would be no harm in changing the subject, at least for a little while.

"Of course. My grandma and one of my great aunts are living up there now. I try to go over and visit every couple of weeks or so and drag my kid along. I guess Shelly finally got around to taking you over there and introducing you around. Who'd you end up talking to? And more importantly, what did they tell you?"

Becca told her about their visit, right up through the story about the rogue wolf and what had happened to her and her family. She paused a minute. "Was that your family, the ones who took in the kids?"

"Yep. My aunt. I knew them a little, growing up. They were grown up by the time I got old enough to tag around after them. Jimmy was a nice enough guy, though he smoked too much pot back then. Sara...Annie was always the dominant personality of the two. Not too surprising that she was picked to change." Lizzie fell silent, her expression thoughtful.

Becca snorted. "You'd think the valley's magic would make better choices. It's had enough practice."

"Well, she wasn't always the Annie you met. Back when she was plain old Sara Ann, she was a pretty decent choice. At least until she really went off the rails about everything and that Anderson asshole made it worse." Lizzie pulled up into the parking lot of the county building and parked. "And don't think I don't know what you're doing. I'm not that easily distracted. You're still on my suspect list, at least until I find out what happened to Erin."

"But in the meantime, I get to look at a mangled corpse," Becca muttered. "Not like I'm being punished or anything."

Lizzie looked at Becca over her glasses. "You're contributing to an ongoing investigation." She paused as they got to the steps and frowned at Becca. Her expression softened a little. "Seriously, are you ready for this?"

"No. But I'll do it anyway. Maybe I can see something your people missed, something to prove that Erin is innocent. Or at least justified." Becca drew in a deep breath and yanked the front door open, letting out a dull chemical cloud that nearly sent her back down the steps, coughing. "All right," she added grimly as she caught her breath. Shallow breaths, that was the way to go. Hopefully. "Let's do this."

Lizzie smiled a little, but turned her face away as if she thought Becca wouldn't notice, and led the way to the morgue. She swung the door open into a sterile lab where a couple of techs bustled around the white sheet-covered tables that Becca had been expecting. Why did they use white? Wouldn't red or black make more sense? Becca had always wondered about that.

But a quick look at the one body that wasn't covered up drove the question clean out of her mind.

"Oh my god," she whispered. Lizzie handed her a trashcan without comment. Becca clutched the metal rim like it was a security blanket, but she didn't throw up. Not yet. After all, hadn't she done something like this herself? *But that was different*, her brain insisted. She closed her eyes and hoped with all her heart that this time was different, too.

Then she opened her eyes and tried to make herself focus. The body—she had trouble thinking of it as Leroy—lay on a table near the door. Lizzie hung back to talk to one of the techs, a lanky red-haired man, leaving Becca to approach the table on her own. It took everything she had to walk up to it.

The techs had been hard at work and a lot of his skin had been peeled back or cut open. Becca took a quick look at body parts she couldn't identify, then looked back into the trashcan. This wasn't getting her anywhere. It was time to use some of her wolf skills.

She closed her eyes again and gave the air a tentative sniff, trying to rouse her wolf senses to process whatever information the corpse could give her. The chemicals made it nearly impossible. Instead, the wolf in her head urged her to run, to race out the doors away from this artificial hell and into the woods.

At least when it wasn't urging her to lose her lunch in the trashcan she was still clutching.

The mix of reactions thudded their way through her until she trembled from trying to control herself. Running was only a temporary solution. Lizzie would only make her come back, or so she told herself. She took her mind away from the morgue for a few moments, imagining green, peaceful places in the woods, sunlight dappling green leaves, a stream nearby.

As her panic subsided, she began to smell familiar scents. Then a wave of memories of the trailer and Annie and Leroy giving her their cure swept through her. The wolf within her got distant, dwindling away, getting lost in the remembered fog that came with the injections. But when it surged back, it came with a vengeance. For a wild horrible second, she thought she was going to change then and there.

She struggled for control until it felt like hours before she dimly realized that Lizzie was holding her arm. "Becca? Becca, you still in there? Stay with me." The deputy's voice was firm, commanding, and it helped steady Becca, giving her an anchor to pull herself from the past to the present as her lids fluttered open.

A glance at her hands showed nails longer and sharper than they should have been, as well as more than a bit of extra hair. She shook her head and twitched all over like a dog, trying to shake it all off. Even she couldn't change in daylight, and she had more control over her change than most of the other wolves. Even with the damage that the cure had done. This was all in her head. She just needed to find her way out.

She met Lizzie's anxious eyes. "Sorry. Too many memories for a minute there. I'm okay. And yes, that's Leroy all right." And other than the fact that his death had gotten Erin into trouble, she couldn't summon a great deal of sorrow over it. But then, Lizzie probably knew that already and might have even shared the sentiment.

Becca closed her eyes and tried not to inhale much. She rolled through the scents she'd already collected in her wolf brain, cataloguing the ones she recognized. Chemicals, techs, Leroy, death: all of these she knew and dismissed. There were other things in the cocktail of smells: a whiff of Erin which sent a pang through her, and something familiar that twisted and braided itself into Erin's familiar smell.

It was elusive, hovering just at the edge of her consciousness, like a name on the tip of her tongue that stubbornly remained out of reach. Not a person, or at least not one she knew. It was a woodsy scent with a whiff of decay, and her wolf whimpered when she insisted on revisiting it.

But she couldn't seem to recognize anything more than that. Her eyes popped open and she glared at Lizzie, directing her frustration at the first face she saw. "What is it?" The deputy shook her arm a little in an impatient gesture. "What did you smell?"

Becca bit back a growl. "That's it: I didn't. There something that smells familiar, but I have no idea where I've smelled it before." She sighed and pulled her arm free from Lizzie's fingers. "It might be nothing."

Lizzie looked like she'd like to shake Becca's entire body, and not just her arm, but she stepped back and nodded instead. "All right. I'll get you back to the store and we'll see if you can remember anything else later. C'mon." With a nod to the techs, she shepherded Becca out of the morgue and back to the cruiser.

# CHAPTER 10

E RIN WOKE UP, MORE OR less, in the sense that her eyes opened
and she started to notice her surroundings. But her mind
was having trouble making sense of what it was seeing. She was
in a large cage, and that cage was sitting on the concrete floor of
a cinderblock room. There were a couple of small windows but
they'd been blocked off with something, wood probably.

She squinted around in the dim illumination provided by
two single bare bulbs that hung from beams at each end of the
cavernous space. It smelled like dust and humans and damp
and something else, something she couldn't quite process yet.
Beneath that, there was a subtle aroma of engine grease and
old cardboard. *Warehouse*, her brain helpfully supplied after a
few whiffs.

Something whirred above her and she jerked back from
the bars, expecting an attack. A wary look upward and she

recognized a rotating security camera. Her thoughts were still hazy...almost as if she'd been drugged.

Adrenalin surged through her then, leaving her trembling in its wake. She scrambled to her feet but found that she couldn't stand up straight because the cage was too short. Without thinking, she reached out and yanked at the cage door.

"Good, you're back with us. We weren't sure how big a dose to give you." The blonde man from the jail was sitting in a chair in the shadows, watching her.

How had she not smelled him or heard him? Panic surged through her, making her limbs tremble. What had they given her? And who was this guy?

*Jim.* It came back to her a moment later. Their new neighbor. One half of the couple who had taken her from one prison only to put her in another. What the hell was going on? She forced a deep breath into her lungs, then another, trying to will her limbs still and her heart calm. After a moment, she settled back on her heels in a crouch, trying to look cool and collected.

It didn't seem to be working. "I can see you're scared and wondering what you're doing here." Jim rose and walked toward the cage. "Sorry about this, by the way, but we didn't want to take any chances." He gestured, then began to wander around her prison, though to inspect her or it, Erin wasn't sure. "Looking at you, I have to admit that I had a lot of trouble believing the stories. Initially, anyway." He laughed, a guffaw that echoed against the stone walls and showed teeth that glowed white in the dim light.

Erin tried to look harmless as her thoughts whirled. "What stories are those?" Her voice was hoarse and all of a sudden, she would have killed for a drink of water. Her mouth was getting all cottony. There was water nearby, she could smell it. But how safe was it? Could she trust her senses to tell her?

Then she noticed the water-filled tube in the corner of the cage. It looked like the kind of thing that they used to give water to the dogs at the town shelter. Or animals at the zoo. Not a cup in sight either: she'd have to stand on all fours or crouch on her heels to drink directly out of it. There was a pile of straw, a dog's food dish and a pan with dirt in it that looked like a litter box. An icy chill shot through her. They knew that she was going to change.

"I'd offer you a glass, but then you'd just destroy it when the moon rises in a couple of hours." Jim smiled, something twisted lurking at the edges of his thin lips. "We thought we'd help you get comfortable in your wolf form now. After all, you'll be wearing it for a while."

Erin stared at him, her brain willing her body to shift, to tear the cage apart. What did he mean, she'd "be wearing it a while"? He couldn't control the moon or the valley's magic. There was nothing either of them could do to keep her in wolf form. Nor could she think of any reason that they'd want to.

Her memory helpfully supplied the image of Annie, trapped by Wolf's Point's magic in a twisted version of a wolf that was also still visibly human. Was that what he meant? Had these people found some way to do that? Or had they found something that was the reverse of the slayer's cure, one that would stop the change after it had happened, instead of before? Whichever way she looked at it, she needed to get out of here before they succeeded in doing whatever it was that they planned to do.

Jim was smiling at her again when she emerged from her thoughts. "We have to give our audience what it wants, even if it doesn't know what that is yet. I think you'll do nicely. I'll check and see if Kari's done with dinner. You must be hungry by now and we can't have you fainting away on us." He walked over and opened a door buried in the basement's shadows, then disappeared through it.

Erin twisted around to watch him leave. *Audience? What audience?* The thought swirled around in her drug-clouded mind. Did Ken and Barbie have some sort of weird kink? She shuddered at the thought of having either of them attempt to touch her again. Even without any kind of sexual threat, they were gross and creepy and smelled funny. Or at least Ken... Jim did.

She drank in a nose full of the air, trying to nudge her wolf brain awake to analyze what she thought she was smelling. It woke up a little and she felt a small shock run through her. Her body responded sluggishly to the muted danger signals that her other self was trying to send her. Erin shook her head, trying to clear it. She knew she was in danger; of course she was. She'd been drugged and kidnapped and...

It took her another couple of minutes to look around and recognize what else she was seeing. After that, the cameras on their tripods and their old-fashioned big lights, currently turned off, leapt into sharp focus. It didn't take a genius to recognize what they'd be doing with those. They meant to film her change. That had to be it. They were going to show everyone that werewolves were real.

And once that happened, the Pack was doomed. They'd be caged up as a tourist attraction at best, hunted down and killed at worst. Erin closed her eyes for a moment, letting her wolf pull her back into the moment, sharpening her focus, clearing the drugs from her brain.

Then she crawled over to the water and ran some into her cupped hands. She sniffed it warily, then drank. Her body shivered in reaction to the cold water, the shock, whatever she'd been dosed with, and she sat down in a meditation pose, breathing deep.

When her head cleared a little more, she crawled over to the lock on the cage door and began examining it. There had to be a way out of this and she had to find it before it was too late.

# CHAPTER 11

LIZZIE DROPPED BECCA OFF IN front of the store and pulled away, leaving her staring after the deputy's car for a long couple of minutes. Then Becca shook herself back to reality and went inside. Pete was working the register and Shelly was with a customer in the electrical aisle, and for an instant, the glorious calm ordinariness of Peterson's Hardware was nearly enough to make Becca burst into tears.

But crying wasn't going to fix anything. She glanced at the clock and tried to guess how many hours they had left until moonrise. Which was silly since she had an app on her phone that could tell her that immediately, not to mention a wolf in the back of her mind who could tell her with even greater accuracy. But there was something about clock watching that was more comforting, safer, as if she could cope better with the movement of the hands on the dial than the cold digital calculations or the fierceness of her other self.

But this couldn't go on forever, not if she didn't want to find herself unemployed. She forced herself to look away and headed over to Pete. "Want me to take over the counter for a while?"

He looked up and stared at her, his expression distant as if he wasn't really seeing her. For a moment, she felt like she was some sort of weird critter that had wandered into the store. Pete's blue eyes were full of worry and some other things she couldn't read. Then his expression shifted to blandly reassuring. He even smiled, though it didn't look all that real to Becca. "I'm sure it will all be okay, Becca. How about you finish the hardware inventory? I'm waiting on some calls about orders."

Becca slunk off to count nails and stay out of the way for a few hours. After the first hour, she realized it was the perfect task for her, since she could fret and worry to her heart's content and still count as long she updated her little crosshatches every ten items. Next to that, she started a list of everything that could have happened to Erin. It covered everything from catastrophic injury to government cover-up to alien abduction, then looped back again. For variety, she let her fears take a new direction and worried that Pete and Shelly would let her go because she brought too much drama to the store.

"That's very comprehensive. Especially the last one." Shelly's voice over her shoulder made her jump and lose count. "Sorry. I should have realized that you were absorbed. I'm not sure we can completely rule out any of those, if it makes you feel better." She gestured at Becca's list and settled into a crouch at her side. "Except for firing you for being a drama queen. I think we can rule that off the list, at least for the time being." She gave Becca a small smile.

Becca grimaced and pushed the nails back into the plastic container again so she could recount them. "It doesn't. Well, except for the last part. I want to be able to rule out the wackier stuff, but living here, I just can't. There was something about Leroy's body at the morgue, some weird smell that I recognized, but for the life of me I can't remember what it was. And I'm sure it's a clue."

"Hmmm…clue to what, though? Did it smell like a person? Or a place?" Shelly cocked her head to one side, the wolf looking out of her eyes with a golden glow.

Becca could feel her own wolf surge inside in response. She was thinking about this like a human would, a human without a wolf inside her with a better memory for scents than she could ever have. She smacked her hand against her forehead. "I'm an idiot. I need to let the wolf do this part."

Shelly frowned. "Well, yes. But you are your wolf and your wolf is you, it's not some alternate personality thing that happens once a month or so. But that aside, that part of you is going to organize and remember scents a lot better than Becca Thornton."

"Okay, I'm on board. How do I go about doing that? I'm pretty sure I'm not up for changing right now."

"Good. Things would be pretty unstable if you could do it that easily. The easiest thing to do is to retrace your steps, only let your wolf guide you, instead of depending on your memory alone."

"Sort of like that meditation thing you and Erin were trying to get me to experiment with a few weeks back?" Becca frowned, trying to follow what Shelly wanted her to do. Where had she been in the last couple of days? House, hardware store, Shelly and Pete's house, jail, morgue and the town streets in between. That about summed up her life right now. Had she met anyone new?

That was harder. There were the store customers and people on the street when she walked Clyde and the techs at the morgue and the lawyer and the Circle and who knew how many others? It would be easier to think about each place first. She stared down at the box of screws that she was holding. "What about inventory?" she asked, worried that she sounded like an eight-year-old, deprived of the fun of counting screws.

"Kira's going to be here in twenty minutes. I asked her to come by and help after school in case Lizzie kept you for a while. Don't worry, it'll still be here tomorrow. Finish up that box and Molly will go with you to retrace your steps. Two noses are better than one, I always say." Shelly rose and gave Becca a gentle pat on the shoulder before she walked away.

Becca grimaced at the nails. Possibly at the thought of spending a lot of time with Molly, too, but she was less sure about that than she had been a few months ago. She just didn't get Molly. And she hadn't tried as hard as she should have. The unfamiliar words "bi" and "poly" danced through her head. Erin just tossed them around like she'd been using them all her life, leaving Becca to look them up on the internet rather than seem ignorant.

Which she had done, but she still wasn't sure that she got it. Hopefully, Molly would be okay with a little awkwardness until she figured it out.

Right now, she had more important things to worry about. She rolled her shoulders and her neck to try and get the muscles to loosen up. Then she tried to empty her mind of everything except the scent of nails and metal. If she could practice on these, then maybe she could find something that might lead to Erin.

The thought sent a warm rush of hope and longing through her, stopping just short of turning into a hot flash. She wouldn't chicken out this time. When she found Erin again, she was going to tell the other woman exactly how she felt. And she wouldn't be taking no for an answer this time, unless that was how Erin really felt.

Maybe Molly would have some tips. She'd known Erin longer, after all, and she was...all those things that Becca had to look up. She snorted at herself. Molly was Pack, and Molly and her partners had helped rescue her after the slayers had kidnapped her. She didn't need to know any more than that about the other woman to appreciate whatever help she could offer.

When Molly showed up a half an hour later to pick her up, Becca had managed to restore her thoughts to some semblance of order and logic. She also knew more about the smell of individual nails and the plastic container that held them than she had ever believed possible. Whenever she blinked, she had a vision of Molly and her running through the woods on all fours following the scent of one of Erin's shirts. When she opened her eyes and looked at the nails again, that seemed like a perfectly reasonable idea.

"Hi," Molly's voice cut through her latest round of nail staring. "Shelly says you're ready for a break."

Becca looked up and blinked again, letting her wolf brain subside enough to talk. "Hi. As usual, she's completely right. Let me put these away, then we can get started." She rose carefully, half expecting her knees to pop and crack, even though she knew that they wouldn't.

Once the nails were back on their shelf and she had logged their total, she followed Molly up to the desk and handed the clipboard off to Kira. "I'm about a quarter of the way through the nails, if that helps any." From the teenager's expression, it didn't. But she nodded to both of them, took the clipboard and walked over to the shelves with a heavy sigh.

Molly gave Becca a sidelong smile and jerked her head toward the door. "I think by now you'd know if whatever or whoever you smelled was here."

Becca nodded, a little reluctantly. It had been so frustrating trying to remember the scent this afternoon that she wasn't really sure that she wanted to keep trying. Except it might be the only way to find Erin. A rush of guilt filled her and she led the way to the front door at a brisk trot. "I think you're right. Maybe we should start at the house?"

Molly said, "How about we retrace your steps from here to home, then go from there, if nothing else turns up?"

Becca took a deep breath, inhaling the scents of Wolf's Point's downtown: car exhaust, perfume, trash, cleaning fluids, humans, pets. How was she supposed to find something in this mess that was more familiar than anything else? She grimaced in frustration and Molly gave her arm a gentle squeeze.

Becca studied her sidelong for a moment. Molly was a good four inches taller than she was and considerably broader and rounder. Her face was wide and freckled and she had a frequent smile that displayed the gap between her front teeth. Her hand on Becca's sleeve was wide and short-fingered, tanned deep brown from all the years that the other woman had spent outside delivering the mail.

After a moment's consideration, Becca decided that she liked the comfort of Molly's touch and smiled up at her. "We're going to find her by tonight, aren't we? I can just feel it in my bones." She forced a cheer she didn't feel into her tone, then turned and began walking before Molly could say a word in response.

"I guess that tells me how you're doing. Listen, Becca, we'll do everything we can. We'll figure this out. We always do." Molly's nostrils flared too as she took in the surrounding scents and the shadow of the wolf gleamed in her eyes.

That was enough to make Becca bite back what she wanted to say: *What about the times they hadn't figured it out? What about Annie and her family? Margaret?* But she bit her tongue and didn't bring any of that up. It wouldn't help right now.

Instead, she drew a deep, trembling breath and let her wolf rise up, just a bit, and let it have her nose. Her next breath staggered her with a wave of unwanted information and she clutched a parking meter for balance as she fought for control.

Molly held her other arm, letting go once it was obvious that Becca was getting a handle on things. "Learning control was really hard for me the first few times I did it too. Once I start to go wolf, I always want to go all the way." She gave a snorting little laugh. "Carlos…Carla says that's how I do everything. Still getting used to that."

Becca shook her head to clear it, then sucked down another wave of scents. She started walking carefully down the same street that she walked each day, trying to remember if she'd run across anything unusual near any of the shops along the way. "How is Carlos…wait, Carla? And…your other friend? Er… partner." She could feel her face turn beet-red. That really hadn't come out the way that she had imagined it would when she was planning that out in her head. And why was Carlos Carla all of a sudden? Was it okay to ask?

"Jonas. And they're both fine, thanks, just recognizing some changes that have been coming for a while. How's Clyde?" Molly was looking down the street, nostrils flaring as she drank in the breeze. Nothing in her expression suggested that she found the conversation unusual or weird.

"He's a little freaked out. I left him at Shelly and Pete's so he'd have some company." *And to make sure I don't eat him.* Becca rolled her eyes at her own uncertainties and followed Molly's lead, drinking in the gentle breeze that blew down the street toward them. After a long moment of silence, she asked, "So why is Carlos now going by Carla? It's not any of my business, but I don't want to be rude or stupid or…something." She trailed off.

Molly gave her a sidelong glance, as if she was considering whether or not to explain what was going on. Then she stopped and sat down on a nearby bench. She patted the seat beside her and Becca sat down. Molly cleared her throat. "Okay, this is going to take a couple of minutes. Polyamory and trans 101, but just the very short recap because we can talk about it more later and we've got important stuff to do. Carla and I are married and Jonas is our partner. This is how we do a polyamorous relationship, but there are lots of other ways to do it too. We talk through all relationship-impacting decisions together and do a lot of negotiating and that's how we've managed to stay together for the last ten years." She took in a deep breath and poked something in the grass with her shoe. Becca couldn't tell if she was fidgeting or really looking at something for a few seconds.

Then she continued, "I think Carlos has known for a long time that she was really Carla, but I don't think she was ready to let the rest of us meet her. Just being able to talk about it and to use a name and a pronoun that feels right to her was a big change. She started taking hormones a few months ago and is looking at surgery. Jonas and I have been doing a lot of reading and going to a support group with her so we can support her.

I'm still wrestling with how I feel about some of it and making sure I've got her real name and pronouns right, so, because I know you're a stickler for being polite and you notice things, remind me when I slip up, okay? I haven't told anyone else yet. Didn't get a chance to tell Erin." She sighed deeply and Becca rested a hand on her shoulder and squeezed lightly.

"Erin was wondering about Carlos…Carla when we were over for dinner a few weeks back, so I think she has a notion. She thought that she was getting ready to come out, but Erin wasn't sure who that new person would be."

Molly smiled, then choked like she was holding back tears. It was funny, Becca thought. She could turn into a wolf with someone and wake up naked with them and still not know if it was okay to hug them. She reached out carefully and put her arm around Molly's shoulders.

"I miss her so much too." Becca choked, then swallowed her tears back down. "And I'll try. Keep reminding me, too. Carla tried to help me when Annie and her men were holding me, not to mention helping find me in that ditch after I got away from them, so I owe hi—her a couple." They leaned into each other in companionable silence, like they did when they were wolves, and drank in the air together.

After a few minutes, Molly cleared her throat. "Mind if I ask you something?"

Becca blinked, immediately on edge. But then, it wasn't as if she could say no, not after what they'd just talked about. "Sure," she responded, trying to ease the hesitation in her voice.

"Are you and Erin together? Or just roommates?" Molly was giving her a very direct look, brown eyes boring into the side of her skull to read her thoughts. No, wait, that was just the hormones talking.

Becca grimaced and thought for a few moments about how best to answer that. "We're...kind of together. Only not very? I've never been with a woman before and I'm still kind of sorting things out. But I really, really like her. And I think she's sexy!" Becca felt her face flush. "Or was that TMI? I don't even know what to call...whatever it is we are. Whatever I am. I don't know if I'm bisexual or lesbian or what." She drew in a deep, quavering breath. "But I think bisexual sounds about right. I just hate not knowing the rules." Once she'd said it, she felt lighter, like all this uncertainty had been weighing on her.

Molly tilted her head, her expression considering. "Well, questioning is always good at this stage. I think you can be someone who likes Erin a lot and is trying to figure out what your relationship will be. I don't know that it requires a label." She paused. "Though I would love to have another out bi gal in the Pack, don't get me wrong. But I don't think my desire for camaraderie has any bearing on how you should identify." She chuckled a little.

There was a brief silence as they both figured out what to say next. Then Molly added, "I was around when Erin's ex dumped her and it frankly sucked for a while. She's such a great person and a good friend and I want her to be happy." She must have sensed Becca's tension because she added, "And I like what I've seen of you too. I'm not wanting to butt in, just hoping you two crazy kids sort it out in a way that makes you both happy, okay?"

Becca studied her for a long couple of minutes. "Thank you. Yes, that helps."

"And you can talk to me about this if you need to."

"That really helps a lot too." Becca grinned at her. "Let's try and find her so I can angst at her in person." Molly gave her a fist bump and they went back to searching for a trace of Erin on the street around them

Nothing except the ordinary scents of downtown Wolf's Point came their way at first. Becca could feel her shoulders slump. If she was better at this, maybe they'd have found Erin by now. Unless Erin was on the run outside the valley. Then maybe—she broke up her thoughts with a fierce shake of her head. "Maybe we should get Clyde for this job. Probably be better at it than I am."

Molly nudged her with one elbow, the gentle contact steadying her. Being with Molly like this reminded her of when she had first changed with the Pack and how scared she'd been until they all laid down together on the floor of the Pack's cave. The pressure of warm wolves around her, the sense that they were all connected, had been enough to center her then. And now—Becca's head shot up, her nostrils flaring to gulp the air in. "There! That smells familiar! Coming from over there." She surged off across the street, Molly at her heels.

# CHAPTER 12

B Y THE TIME BECCA GOT back to the house, she was exhausted. She and Molly had been running for hours: lope, stop, sniff, analyze, repeat. It had happened so often that she was beginning to be afraid that she'd never smell anything again. They kept thinking they had found a trail, only to lose those elusive scents and end up running around in circles. All that work to come up with a big fat zero.

Becca dropped into the swing on the porch and rubbed her face hard, trying not to cry. Why was this so hard? It was as if whoever took Erin knew how to cover their trail. What if she was dead or injured? Or maybe she had escaped on her own and didn't want to be found. That thought hit her just below the solar plexus.

She blinked back her tears and looked around without really seeing the garden beds that needed some work, the red paint chipping on the porch wall, the crooked third step. All the things that she and Erin had been planning to fix. What was she going to do if Erin wasn't coming back? This wasn't her house, not really. Erin's name was on the title, not hers. She didn't even have a lease, let alone a legal right to keep this place.

At least if the worst happened, she'd be able to buy herself a condo or another place to live with the cash she got from Ed, but leaving this house felt like it meant giving up on Erin too. A few more minutes of this and Becca thumped the back of her head gently against the wooden back of the swing. At this rate, she was going to worry herself into an early grave, and much good that would do anyone.

A sound from the empty house behind her broke into her thoughts before her attention could drift any further. All at once, Becca was on red alert, ears and nose working overtime. Had Erin escaped and come here to hide out? That didn't make any sense, but her heart leapt anyway, alive with hope and longing for an instant. It hurt to let go of that, especially to replace it with the realization that if Erin had escaped on her own, she'd have gone to the mountains, maybe some place near the Pack's cave. That was the only sensible thing to do.

So it had to be someone else. Family member or friend of Erin's she hadn't met, maybe? A Pack member with a key who had forgotten to mention that she was stopping by? Or just a run-of-the-mill break-in? The thought that this horrible day could end with something as mundane as a burglary almost nearly made Becca laugh out loud. That impulse died away quickly, leaving her shaking with reaction. Maybe she should go get Gladys, since she was the Pack member who lived closest. It would be good to have company to confront the intruder or whoever this was.

The sound moved further away from her, as if the intruder was working their way toward the back door. Becca's hesitation vanished and she rose quietly from the swing and tiptoed off the porch, carefully avoiding the creaking step. If she wanted to find out who this was, there wasn't time to go get help. She'd have to go check it out on her own.

Bent low, she dashed to the side of the house and began creeping down the path to the backyard. A couple of scraggly bushes alongside the house provided some cover for her as she tried to peer into the side windows. A quick glance at their next-door neighbors showed no lights in their windows, so at least they wouldn't wonder what she was up to. Of course, they wouldn't be around to help, either. Becca swallowed hard and kept moving. If she was sneaky enough, she could hide in the bushes or behind the backyard tree and see who this was without being seen herself.

Part of her wanted to go on the offensive and attack the minute they emerged from the house. More than a part, if she was being honest. All of her fears about Erin, her rage about what had happened, boiled up. She wanted to punch something. No, that wasn't it. She wanted to rend someone's throat with her teeth.

She blinked and shook her head as a blood-red haze settled over her vision at the thought. Her heart pounded as if she'd been running and she trembled with the effort it took not to give in. Becca stuck her fingers into the lawn and tried to send all the energy surging through her downward, into the earth. She wasn't going to maul someone for trying to take the TV, if that's what they were up to, she promised herself that much.

The sounds from inside the house got quiet, as if the intruder was closer to the back door, maybe looking outside.

Or perhaps headed for the basement or upstairs. Becca yanked her fingers out of the dirt and shot forward to the edge of the house in a crouch. Her whole body trembled with conflicting impulses: attack, stalk, run for help, hide. She forced one breath after another into her lungs and pressed up against the corner of the house, listening and sniffing, before she risked a glance around the corner.

The backyard was empty and the back door was still closed, but she could hear noises in the kitchen again. What the hell were they doing in there? She added impatience to the list of things she was feeling right now and forced herself to wait, forced her body into stillness. *Hunting. We are hunting.* Her wolf grinned in the back of her mind, settling in to wait.

Finally, just as if felt like she was about to lose control of her human self, the back door swung open slowly. She pulled her head back as someone stepped out to look around. They closed the door quietly behind them and walked down the steps, clearly taking the time to be quiet and avoid notice.

Becca glanced at the neighbors across the alley, but realized they probably couldn't see anything beyond their hedge. She wondered whose attention this person was trying to avoid if their neighbors were out or out of sight. Maybe they had seen her in the yard. She gulped in a big breath and jerked upright. Enough of this, she was going to confront them, whoever they were.

An instant later, doubt set in. She wasn't much of a fighter, not as a human anyway. What was she going to do, chase them around the yard at better-than-average middle-aged lady speed, then nibble on them, after she knocked them over, assuming she could manage that much? She pulled her phone quietly from her pocket and unlocked it to turn on the camera. Picture, then call Lizzie, then Shelly: that sounded a lot more feasible.

She heard them reach the bottom step and spun around the corner, camera in hand.

That, of course, was when the Sanchez family next door got home. "Hey, Becca," George Sanchez yelled from outside his garage. "What's going on?"

Becca yelled, "Burglar!" in response as she scrambled after the intruder, now racing away on the uneven brickwork of their back garden path. Whoever they were, they wore a black hoodie and maybe a mask, she couldn't be sure in the dim light, even with wolf-enhanced vision. And they were faster than she was, at least in this form. She snapped as many photos as she could, hoping the camera would catch something she hadn't yet.

She stopped at the back gate, cursing quietly under her breath as she sucked in a deep whiff of their scent, trying to imprint it on her brain. Mr. Sanchez dashed around the garage into the back alley they all used as a driveway, whether to try to catch a glimpse of the fleeing burglar or to catch them, Becca couldn't be sure, but she gave him points for effort. She could hear Cecilia Sanchez calling the Sheriff's Department, their kids shrieking in excitement as they piled out of the car, but it all came from far away, as if she were dreaming.

Her wolf brain was telling her something now that couldn't be true and she kept rejecting it, over and over again, until she realized what she was doing. She exhaled with a trembling sigh, trying to accept this weird new bit of information: the burglar smelled like Erin.

# CHAPTER 13

E RIN SAT UP CAUTIOUSLY AND banged her head against the metal bars that surrounded her. With a quiet curse, she got on all fours and crawled across the cage to splash water on her face, hoping it would clear her aching head. Then she started circling, wincing a little as the bars dug into her knees. It was on her fourth uncomfortable, cramped trip around the cage that a glimmer of an idea began to occur to her. It vanished as quickly as it appeared and she cursed softly again. It was still so hard to focus or even to really look around; her vision was only slightly less fuzzy than her brain.

Start with food and water, she decided. That would tell her something about what her captors had planned. She crawled over to the water and studied it. The cage's plastic water tank was attached to a hose that led to a nearby utility sink. She unplugged the plastic tube that hung into the cage, then plugged it and unplugged it again. The water kept running. At least they weren't going to let her die of thirst, so that was something. She sniffed cautiously, then drank a few thirsty gulps from the tube.

Food was less plentiful. There was a bowl of jerky and dried fruit under the water container. After a covert lick or two to test it for, well, whatever they might have put in it, she sat down and devoured its contents. If it was drugged, it was nothing she could smell or taste; she'd have to hope for the best if she wanted to be ready for...whatever was going to happen next.

Erin finished eating and rolled her head slowly from side to side, both to loosen up her neck and to make sure that her sense of disorientation had faded. Then she took another good look at her surroundings. At first, there wasn't much to see that she hadn't seen before. The warehouse was set up like a TV studio, or at least what she thought a TV studio looked like, complete with big lights and cameras, their cords running all around the floor. Metal cabinets lined the far wall and there were a couple of broken chairs and a table.

There were no windows and only one door that she could see. *Limited escape routes.* She added that to the list of things she needed a solution for. *Drugged werewolf. Weird kidnappers who knew what she was. Moonrise coming soon. Was, no, might be, a murderer and definitely the target of a police hunt by now.* Maybe she should quit while she was ahead. At least Ken, or whatever his name was, wasn't sitting in a chair watching her now.

Then she spotted the red gleaming light of a camera on the wall pointed at her cage. So they were keeping an eye on her after all. She drew a deep breath and tried to steady her nerves, trying to find some reassurance to dampen the rising flood of panic that was beginning to fill her. A treacherous part of her mind suggested that a drink might calm her down; she tried to stifle that as fast as she could. Good thing that wasn't an option right now, at least.

Her panicked brain found a momentarily comforting thought to fill its place: there had been cameras at the jail too; Shelly and the Pack would figure out what happened and they would come for her. *Becca* would come for her, somehow. Erin clung to that idea, wrapping herself in it like a cocoon for a few moments. Maybe she could figure out where she was. That might tell her how likely a speedy rescue was coming. If nothing else, it would distract her.

She closed her eyes and stretched out her other human senses, as far as they would go. When that didn't yield much, she let her wolf out as far as she could. The moon called her, but not as sharply as it had back at the jail. Past midnight and heading for morning, then, assuming she was functioning at something close to normal.

They'd taken her after dark and she'd been out long enough for them to haul her unconscious body from her cell and drive somewhere. They had to be close to Wolf's Point. There hadn't been enough time to get to Mountainview or one of the other towns. So they were somewhere not too far away from town in an old warehouse. Maybe an abandoned building?

She wracked her brain trying to remember where there were old and unused warehouses near the jail. There had been that lumber place out on the highway, the one that had closed up three years ago. Could this be it? She inhaled deeply, trying to smell the ghosts of trees turned into planks.

Sure enough, there was something there, just a hint of what might have been here before. But she couldn't be sure. Maybe it was a different warehouse. Or maybe they just hadn't processed or stored lumber in this room. Regardless of which building she was in, the Pack would need time to find her, no matter what. She drank in another deep, shuddering breath to calm her nerves and find her resolve. She would have to find some way to buy them that time.

And that was when that snippet of an idea came back to her, crystal clear this time around. Erin opened her eyes and looked straight at the camera. She'd start with the easiest thing she could do, then ramp up from there until something worked. "Hey! Hey! I need to use the john! Give me a break—I ain't pissing in here and I don't want to drop my pants for your entertainment." She scowled at the red light and drummed her fingers impatiently against the cage's metal floor. "Isn't this against the Geneva Convention or something?"

She tried to look as pathetic as she could and scrunched down into a ball. Pathetic was coming pretty easy to her right now, what with how this night was going. Before she could stop it, a tear rolled down her cheek. She wrapped her knees in her arms and lowered her head, letting out a sob that was only partially faked.

It took a long couple of minutes to get a response, and when it came, it showed up in the form of Barbie with a taser. The blonde woman glared warily into the cage. "Don't you try anything. I'm not afraid to use this." She gestured with the taser and Erin nodded warily, holding her hands up in a gesture of surrender.

Barbie unlocked the cage door and stood back as Erin crawled out and tried to stand. It took a couple of tries and by the time she was upright, her bladder was screaming. She lurched forward in the direction that her captor gestured, stumbling across the obstacles in her path until she could see a second door on the other side of the cabinets. Barbie herded her through it into a short, dark hallway and then into a spare industrial style bathroom with concrete walls and an open stall.

She hit a switch and a bare light bulb blazed from the ceiling. "Hurry up."

Erin lurched into the stall, not even caring that there wasn't a door. At least her captor had the good grace to look away when she dropped her trousers. A moment of clarity came along with her sense of relief: Ken didn't know Barbie was doing this. There was something in the woman's tone, the way she shifted from foot to foot and kept glancing nervously at the door that gave her away.

Erin finished and stood up, pulling her pants back on while leaning against the stall wall to keep her balance. Now to try Plan A. "Thanks." She tucked her shirt back in and walked out, moving slowly and carefully. "Mind if I wash my hands?"

Barbie nodded, a little frown knitting her eyebrows together. "You're not what I expected."

Erin gave the other woman's reflection in the broken mirror a wry smile. "I can't even imagine what you think I am. I'm not worth much, you know. No one's going to pay a ransom."

"We're not waiting on a ransom." Barbie's face had gone blank again and she gestured at the door with the taser. "Let's go back now."

Erin staggered a little, catching herself on the wall before she reached for the door. Maybe she could tackle her captor? A quick assessment of her balance and reflexes told her she was still fighting off the drugs. She'd just get herself tased for nothing. Keep talking then, and see what she could find out. "So why are you doing this? You might as well tell me."

She trailed her hand along the cold hallway wall as she moved slowly back toward the room with the cage in it. The point between her shoulder blades prickled and she wondered for a terrifying instant if Barbie was going to zap her for asking too many questions. Her feet wove an unsteady path forward as she tried to look around. The cameras and equipment were older than they had looked at first. There was a lot of electrical tape on the wires and the lights and cameras didn't match each other, some clearly older than others. This was a low budget operation, whatever it was.

"We're doing this to get rich. You're going to make us reality TV rock stars, pumpkin. Now get back in the damn cage before I have to use this thing." Barbie's voice was distant, cold, and Erin glanced sidelong at the camera. It blinked. Ken must be back from where ever he had gone. Or maybe they had a whole crew with them.

Reality TV stars. *Oh shit.* It confirmed all of her worst fears and her brain chased its thoughts like a tail all over the place as Barbie opened the cage back up. She had to do something to stop them, but what?

She clambered awkwardly back inside and watched Barbie lock her back in. She slumped against the far side away from the door and tilted her head back to catch the other woman's gaze. *Something. There had to be a way to sidetrack this.* "No one is ever going to believe it, you know. They'll just think it's bad special effects and you won't make anything off that."

She had the satisfaction of seeing her captor flinch before she stomped off. Erin closed her eyes, trying to make the last of the fuzziness leave her brain and body. She was going to have to be alert for whatever she decided to do next. If she wasn't up for fighting her way out, maybe she could send a signal to the Pack. But how? Her brain swirled with what little she'd seen of the warehouse on the way to and from the bathroom. There had to be something she could use, somehow.

She tilted her head back, and after a few minutes, fell into a light doze. When she woke up again, her head was clear. She crawled over to the water tube and took a long drink before plugging it back up. Something caught her eye: a glint of copper wire that had worked free from the tape on one of the electrical cords that surrounded her cage. It was a couple of feet away but as she squinted at it, she realized that she could see other worn spots on some of the other cords.

The water tube squeaked beneath her fingers and she looked up, following the path of the plastic tubing up the bars, then out to the distant sink on the wall. The tube was fastened to the bars with plastic ties, nothing fancy. Or particularly sturdy. She leaned over so that her body blocked the camera and tested one of them. It took a few minutes of twisting and pulling, but the lowest tie broke fairly easily. She could stretch the water tube a few inches in and out of the cage now.

Erin grinned, sat up and stretched as well as she could within the confines of her prison. She twisted around like she was trying to work out a kink in her back and snapped the next lowest tie, then the one above it. Then she pulled the stopper from the tube and stuck it as far outside the cage as she could, sending a small stream of water cascading over the floor toward the electrical cords.

Fortunately for her, the floor sloped just enough to carry the water toward her target and not back into the cage. She propped the tube on one of the lower bars and watched a pool form under one of the light stands, gradually expanding out toward the cords. She let the water run long enough to soak the area, then pulled the tube back in and plugged it. Then she twisted a few of the broken ties around it to make it look like nothing had changed. Maybe they'd think they had a broken pipe or something.

Now there was nothing to do but wait for the water to do its thing. She dropped her head down onto her knees to make it look like she had fallen asleep again. After a few minutes, a sharp burnt smell drifted her way and Erin grinned quietly, then grimaced. Hopefully, Ken and Barbie would come back and save her from an actual fire, because if they didn't, she was in a lot of trouble. But if this worked, a few shorts in the warehouse's electrical system should be enough to send their little reality television dreams up in smoke.

She pulled her shirt up over her nose and waited for the slight burning smell to intensify. There was a small shower of sparks and a cloud of burning metal and plastic began to overwhelm her wolf-sensitive nose. She took a few shallow breaths, and when she could stop coughing, she started yelling and waving her arms at the camera.

# CHAPTER 14

BECCA SCOWLED AT GLADYS ACROSS Shelly's dining room table. "I don't know why the burglar smelled like Erin. They didn't look like Erin, at least not from what I could see. Which wasn't much. And yes, I tried to follow the scent, but they ran really fast, then took off in a car." This was the third time she'd gone over what had happened and she was beginning to get cranky about it.

Who knew? Maybe the burglar had rubbed Erin's clothes behind his ears or something for some weird reason. For that matter, all he appeared to have taken were some of Erin's clothes. It was creepy as all get out, the more she thought about it. But going over and over it wasn't helping a bit.

Wait, why did she suddenly think that the intruder had been a he?

"What is it? What did you just remember?" Mrs. Hui leaned forward, staring intently at her.

*Lin. She said to call her "Lin."* Becca frowned, trying to focus. "I might be just assuming this, but I think the intruder was a guy, now that I'm thinking about it. There was something about the way he moved and carried himself. I'm not absolutely sure though."

Shelly rubbed her eyes, then ran her fingers down her cheeks and let them come to rest under her chin. She looked exhausted. Molly silently poured a cup of coffee from the pot in the middle of the table and pushed it over to her. Shelly gave her a grin of thanks, then turned back to Becca. "You said that whoever it was, they moved faster than a normal human?"

Becca nodded, reaching for the coffee pot after Molly put it back. Her stomach growled loudly, reminding them that lunch was overdue. Shelly grimaced. "Right. Let's a take a break and eat something. We're running out of time; hopefully, food shakes loose some inspiration or memories." She shoved her chair back and they all trailed after her into the kitchen.

Before Becca knew it, she found herself participating in an assembly line that was cranking out sandwiches and putting them on plates, slicing fruit, pulling out handfuls of tortilla chips and more. Gladys caught her eye and mouthed "teenagers" and Becca giggled despite herself. Maybe Gladys had her moments, after all. Shelly and Pete's kids, Kira and the twins, were some of the best-behaved kids in Wolf's Point. Looking at how Shelly was organizing the Pack now, it wasn't hard to see why.

Becca followed Molly out and sat back down at the table with her plate. They all passed around the water pitcher and condiments before settling in to eat in silence, something that made her pretty happy after all the questions. She tried to not make herself think about the burglar anymore. Maybe if she stopped thinking so hard, she'd remember something more useful.

Molly was the first to speak up and break up the quiet. "You know, it feels like we just run from crisis to crisis, and sometimes I think we all don't know each other as well we should, apart from emergencies. Why don't we try going around and sharing something about our lives, something that doesn't have anything to do with the Pack?" She caught Shelly's eye and added, "Really short shares."

Shelly frowned and Becca watched her glance dart toward the clock. They were all thinking it: *there was no time, Erin was in trouble, they had to do something.* Shelly wrinkled her nose as if she could hear what they were all thinking, then shrugged. "You have a point, Molly. But you're right about keeping it short too. We can try a longer version after we...get Erin back."

Molly nodded. "I'll start. When I'm not working at the Post Office or, you know, doing stuff with you fine ladies, I play the ukulele with my partner who some of you know as Carlos, but who now goes by Carla, and who I'll be referring to as my wife in the future. Our boyfriend Jonas and some other friends play instruments too and we have a super casual band." She gave them all a cheerful gap-toothed grin. "Who's next?"

Becca saw a few blinks and one or two puzzled frowns, but no one asked anything. She caught Molly's eye and smiled at her, catching Shelly's approving nod from the corner of her eye. Had her previous jealousy been that obvious? Or was Shelly just glad that she was being supportive? She winced a little, then made herself focus on the other members of the Pack.

Lin Hui was next, as it turned out. White-haired and poised, she met each woman's eyes as she looked around the table. "I speak Mandarin, Vietnamese and French and a bit of several other languages. When the hospital in Mountainview needs a backup translator, they call me. I also volunteer at Circle House when I'm not working at our restaurant or on Pack business or spending time with my family." After a moment of silence, she added, "I believe that this will be my last season of running with the Pack. I'm feeling more fragile and Circle House is calling to my spirit." There was a moment of stunned silence, suggesting that several Pack members were holding their breath.

The moment passed, leaving a sense of quiet shock in its wake, and Lin nodded to the woman on her right before anyone could say anything else. Gladys went after that. She, it turned out, belonged to a Scrabble club and had played at tournaments. Shelly had been a star basketball player in high school and college, until an injury sidelined her. She still played pick-up games with Kira and her friends and did some volunteering with the high school girls' basketball team. Adelía Rodriguez made pottery in her family's garage and hoped to get good enough at it to sell her work one day.

And then everyone was looking at Becca. *Oh crap, I've got nothing.* The realization gave a sinking feeling in the pit of her stomach. She worked at the hardware store, she lived with Erin and Clyde, she had volunteered at the Women's Club before it burned down and she turned into a wolf once a month: wasn't that enough? "I like to read books? Mysteries, fantasies, romances and whatever else looks good, things like that." She could hear her voice tilt up when she said it, like she was nervous and asking for approval.

"Cool," Molly responded. "We used to have a good book club at the Women's Club before, well, it went up in smoke. We should start that up again. Speaking of which, any word on the insurance settlement?"

Lin nodded. "The Board should have an update in a couple of weeks. We've been talking to architects and contractors about what it will take to rebuild. I'll be able to tell you more soon."

A chorus of happy responses swept the room. Becca didn't realize that anyone missed the Club as much as she did. It was good to be proven wrong. But if they didn't get Erin back safely, it wouldn't be the same. Nothing would. She chewed her lip, anxiety warring with the general warm fuzzies that everyone was still expressing about the Club news.

Shelly caught her eye and nodded. "Everyone done eating? Okay, I know we'll need to continue some of these conversations, but for now let's clean up. I think I have an idea that might be helpful for getting Erin back from wherever she is." A few moments later, the dishes were in the dishwasher and they were all assembled in the living room.

Shelly pushed aside a woven rug on one of the walls to reveal a whiteboard. "Sometimes it helps to be old-fashioned." She made a quick list of what they already knew and what Becca had told them. "I think we've established that either Erin escaped on her own, which looks unlikely, or she was taken from the jail. Becca's burglar suggests the latter, like someone knows about her and is trying to found out more. If they're holding her someplace, they'd want her to have clothes to change into. At this point, I want to split those of us who don't have to get back to work right away into three teams: one to look at all the locations near town where you could hide out or hide someone else, one to go to the cave, and one to go check out Erin and Becca's place from top to bottom and see what we can find. Any questions or other thoughts?"

Molly nodded. "I do need to get back to work, but I can help with whatever needs doing when I get off shift again. I'll ask around at the Post Office about businesses and homes that have stopped getting mail or that look unoccupied." She left, leaving the others to their tasks. Lin pulled up some county maps on the Pack laptop and started comparing the real estate listings.

Becca turned over her house keys to Gladys and Adelía, somewhat reluctantly. She realized that Shelly was right and they needed a fresh set of noses, but a little irrational voice in her mind howled, *Any clues are mine. I get to find Erin. I get to save Erin.* And she wasn't that eager to get back to the cave, with its weight of ritual and magic and other things that she didn't understand as well as she wanted to. But Shelly had picked her as her teammate for that task so there wasn't much she could say about that.

She trailed after Shelly to the cars, and they had started to get into Shelly's truck when she got a call from Lizzie. Becca went over to give Clyde a skritch, relieved to see that he looked happy and playful, clearly enjoying the company of the other dogs, but glad to see her anyway. By the time she wandered back, Shelly was still talking to Lizzie, but they'd switched languages to the one their tribe spoke and Becca no longer understood what was going on.

Shelly handed her the keys and they climbed in as she kept talking to Lizzie. Becca started driving as Shelly's voice reached a frustrated higher pitch. It wasn't too hard to figure out that Lizzie was pushing her to reveal what she know about Erin and Shelly was pushing back. Becca sighed quietly. Even after they got Erin back, they'd still have to deal with the body and the murder charges and the lawyer and...

The phone conversation ended with an exasperated growl from Shelly as she clicked off and put her phone back in her pocket. "It shouldn't be this hard. We all know how badly she wants to be in the Pack, but if this is how it's going to be when the Pack and Sheriff's Department are in conflict, I don't see how she'll be able to balance the two. Especially not if she decides to run for sheriff." Shelly rubbed her eyes and closed them for a moment.

"She thinking about that?" Becca gave her a surprised quick glance. Sheriff Henderson had had his position since long before she moved to town and he looked to be pretty entrenched.

"She is, and that would make her a lot of firsts if she won. So there's a lot riding on solving this murder from her perspective and she's feeling the pressure. I know she doesn't want it to be Erin, but she's torn."

"I don't understand why Erin confessed. And if she did do it, why kill Leroy now? There's gotta be something more going on here." Becca's frustration was calling up her wolf. The full moon was too close, there were too many questions unanswered, they had to find Erin—a growl popped out of her mouth, startling both of them.

"That does sum it up, yep." Shelly rolled down the window and took a deep breath as Becca turned off onto the road that led up toward the path to the Pack's cave. They sat in silence for a few moments until they got to the turnoff and Becca parked the truck.

"Did you ever find out what happened to Annie, I mean, *after* what happened to Annie?" She grabbed the daypack with the water bottles and supplies and slung it over her shoulder as they locked up and started hiking.

Shelly glanced back at her. "You remember what they told us at Circle House? We all hoped that she'd turn out okay, back in the beginning, despite everything. Poor Margaret." They hiked in silence for a few minutes before Shelly continued, "We've been looking for her since she changed and there's been a sighting here and there. A missing chicken or some stolen food. But that's been it so far. She's definitely still alive."

Becca tried to decide if this was the best time to ask about Margaret, but realized that she needed to save her breath for the trail. They hiked in silence, each lost in her own thoughts, stopping only to drink some water at the halfway mark before continuing upward. Becca wondered what Shelly hoped to find in the cave: spiritual guidance, perhaps? Erin hiding out?

That last thought made her heart leap. That would solve all...well, some of their problems. They could keep her safe somewhere nearby until they figured out who killed Leroy or the lawyers found a solution or...

They arrived at the ledge outside the cave, distracted and slightly out of breath. Neither was expecting a hurtling furry body to charge out of the opening. It knocked Shelly over and pushed Becca dangerously close to the cliff edge as the snarling mouth and ferocious claws sent them scrambling out of the way. The creature paused for a moment and studied them from a few feet away, as if it was thinking about attacking them.

Shelly answered with a snarl of her own that turned her eyes golden and sent a ripple of dark fur growing over her skin. She started to scramble to her feet as Becca recovered her balance and grabbed a loose rock from the ground nearby. The creature stared at them for a heartbeat more, then bolted off on the narrow and treacherous path that led up the mountain. An instant later, it vanished from view.

"Annie?" Becca gasped. The creature smelled like her, and how many other half-wolf monsters were there in the valley? The moment she had the thought, she regretted it. Given all the things she didn't know yet and all that she had recently, it was likely that there was more than one and no one had mentioned it yet.

Shelly was shivering all over and staring upward with golden eyes. She'd stopped changing for the moment, but it was clear that she wanted to pursue Annie or whoever that had been. In another moment, she'd be lost to anything that Becca could suggest.

"Maybe just follow their trail while I check out the cave? It would be safer to save any attacks for when the whole Pack is here." Becca's voice trembled. The wolf called her too, but not enough to transform, even if she'd had Shelly's level of control. She just knew that they couldn't lose Shelly, not now. Annie was dangerous no matter what form she took.

Her Alpha growled something that might have been agreement and let the change take her. A few moments later, a medium-sized wolf, brown and black with silver highlights, stood in front of Becca. An instant after that, the wolf was loping up the mountain at a ground-covering, but cautious, pace. Becca watched her for a moment, then sighed. "Right. I'll go try and figure out what she or they were doing in here, if I can."

She picked up the pack and walked into the cave, letting the cool dimly lit darkness pull her in until it was ready to reveal what it knew.

# CHAPTER 15

**M**OONRISE WAS COMING. ERIN COULD feel it in her blood, even though her captors had locked her away in a concrete room without windows after the mysterious flood. They had come in with a fire extinguisher when the sparks turned to flames and they put them out before all the equipment caught fire. Unfortunately. But at least it looked like it had been enough to take out a few of the big lights and damage the camera wiring, as far as Erin could tell. She could only hope that would be enough to set their schedule, whatever it was, back, and for her to get out of here.

Since she had had plenty of time to think in her new prison, she started mulling over what would happen if they did actually manage to film her change. Most people would dismiss it out of hand as a trick, but that wouldn't do her much good. It likely wouldn't be great for her accounting business or for Becca either. And then there was the pesky matter of the murder charges that she was facing. She couldn't imagine that Lizzie and the other deputies wouldn't be all over a video like that if it went viral or something. Maybe she could get Barbie and Ken busted for harboring a fugitive, with no effort on her part.

A dry laugh shook her shoulders and she went back to pacing around the room. Four paces down one side, seven paces down the other and she was ready to change right now. Frustration, anger, much of it at herself, as well as fear for her friends: all of it roiled inside her, driving her wolf from its sleep until she was ready to sprout fur. She growled softly. Stress made her volatile and the wolf running through her head made that worse.

But at least she wasn't craving a drink. No more than usual, anyway. She stopped pacing and rubbed her hands over her face. If this entire situation wasn't enough to make her seriously want to fall off the wagon, what was? If she'd had a blackout up in the mountains, what was it from? Where did she get the booze?

Her memory helpfully pulled up a picture of the bloody body in the trunk and she shied away from it. She knew the taste of bloodlust, the flavor of the hunt, the rage of fighting a threat to her Alpha, her Pack, her loved ones...but this? It wasn't as if she'd ever been an angry drunk, so even if she had somehow managed to get drunk enough to black out, why did she do this?

Now that she'd had a nice long stretch to do nothing but think about it, calling Lizzie and confessing hadn't been her smartest move. She remembered how freaked out Becca and Shelly had been, how they'd tried to reach her and how she'd tried to drive them away. A huge wave of guilt and remorse swept over her. She dropped into the sagging army cot that served her for both bed and couch in her cell and bent over to bury her head in her hands.

She whispered all the things she learned in recovery that made her feel better: poetry, prayers, song lyrics. Not one of them was enough to deal with her wave of emotion on their own, but twenty minutes of them, melded together like a mix tape in her head, were oddly soothing. Her emotions and thoughts began to slow down, enough to think anyway.

What emerged from that was the startling suspicion that maybe she'd been played. Maybe she'd blacked out for some other reason and someone stashed a body in her trunk while she was out of it? The thought staggered her. She'd been up in the mountains for a day's hike. Who could have known that she was there? Did they just have a body handy or did they kill someone, then realize that she was there to frame for it? Was she just convenient?

The sound of the lock turning yanked her out of her head. Ken...*Jim* walked in carrying a plastic tray, a taser conspicuously sticking out underneath it. "Only two more hours until the fireworks start! We thought you might want a solid meal in your stomach for all the commotion." He grinned, white teeth perfectly straight in a smile that could only have had dental assistance. There was a cloud of scent around him too, like he bathed in essential oils or cologne before deciding to inflict his company on her.

Erin wrinkled her nose at him, then glanced at the tray and took a quick sniff of that instead. Meat, potatoes, some green vegetables, all formerly frozen and reheated. Nothing that would drug her or slow her down, which surprised her. They must be hoping that she would be a classic monster putting on a good show when the moon rose.

A memory of the body in her trunk flashed through her mind and she flinched. Maybe they were right and she was a monster. Maybe she deserved this.

"Cat got your tongue?" He kept grinning and moved a little closer, taser now leveled at her. "Catching you was quite the coup. You're going to make us rich, little lady." Erin tilted her sideways and looked up at him. Something in her face made him step back and she bared her teeth in an expression that might have been a smile, but clearly wasn't.

"I don't know what you two think is going to happen, but let's say that I do turn into something, maybe the monster that you think I'll become. Who's going to believe that you didn't edit a video, that it isn't fake? Who's going to pay attention to you two, whatever you are…failed newscasters? Ex-models? Disgraced politicians?" A dim memory awakened; she had seen Jim and Kari before, a long time ago. They had been on television for…something, but she couldn't remember what.

Jim glared at her, pale skin flushing, eyes narrowing. "You think you're so clever, don't you? We'll see how smart you look when the moon comes up!" He glanced at his wrist. "Only two more hours to go before everyone gets to see you as you really are."

"As I really am?" Erin sat down on the bed and leaned back against the wall. This was getting weird and he was starting to sweat. She could see his hand begin to shake. He held all the cards here, what did he have to be nervous about?

She decided to try and find out, if she could. "What did I ever do to you? I've never met you before, as far as I know, so why are you so focused on me?" She clasped her hands over her belly and tilted her head to eye him sidelong. If she reached out with her wolf senses, she could smell something familiar about him, something that stood out under all the other stuff he was wearing, the sweat that was beginning to show under his arms. What was wrong with him?

"We've studied you for months, ever since we heard about this town from my high school buddy, Leroy. Yeah, I saw you flinch. I know you knew Leroy. He and his crazy friends had some big holy mission about curing you and making you human again." He snorted in contempt. "But we know where the real money is. You're worth a lot more turning into a monster once a month than you are cured. And the best part is that if you don't cooperate and we have to take you out, there's more where you came from. Aren't there?" He pulled a bandanna out of his pocket and waved it at her. A familiar scent wafted across the room.

*Becca! He knew what Becca was.* Adrenaline shot through Erin's system until she had to clench her hands together to control their trembling. Rage was coming next and once that hit, she wasn't going to care about the taser. Especially if she could somehow make herself change before he fired it. *Keep him talking, keep him talking. It won't be that much longer.* Her wolf was practically whispering the words in her ear now.

"I'm not sure what I'm supposed to make of an old bandanna. More of what I am? You're going to have to humor my aging brain with a bit more information." She let her voice slip into the slower, backcountry accent she'd left behind years ago, hoping he'd let his guard down, underestimate her. Her body was rigid with the effort it took to stay still on the bed.

"I don't believe you. Besides..." He inched closer as he spoke, taser in hand. "I can *smell* you." His blue eyes were darker now, a shadow that might have been hair creeping down his forehead in a long V. The fingers on his free hand clenched and unclenched rapidly, as though there was an electric current running through his hand.

Some part of him was aware that something was wrong. He rubbed his free hand over his jeans with a jerky motion and seemed to be trying to catch his breath. He turned away from her and glanced at the door, murmuring, "No! It's not supposed to happen again!" His body shook as he stepped back and yelled for his wife.

Erin sat up slowly. She could smell something that wasn't wolf, wasn't human, sharp and sour, coming off him now, no longer buried under the cologne or whatever it was he was wearing to try to cover it. The combination of smells made her human stomach feel queasy but sent her wolf surging to the surface of her mind. *Danger. Enemy.* She gripped the edge of the bed, felt it bend under her fingers. If Becca could exert control over her change, she could too. She had to.

Jim looked different now. He seemed to be responding to something that only he could hear and feel. His head shifted from side to side, skin moving in odd ripples under his clothes. He clenched his fists and tightened his features as if he was in pain. Erin hoped he was but that thought was fleeting. Her wolf was awake and fighting for control now. She could feel her own transformation rippling under her skin, transforming her bones.

And the more that she saw of what was going on with Jim, the less she wanted to exert any more self-control than she had to.

He was losing his battle with whatever was inside him. Suddenly, his body stretched up and out and he loomed over her. His face stretched like something out of a bad horror film and fur sprouted in tufts on his exposed skin. Claws burst from his fingers and inhuman growls poured from his throat as his face changed itself into a muzzle. The taser fell to the floor with a clunk as his clothing split around his rapidly expanding body.

*Bear!* Erin's wolf screamed to the surface, in full control now as it forced past her human self, taking over. She rolled off the bed and over to the far wall as her own body completed its transformation. Changing had gotten easier as she'd gotten used to it, an almost effortless flow between one form and the other when the full moon called her wolf out each month.

But not this time. Her human self was terrified and her wolf was enraged and the moon wasn't up high enough yet to send the true call to change coursing through her. This transformation was fueled by anger, adrenaline and terror, and it wrenched Erin's body into a shape that was neither wolf nor human.

One howl from her and an answering snarl from the bear and they leapt at each other, claws flashing. She was faster than the bear but he was larger and stronger. One swipe of a massive paw sent her tumbling to the other side of the room, slamming into the wall next to the door. Her human half struggled to assert herself to grab for the taser on the floor, but her wolf was too far gone in fear and rage. When she hit the floor, she scrambled to her feet and charged the bear. This time, blood splashed on the floor as their bodies collided and their howls and snarls of pain echoed through the room.

There was a sound in the hallway and a human female appeared in the doorway shouting and sending out flashes of light. Erin pulled her head behind the bear so that he blocked whatever the human was shooting at them. The bear swung his head from side to side, trying to watch her and the human through small cold eyes. Erin seized the moment that he was off balance to shove him backward as hard as she could. He went down on his back in a tangle of paws and fur and Erin zigzagged toward the door, racing as fast as she could. The human frantically fired something at them both, but Erin twisted midair and whatever it was passed her and struck the bear.

Erin swatted the screaming woman out of the doorway and bolted into the warehouse corridor, the bear's roars echoing behind her. She ran toward the outside door at the end of the hallway, moving as fast as she could on two legs when she wanted to run on four. But there was no time to finish shifting. And she was wounded and running out of time.

The human was out in the corridor behind her now, fumbling with the thing in her hands, and Erin knew with both halves of her brain that if she managed to fire more little missiles, she would never get free. She threw herself forward, weaving back and forth to make herself less of a target, and struck the metal door full force, only to bounce off its locked surface. A loud clanging alarm began to shriek, tormenting her wolf hearing.

She rolled backward, looking for another route to freedom. The glint of moonlight to her right caught her eye and she ran into another room off the corridor, this one an office with a big window. The moon and the idea struck her at the same time and she hurtled through the window, shifting so she hit it in wolf form, sending a shower of glass into the parking lot outside. With a mighty surge, she jumped across what she could of the sea of broken glass, forcing herself to ignore the sharp pains from the slivers in her paws as she raced into the woods. She sought the deep shadows before she stopped to lick her bleeding paws and her wounded side and listen for pursuit.

# CHAPTER 16

THE CAVE SWALLOWED BECCA LIKE a big dry mouth, the sensation tempting her to close her eyes and stay very still and hope that whatever it was moved on and found itself other prey. But there was no time. She could hear Shelly scrambling up the hill, pursuing Annie, and moonrise was coming very soon. Her wolf was boiling in her blood, frantic to break free and follow her Alpha.

The paintings on the walls seemed to be moving, racing forward to follow each other around the rough stone walls. Becca flinched and blinked. Nothing moved. Her imagination was running away with her. Or…another thought occurred. Had Annie come back to call them to life? Was she seeing the aftereffects of new magic or old magic? She forced herself to walk to the cave's center where something lay piled up on the floor, partially revealed in the dim light from the entrance.

She paused a few steps away and sniffed cautiously, letting her wolf explore what she could of whatever it was. A bundle of mixed scents met her nose, making her wrinkle her face up in distaste: fear, sweat, sage, herbs, other less savory things. Why could she smell those things now and not when they were outside? It made no sense.

Becca pulled a small flashlight from her bag and, with a silent apology to the cave's guardians, turned it on to examine the pile. Electric light never felt right in here, like there was an unwritten rule that they should only use candles or wolf sight. A ragged cloth, part of a shirt, perhaps, lay in the middle of the floor. There was some blood and hair scattered around it, its texture definitely not human. Next to that, a candle stub lay on its side and something gritty was spread around in a very rough circle. She bent down, forcing herself to breathe in more of the scent, to make it familiar. *Annie*. She was sure this time.

She pictured the leader of the werewolf hunters as she had seen her last, transformed into a monster stuck somewhere between wolf and human by the cave's magic. Remembered her running off into the night, just like she had done when they hiked up here just now. But why come back tonight? Was she looking for a way to change back into a human? Or something else?

Annie hadn't wanted to be a wolf in the first place, as far as Becca could tell from their conversations, if you could call them that. She had blitzed into Wolf's Point with her pack of werewolf hunters, kidnapped Shelly, held Becca prisoner, experimented on them with a werewolf "cure" that her medic, Leroy, had concocted, almost killed Erin. Had even killed Margaret before all of that. So why had the valley's magic changed her instead of killing her?

Becca shivered, remembering how the paintings had come to life and consumed Annie's colleague or lover or whatever he was, Anderson. If he was a danger to the wolves and the town, why wasn't she? But now her thoughts were getting jumbled up. The moon was calling her and she could hear the others on the trail outside. She could wonder about Annie and get undressed at the same time. Or at least, she could wonder until she changed, then worry about it when she was human again.

As she shed her clothes and put them in a neat pile, she remembered the first time that she had changed in this cave, the press of the bodies of the other wolves against hers. Remembered the fear, followed by the comfort and newfound sense of belonging. She bit back a small howl of grief. She didn't want to change alone.

*Erin.* What was Erin doing right now? How could she be wasting time wondering about Annie when Erin was in who knew what danger? She drank in a deep breath, then another, as if she could taste Erin on the wind if she just inhaled hard enough. Her sense of smell would be better soon, her other senses stronger. She promised herself that if Shelly wouldn't take the Pack to go look for Erin, she'd do it herself. Tonight. Even if she had to go alone.

Becca crouched on the floor, waiting for the others. Her instinct told her that the moon would be well above the horizon in a few minutes, and on the heels of that thought, the other Pack members poured into the cave. Molly squeezed her shoulder, her words suggesting that she knew exactly what Becca had been thinking. "We'll find her tonight." Becca gulped down a sudden urge to cry at her reassurance and nodded.

The wolf inside her surged to the surface a moment later, bending and twisting her body into its still new moon-called shape. A howl from outside drew an answering one from her, echoing out into the newly darkened sky. Within moments, a pack of wolves was waiting at the cliff mouth for Shelly.

They didn't have long to wait. It had been her howl that Becca had heard outside, calling them out to follow her up on a roundabout, treacherous trail that led up and around the mountain. They moved swiftly despite the shale and pebbles sliding under their paws. Wherever they were headed, their Alpha wanted them to get there quickly.

*Erin.* Becca's heart sang, wolf and human entwined and hopeful. Afterward, she couldn't have said why she was so sure, why she was so suddenly filled with certainty that they were going to get Erin back. After all, Shelly had chased after Annie, and unless Annie had something to do with Erin's disappearance...the thought vanished as Becca went all wolf, leaving her human self in the quiet, dark part of her mind where most of her human self slept on full moon nights.

The Pack surged along, exchanging soft yips of encouragement or warning to each other. Lin slipped and went down, but scrambled up when Becca went back for her and nosed her at her to see if she was okay. She lagged behind the rest of the Pack at first, limping a little after her stumble, but Adelía and Carly hung back too, encouraging her, and soon she was running faster, keeping up with the others. Shelly paused on a ledge next to a big boulder and looked out over the valley below until they all caught up.

Becca drank in the air, tasting humans and prey and car exhaust and all the other scents of the valley, searching for something familiar. There were a few twinkling lights in the trees and along the roads below them, humans in cars and buildings, probably. They were too far up for the rancid clouds of exhaust to cloud their senses. Shelly had led them away from Wolf's Point, out toward the highway and the scattered buildings that lay along it.

Their Alpha paused, then her ears went flat. She growled softly, sending a ripple of alarm through the others. Then she took off at a dead run downhill, Becca and the others who could keep up with her at her heels. The wind tore through their fur so that a few tufts of it sailed behind them or were stuck in the underbrush. Becca panted as she ran, drinking the air in gulps, wolf thoughts processing prey and potential danger and the comforting nearness of the others.

She was getting hungry and thirsty when they began to gradually slow down. Shelly slowed from a run to a trot, turning their motion sideways to a nearby creek. The entire Pack caught up with them and slurped quick drinks from the fast-moving trickle as it ran over the rocks. Shelly sat and waited for them, her stance seeming relaxed, but Becca could smell tension coming off her in waves. She walked over and sat nearby, letting her senses wander, trying to discover what had Shelly so on edge.

There was something alien, yet familiar. Close, even though they couldn't see it yet. The wind shifted and its scent washed over them in a wave. *Intruder. Enemy.* Becca's wolf senses howled through her head. Molly began to growl. Next to her, Shelly began to shift into a hybrid of wolf and human. Whatever it was coming toward them reeked of blood and rage and a terrifying wrongness. Some new kind of monster had invaded Wolf's Point and it was coming for them.

Becca scrambled to her feet, hesitating. Her wolf self demanded that she support Shelly and follow her lead, but a memory of being caught halfway between forms wandered through her mind. Her human self grumbled sleepily from its den until she silenced it again. No matter what she did, the Pack were going to a battle tonight and she needed to help them win.

A tiny cub thought whimpered through her: *Erin?* Then that thought was gone, replaced with a primal rage and bloodlust. She drank in a gulp of air, drawing with it a new scent along with the creature's. It brought up a memory of Erin's room and the burglar, this time to her werewolf senses, and she growled. Her brain whirled with emotions, smells, sounds, the feel of the Pack nearby, and a picture in her head of Erin, Erin's room, something familiar…

And then it was gone and they were moving, a flowing river of grey and black and brown pouring down the hillside after Shelly. Their enemy lumbered out of the woods to face them with a roar. *Bear.* Becca's human brain woke suddenly. *Not bear,* responded her wolf self. *Monster. Wrong.* All around, wolves were snarling and growling, as if they were all thinking the same thing at the same time.

Shelly was closest to the creature and reared up on her furry hind legs before charging at it. A huge paw swiped out at her as the beast that was more than a beast rose to its hind paws to meet her. She darted under the blow, landing one of her own with a clawed hand before twisting away. Becca circled them before throwing herself at its enormous back leg and sinking her teeth into its flesh. The creature bellowed in pain, a giant paw flailing backward to knock her loose, but she twisted to duck under the blow without losing her grip and bit harder.

Now the others were circling it, snapping at it, lunging at it. It didn't know where to strike first and it roared in pain, waving its immense paws in the air. Brown fur rippled in the wind and its eyes gleamed reddish black in the moonlight. Becca caught glimpses of it as it dropped to all fours, still trying to kick her loose. But now Shelly was lunging at it, then Molly and Adelía and Mrs. Hui and the others came on in a wave, striking from all sides.

Becca's teeth sank through its thick fur and into its flesh, sending a warm rush of hot blood into her mouth. It tasted metallic and tainted with human interference. Someone had given this beast a drug of some kind and whatever it was coursed through it, slowing it down. The thought distracted her for a critical instant and she loosened her grip. It turned and swiped at her again, this time succeeding in knocking her loose from her grip on its leg. She flew through the air, twisting as she went in hopes of landing on her paws.

She landed hard with a yelp just as a shrill whistle echoed through the clearing. The bear shook its head as if trying to clear the noise away, but it only got louder. One of the wolves whimpered as the sound impacted the Pack's sensitive hearing and several of them pulled back, burying their heads in their paws. The bear ignored them, instead spinning around as it dropped to all fours and began a lumbering run toward the sound.

Shelly shook her head, snarling after it. But the sound was too much and she stayed still, and the other wolves stayed with her. After a few minutes, the sounds of the bear crashing through the woods faded and the whistle faded with it. They picked themselves up and ran after it, following the clear trail of blood spatter and broken branches down past the winding creek to the edge of a human road. There, they halted, alert for signs of danger as much as to catch the scent again.

The bear's trail went up to the edge of the asphalt, then stopped abruptly. They ran up and down the road in ones and twos trying to find its scent again but found nothing but human and car smells. Someone had come and taken their enemy away. After a few moments of fruitless searching, Shelly gave a short bark and turned away. They all faded into the woods after her.

After that, Becca's memory got hazy. They ran through the woods following Shelly. They circled buildings on the outskirts of Wolf's Point. They loped silently down gravel roads, making the braver local dogs howl and bark. They circled the Wolf Preserve, running along the fence line with the resident wolves matching them stride for stride until they ran out of enclosure. She had a vague memory of the squeal of prey and the snap of bones some time after that, but fortunately no more than her human brain could handle.

The moon was beginning to set when a pack of tired, dirty wolves trailed after Shelly into the cave. Becca barely noticed a new scent as they piled in together. A familiar gray form curled up next to her and she leaned into it, seeking comfort before they all fell asleep. The others packed in around them, sniffing her companion happily before they all curled up together. She fell asleep as her human brain woke up briefly and tried to tell her something important.

# CHAPTER 17

D AWN WAS COOL AND QUIET, bringing a light rain with it. Inside the dry cave, a group of middle-aged and a few older-than-middle-aged women awoke naked on the stone floor. Lin sat up slowly with an audible groan. "Dammit, Shelly, when is that insurance money coming? We need to rebuild the Women's Club. My bones are getting too old for cold stone." She stretched with a few quiet creaks and cracks, as if to demonstrate her point.

But Shelly wasn't paying much attention and neither were the others. Instead, all eyes turned to a battered but familiar lean figure curled up against Becca. Becca herself woke with a start, aware of being watched and of someone pressing closer to her than any Pack member normally did after they changed. *What the...*she twisted around with a thump. "Erin!"

One gray eye opened slowly. The other one looked swollen and stayed shut. Erin blinked her good eye slowly, then brought up her hand to rub it over her face. There were scabs and dried blood all up and down her arms, her legs, her naked torso. Molly scrambled over with some water, a First Aid kit and an energy bar from one of the packs they had brought. Without saying a word, she put them all down next to Erin and began cautiously cleaning her legs.

Becca was breathing hard just looking at her. How could she have done...where had she...why hadn't she come back sooner... it all whirled up until it came out as a choked sob. She forced herself to reach out and unscrew the cap on the water bottle, then hold it out to Erin. Slowly, so slowly, the other woman sat up and took it. She drank long and deep, the sound breaking the spell of stillness that had settled on the others.

Quietly, the others fetched their own water and food and began to scramble into their clothes. Clothes, more water and some jerky appeared next to Becca as if by magic. She drank and ate, but she didn't taste a thing until Erin splashed some water on her hand and used it to wipe her swollen eye. The lid cracked open a little and Erin gasped as the light hit it. Molly drew back, looking concerned.

That was when Becca snapped and grabbed Erin in a fierce hug. "Where have you been? What happened to you?" She growled the words in Erin's ear, ignoring the shudder that went through the other woman when she first touched her.

Erin twisted her face into Becca's neck and gave a wrenching sob. Becca immediately loosened her grip. "What's the matter? Did I hurt you? Oh baby, I'm so sorry!" She kissed Erin's forehead gently as she looked up over Erin's head to meet Shelly's eyes.

Shelly dropped to the floor in front of them, sitting cross-legged, eyes narrow as if she was thinking thoughts she'd rather not be considering. "Normally, I wouldn't interrupt, but I think we're way past normal. What happened to you, Erin?"

She paused and looked at both of them again. "Maybe put some clothes on first, though."

Becca could feel her face flush. Hot flash or blush? Did it matter? Her skin was tingling from where she had pressed up against Erin and there was a deep ache inside her that she hadn't felt in a long, long time. So clearly Shelly had a point about them getting dressed. Some things would be easier to handle with clothes on. She could puzzle over her thoughts on that later.

She turned away and they scrambled into their clothes. The Pack gathered around in a loose circle, looking at Erin expectantly. She finished dressing, then sat back down with a sigh in front of Shelly, the wet cloth pressed to her injured eye. Becca scrambled off to the side and joined the circle, after a moment of hesitation. She wanted to support Erin but this was also Pack business and Erin needed to tell them what happened and…she took another bite of a protein bar, trying to calm her whirling thoughts.

What would have happened if the Pack hadn't been here? If she and Erin had woken up just like this? A warm sensation travelled up her at the thought. *Great. I couldn't have just thrown myself at her when she wasn't a fugitive?* The sound of Erin's weary voice yanked her from her fantasies and regrets.

She was telling the story of what had happened to her, and for a moment, Becca thought she was still fantasizing. Their new neighbors, Jim and Kari, were trying to make a reality TV show out of the Pack? And Jim was some sort of werebear? She tried desperately to remember what she could of them. Had they smelled unusual, done anything that suggested that they weren't exactly what they seemed to be? They had already seemed fake to her, so it was hard to remember anything more unusual than that. Where had Ed found these people anyway?

Then she remembered the break-in at their house. Could the burglar have been Jim? But why? What had they been looking for? She reined in her thoughts with an effort to focus on what Erin was saying. She could tell them all about the break-in after that.

That was when Shelly asked the question that Becca had been asking herself for days. "Could this bear or Annie, for that matter, have killed Leroy? Did you remember anything more of what happened to you before you found his body in the trunk of your car?"

Erin frowned, good eye squinting with effort. The cuts and bruises on her arms and face had begun to heal already, but not as fast as normal. Drugs and shock and stress must be slowing the process down, Becca thought, with a flash of rage. Erin dropped her face into her hands, rested her elbows on her knees, whole body wrestling with memories and loss. Becca crawled over to her and wrapped an arm around her shoulders. "Shh…it'll come back to you. Try to relax," she crooned softly.

To take some of the pressure off Erin, she told Shelly and the Pack about the break-in, then told the Pack about finding Annie in the cave when they got there. She gestured over the remains of the other woman's ritual or whatever it was, miraculously undisturbed by all of their scrambling around. "Anyone remember seeing anything like this before? Any ideas on what she might have been doing?"

They all looked at the center of the cave and what remained of the candle and the sand, or whatever the gritty stuff was. Lin and Gladys got to their feet and walked over to look at it more closely. Adelía pulled a flashlight from her bag and clicked it on to show the darker corners. Soon, they were all on their feet except Becca and Erin, sniffing and checking out the entire area.

Erin glanced over after a few moments. "Do you think she's trying to change back? It must be horrible to be stuck like that!" Her eyes looked haunted, at least to Becca, and she held her a little closer. That was when she noticed that one of Erin's arms had started bleeding and let go of her to grab some bandages in the first aid kit. Thank goodness someone thought to stash a couple here after they had their big dustup with the slayers.

It was funny, Becca thought, that whatever Annie had been doing hadn't activated any of the paintings. That sparked the beginning of an idea, one that percolated as she patched up Erin's wound. It looked like it might have some glass in it, and she pulled out a small pair of tweezers and began removing slivers by flashlight as she talked. "And if she was trying to change back," Becca said, her tone thoughtful as she worked out what she was trying to say, "is there some way that we could see what she was doing? Like a hidden camera or something?"

No one said anything, but Shelly frowned and looked around. "I wonder…" She got up and walked over to the paintings that swept around the walls from entrance to just short of the entrance on the other side, each showing wolf-women and women changing to and from their wolf forms. Once, not so long ago, she, Erin and Becca had called them to life to protect the Pack and their home. Shelly reached out and touched the one that her daughter Kira had done of her, fingers trailing over the paint thoughtfully.

Becca watched Shelly carefully, waiting for her to confirm her suspicions. If the paintings could be called off the wall to attack, why not to witness as well? Maybe they could function as some kind of magical security cameras. She could see her thoughts mirrored on Shelly's face, along with doubt. Her spirits sank along with that shift. It wasn't like they had a handy library of Pack rituals and history to refer to.

Or did they? "I don't think we can do anything right now, but how about I go over to Circle House later and ask there? We could meet up here after that and see what we can do then."

Becca was hesitant about speaking up, but if not now, when? Shelly wasn't the kind of leader who insisted on claiming all the ideas for herself. Not that that was the real reason. Now that Erin was back and awake, she was feeling torn, wanting to spend the time nursing her instead.

Erin shifted and Becca reached out to sooth her with a touch, only to find herself drawing back. What were they going to do about Erin if they all left? Would she be safe? She couldn't think of anywhere to hide her that Lizzie wouldn't know about or might suddenly decide to search. And who knew how long this might need to go on? *Do I really think she did it?* She quelled a wave of nausea and confusion.

Gladys cleared her throat and spoke as if she could read Becca's thoughts, "Lin and I can take shifts with Erin today until she's back on her paws...feet. But we need something longer term than that."

Molly cleared her throat. "Would you be okay with Carla doing a shift or two? This isn't the best season for surveying and Erin knows her. At any rate, she's got some flexibility in her schedule. And she's fascinated with all this." Molly gestured at the walls. "Not a long-term solution either, but I know she'd be up for staying here a couple of days."

"That's an idea; can you check in and see when she's available? I'm not sure I want to ask many of our friends and relatives, because we don't know how dangerous it is, but Carla went up against the hunters and she knows when to call for help. And yes," Shelly responded, her tone thoughtful, "we do need something more effective than just sitting around here. Proving Erin's innocence would solve many of our problems. But if we can't do that right away, maybe Lizzie would be open to some new suspects and could convince the Sheriff's Department to check them out in the meantime."

All around the cave, Becca could hear invisible ears prick up. She knew who her favorite choice was. She wondered if she was the only one who'd been wondering what had become of Annie, at least until today. But then, she'd spent more time around the other woman recently than anyone else. Lucky her. But maybe Annie had a good reason to want Leroy dead. Maybe he wouldn't help change her back.

Erin cleared her throat and Becca put a protective arm on her shoulder again. "Maybe they'd settle for the bear," Erin croaked into the stillness. "I still don't know what happened up on the mountain, but maybe they'd like to find out what that werebear's been up to. I know I would."

Jim and Kari would suit just fine…except that if local TV and law enforcement got ahold of one shifter, why not go looking for more? The less attention on the Pack, the better. Plus, there was the whole kidnapping Erin and hurting her thing. If they were around when Becca got home, she wasn't planning on showing them the Welcome Wagon. There were other ways to deal with trespassers in their valley. She growled softly at the thought.

When she checked back in, Shelly was getting them organized. She gave Becca and Gladys a stern look and added, "Since I'm going to talk to Lizzie about them, steer clear of Jim and Kari if you see them around town. Apparently, they'll remind you of Ken and Barbie, which should make them stand out a bit. That goes double for those of you who live near them." She frowned thoughtfully. "In fact, given the break-in, Gladys, can you put Becca up tonight and maybe tomorrow as well? Just until we get a handle on this."

Becca bit back a groan. So far, she'd gathered that she was going to work, going to Circle House and then not coming back to the cave to check on Erin, as she thought she might, but hiding out at…Gladys' house instead? A flood of protest welled up inside her, only to get swallowed back down by a realization or two.

Shelly couldn't read her mind, but didn't want her hanging around the cave while Erin was there. Why? Too distracting? Too fraught? Ah, too noticeable. It would draw too much attention. Lizzie knew about them, Jim and Kari knew about them. Hell, Annie knew about them.

The only person who apparently hadn't really noticed how much "them" there was to notice was Becca herself. But at least she was starting to catch up. She caught Gladys' reluctant nod from the corner of her eye. Apparently, no one was excited about this.

Erin's eyelids drooped and Becca kicked herself mentally for being selfish and thoughtless. She got up and took some extra clothes from the Pack's emergency stash and made a nest out of them in the back of the cave. There was a little alcove back there, sheltered from view from the entrance. Then she guided Erin over to it and covered her as best she could with a couple of old blankets. A gentle wheeze told her that the other woman was asleep for the moment, and she patted her shoulder gently before going over to stand by Shelly and Gladys.

"Lin went down to her car to get her emergency blanket. She'll take the first shift and Gladys will take you to her place to get settled in. She can walk you over to your place to pack up what you need, too." Shelly studied Becca for a long moment. "There's a lot going on. Give yourself some time."

Was she being that obvious? Of course she was. Becca bit back a sigh and fanned herself with her hand as a mild hot flash crept up on her. Unbidden, a memory of Leroy as he had been, alive and well and dosing werewolves with a supposed cure, popped into her head. Had she hated his guts? Sure, him and the rest of that crew. Would she have killed him, given the chance? More importantly, would she have done it deliberately, then tried to pin the murder on someone else, if she had killed him? That notion gave her a little chill up the spine. She glanced over at Erin and frowned, juggling her mixed emotions.

Lin appeared at the cave entrance a few moments later, scattering her thoughts. She put a blanket over Erin carefully, so as not to waken her, then went to join the others. Becca noticed that she'd brought a cushion to sit on and what looked to be an e-reader. Clearly, she was prepared for the long haul, but now Becca found that she wasn't so sure she wanted to leave. Maybe she should stay for a bit in case Erin woke up. Maybe she'd remember something and then Becca would know for sure what to do next.

But Gladys was herding her outside and down the hill before she knew it. Protesting would get her nowhere, that much was clear. She followed the other woman down the steep trail to the cars. "Is your car at Shelly's or at home?" Gladys gave her a sidelong glance, as if she expected her to freak out or do something weird.

With a sigh, Becca drew in a deep breath. "It's at Shelly's. Would you mind dropping me off there? I'll park it at our house so it looks like someone's home." She added with asperity, "And no, I won't go inside until you get there. I understood what Shelly was getting at and I don't want to face that bear on my own either."

Gladys grimaced and walked over to a old sedan with a sigh. She opened the doors and made a sweeping gesture at Becca. They drove away in silence.

# CHAPTER 18

E RIN COULDN'T REMEMBER WHERE SHE was when she woke up, not at first. Her brain whirled with bears and cameras and dead bodies in a potent and unpleasant mix. Now she was blinking in the dim light of…the cave, that was it. From the angle of the light, it looked like most of the day had passed while she'd been asleep. Someone nearby was looking at something with a glowing screen. It reflected on the paintings above them, giving them an otherworldly gleam.

She rolled over onto her back, wincing as a not quite healed bruise met a small rock on the floor, and kept rolling until she lay on her side. A t-shirt with an ad for a local painting company lying on top of the small pile of women's clothes caught her eye when she looked down. No wonder she could feel the rocks on the floor if all she was sleeping on was a pile of old t-shirts. They needed an air mattress or something up here if they were going to be using it as a hideout.

Or, maybe, they needed not to need to use it as a hideout. Of course, where did that leave her then? She'd come back here because she hoped they'd all be here, that it would be safe. Normal. But that clearly wasn't going to be how things worked. Even waking up was weird.

She took a long minute to assess her dreams, turning them over for clues on what had happened to her, what might happen next. Ordinarily, it wasn't something she would do, but then, nothing that had happened lately was. She gave the air a tentative sniff and closed her eyes, trying to decide if she was ready for company. Whoever it was that was reading nearby didn't smell very familiar, but wasn't a stranger, either.

And wasn't Becca. A quiet ache filled her with that thought. She had encouraged Becca to move in, had been clear about her own feelings, then rejected the other woman's overtures and then followed that up by confessing to murder without any warning. Then she'd gotten kidnapped by a werebear and his consort eager to expose the Pack on reality television for a profit and doom them all in the process. If there was some kind of manual on how to kick off a lesbian romance wrong, she was ticking off a bunch of boxes right now, even if it wasn't all her fault. She smacked her hands over her eyes with a groan.

At least most of her cuts and bruises felt like they'd healed. She'd be all healthy and ready to tackle werebears soon. Or as healthy and ready as she'd been the last time. It wasn't a thought that filled her with a ton of confidence. So choosing not to think about that just left the disaster that was the rest of her life. And her accounting business, if she still had one. This was not getting any better.

"How are you feeling? Do you want some water?" The voice was familiar, but pitched a little higher than she was used to hearing it. And considerably closer than they had been a minute ago. She sat up slowly and squinted at the other person, then took the water bottle they were offering and took a deep swig.

"I need to pee," she croaked when she put the bottle back down. "Am I allowed to go outside on my own or do you need to come with me?" She scrambled to her feet, wincing a little at a few rediscovered bruises, and took a closer look at her companion. "Carl...? Hi. What's up? No, wait, I think that's a longer discussion than I have time for right now. Let me pee first. Got any food with you? And coffee? Yay. Back in a few."

She wove her way unsteadily toward the entrance without giving her companion a chance to do more than wave a thermos, but they caught up with her just before she went outside. "Here." They handed Erin a couple of clean pieces of cloth and a plastic bag. "Shelly said to use the next ledge up, behind the big rock, if you can make it up there. I can help you...if you like."

Erin squinted outside, then nodded when the bright light felt like it was stabbing her brain. "If you wouldn't mind. I'm still pretty loopy."

Her companion guided her up to the next ledge, then turned away and walked back down a few paces to give her some privacy. "There's a thermos of coffee and a cooler with food in the cave when you're ready."

"You are a magical being and I'm thrilled that you're here," Erin remarked as she pulled her pants back up and leaned against the boulder to make sure that she was ready to stand up. The other person's ears turned very pink, which made her smile. She rubbed some sanitizer from the bag onto her hands and cleaned up after herself before sliding down the trail a couple of steps. Then she put her hand on her companion's shoulder. "Lead on."

She glanced around as they walked carefully downhill. The woods around them were quiet but she could hear small animals and birds settling in for the night, or in some cases, waking up and beginning to search for food. She stretched her senses, but there was nothing nearby that smelled or sounded like a strange wolf or a bear of any variety, familiar or otherwise. Or like an employee of the Sheriff's Department, so that was good, too. The question was: how long would this happy state of affairs last?

They went back into the cave and stashed Erin's plastic bag in a bigger bag, then sat down to coffee and buttered rolls and fruit. There were a couple of pieces of jerky and some other miscellaneous edibles in the cooler and Erin tucked in like she hadn't eaten in days. Between bites, she studied the person sitting across from her. She knew that some changes were probably coming, but she hadn't known Carlos as well as she did Molly to begin with, so she wanted to make sure that she wasn't being rude or obnoxious.

The short, muscular, dark-haired brown-skinned man had fallen away to reveal a medium-sized, well made-up and handsome middle-aged person. Well, it wasn't like she hadn't seen a transformation or two in her time. She could certainly handle this one, especially since her only role in it was to try to not be a jerk.

After a few minutes of chewing, she cleared her throat. "So," she gestured with a roll, "I like what you did with your makeup. I was always terrible with that. Now, just so I've got this right, what do you want me to call you and what pronouns should I use?"

They cleared their throat and took a sip from the water bottle. "I'm going by Carla, which I know will be a challenge with my old name and whenever Carli is around, but I've always liked it. I'd like it if you used she and her, but I'm okay with they or them and…maybe I should have talked to you and Becca more about this last time you were over?" She paused and looked worried, like she wasn't sure how Erin was going to react.

Erin started to tell her that everything was fine when Carla's phone broke into a few bars of a lively pop song, making them both jump. Carla glanced down and grabbed the phone. "It's the boss. Hi, Shelly. She just woke up. Right, here she is."

Erin took the phone, despite a wave of trepidation that made her want to run out of the cave, never to be seen again. What had gone wrong now? "Hey. Yep, I'm feeling better. Just finished eating and Carla and I were getting caught up. What's happening?" She frowned at what Shelly said next, cursed softly, protested, then finally, reluctantly, agreed. She turned the phone off when they were done and handed it back to Carla. Then she dug her fingers into her short-cropped hair, making it stand on end. Memories of Becca smoothing it down when it got like this make her choke a little. But now wasn't the time for this. She had her orders and Carla was waiting to hear them too.

"Well, the sheriff apparently likes me *and* Annie *and* Jim *and* Kari, all working together, for Leroy's killing. Says maybe it was some kind of revenge pact or a sex thing, which tells you how well he knows me. Annie, you already know. Kari and Jim are our new neighbors and Jim just happens to be a werebear, which you probably don't know. Leroy, you met and had a gun battle with."

Carla's dark eyes were very wide. "Wait, go back to the werebear thing. No, wait, on second thought, I thought Annie died when the paintings did their thing?"

"Nope. The magic sort of blended her halves together and now she's running around the mountains as a human-wolf hybrid. Shelly and Becca found her here at the cave yesterday. The werebear is a bonus of sorts, unless Becca's ex sold the house to him and his partner on purpose, which seems somewhat unlikely. Ed's not a big believer in the supernatural. I don't know if she turns into anything too, but I'm hoping not. This is already one hell of a week without that happening too."

"I'll say. You gals always know how to put anything I'm going through in perspective. Not that I'm comparing or anything." Carla shook her head in amazement. "So does Shelly want us to do anything right now or should we stay put and wait for more news?"

"She wants us to go werebear hunting." Erin grimaced, then noticed Carla's expression. "No, not like going head-to-head with it, but if we can figure out where he is now and where his partner is, we can try and check out what else they might be up to. Shelly doesn't want me in town for obvious reasons, so if you're up for it, you get to come with while we follow my trail back through the woods to where they were holding me and see what we can find. Think you're up for that?"

Carla's eyes shone. "You mean I can go on a Pack mission? I'd love to! I've been kind of jealous of Molly since she told Jonas and me about all this." She waved a hand at the cave walls and gave Erin a smile that practically glowed. "I know it doesn't mean I'll be called to join or anything, but just being closer to you all like this is something I've wanted for ages now." She gave the paintings a dreamy stare, then blinked and got up and grabbed her pack.

"Huh. Well, don't get all fangirl on me. There are some downsides too, as you know. But we can talk more while we're tracking. We just have to be quiet and careful about it. And if I tell you to run or hide, you do it right away. Understand?"

Carla nodded solemnly. She opened her pack and showed Erin the gun inside. "Just in case something goes very wrong. I'm licensed to carry and I'm a decent shot. No silver bullets though, so we'll have to hope we don't run into anything really interesting." She pulled out some pants and hiking shoes and changed into them while Erin grabbed a couple of water bottles and a pack of her own from the Pack's stash.

In a few minutes, they were ready to head out into the twilight. Erin was fully alert now, the fogginess that had been slowing her down since she woke up finally fading. Now she noticed the scents and sounds around them, each one clearer and sharper than they had been an hour before. Her better-than-human night vision had kicked in, and soon she was guiding Carla in the darker patches of woods, finding a broken branch here, a pawprint there that told her where the Pack had been. It took some looking around to find her trail in all that.

Carla was studying the woods around them like she was looking for a bear. Erin gave her a small smile and went back to studying the ground. After a few minutes, she found a lone wolf's trail, and a quick breath told even her human senses that it was hers. "This way." She pointed toward the valley and they started following her tracks.

"How did they catch you anyway?"

"They came to the jail with something, a drug, maybe. I don't know how they fooled the guards and the deputies, maybe some kind of hypnosis thing? Or they drugged them first? I gather they think I just vanished and Lizzie thinks that the Pack helped." Erin kept her voice pitched low and soft, just enough to be heard.

"You know they would have, given the chance. They had a couple of different plans, depending on how things turned out. Molly couldn't tell us the details, but I figured some of it out by seeing what she was prepping and who was calling the house. I know that it's not really any of my business unless she tells me about it, but I worry about her. The rest of you, too. So I try to be prepared, you know? In case I'm needed."

Erin gave her a long, considering look. Not for the first time, she wished the magic that changed them and made them what they were would let the Pack make nominations or, at least, suggestions. She had kept a mental list of preferred candidates since she first started to change, but who changed and who didn't was never all that predictable. Still, one could hope. She added another name to her list and smiled at Carla. "You've been a huge help and I'm so glad that Molly has folks watching her back. And ours too."

Carla looked relieved and grinned back at her. "Thanks! So…are we looking for paw prints or footprints or anything in particular? Please tell me that we're not looking for an actual bear?"

"Not yet, though we'll have to get to some version of that soon. Right now, we just want to go back to where they held me and check it out if it's not occupied. Shelly wants more intel on our new adversaries." *And she wants me out of the way, away from Becca, the Pack and the cave, for a bunch of reasons.* She kept that thought to herself. There were plenty of good reasons for Shelly to want those things, even if she didn't like the results.

But she had seen what Shelly saw, seen a whole parade of emotions cross Becca's face, seen the traces of Annie in the cave. If Annie or Lizzie was going to turn up there, it was better that she was away. As for Erin, the sooner they proved that she hadn't killed Leroy, the better off they were all going to be. She rubbed a hand across her cheek and pointed northward. "That seems vaguely familiar. Let's start over there."

They walked quietly, following a nearly invisible trail looking for broken branches and crushed leaves. It was a bit of a challenge in the twilight, but they were relying on Erin's sense of smell as much as what they could see. But after a mile or so of trekking through the woods, Erin could see that Carla was getting restless. She kept looking off to the woods on their left, then away, then back again.

"What is it?" she asked softly, pausing to study the same set of trees that was holding her companion's attention.

"I'm not sure. I thought I saw something move up there. Could just be a deer or something. But it's being kinda sneaky for prey. I would have thought it would take off by now. We're not that quiet."

Erin took in a deep breath, then let it out. "Wind's in the wrong direction. I'm getting a mix of scents, but nothing from that direction." She wasn't hearing anything either, which suggested that whatever they were looking at was staying very still. Or was a figment of Carla's imagination. The woods were shadowy and full of bird noise and leaf movements. It would be easy to think that you had seen something that wasn't there.

But best to be cautious. "Let's go up there," she whispered as she pointed a few yards ahead of them, "to those trees with the bushes around them. We can see if we can see more from a good hiding spot than we can out here."

Carla bit her lip, as if there was something else she wanted to say, but she was silent and nodded. They walked on as if they had just paused for a rest and Carla started some quiet chitchat about the new café in Wolf's Point. Much as they all loved Millie's, it was nice to have another place to go. That topic was enough to carry them into the trees that Erin had selected.

She nodded and Carla slipped quietly behind a tree and looked back the way they had come. Erin walked a few paces further, then ducked into the bushes around another tree. Belatedly, she wondered if any of them were poisonous, but it was a bit late to worry about that now. Still, a werewolf with poison ivy or poison oak was a grim picture, and even grimmer if that werewolf was her. But she'd worry about that later.

Time to stop moving and see what their watcher did, if indeed they had one. She wondered how long Carla could wait, standing quietly in the woods watching for someone or something that might not be there, waiting for it to move. Erin sucked in a slow, deep breath then let it out gradually, letting her body relax into a martial arts stance. If she had to, she could stand like this for an hour or more, back straight, knees apart and gently bent. But truth be told, it had been a hard couple of days and she hoped she wouldn't have to.

It took about ten minutes. There was a slight movement in the branches toward the bottom of the trees, as if something small or travelling low to the ground was moving through them. Whatever it was followed the cover for a few yards, then made a quick dash for the concealment of a boulder. There in the moonlight, Erin saw Annie and snarled, the sound barely audible, but more than audible to more than human ears.

The creature that was Shelly's cousin tilted her head as if she could hear the noise, then bolted into the rocks, scrambling away from them. Whatever she was up, she didn't seem to be a threat tonight. But Erin still wanted to follow her, wanted to see where she went and what she was doing. Maybe find out if she had any of Leroy's blood under her claws.

Erin straightened up silently. After a moment of studying the distant stand of trees, she turned back to Carla with a sigh. Tonight wasn't the night for that kind of pursuit and she had a different set of instructions to follow. She blew out a breath she'd been holding and motioned to Carla. "She's gone now. Since she's not on our list of things to deal with tonight, I think we better stick with Shelly's plan. Let's get back to it."

# CHAPTER 19

B ECCA STARED BLEAKLY AT THE rest home from her car window. She suspected that she knew why Shelly had sent her here instead of letting her stay with Erin. She hadn't thought her doubts and fears had been that obvious, but clearly Shelly had seen something. Or maybe she thought that Lizzie and the other deputies were watching her and the house. Or maybe Shelly wasn't sure about what Erin had been up to, either. The possibilities were endless.

As if on queue, a Sheriff's Department car drove by on the next street, a deputy that she didn't recognize behind the wheel. So Shelly probably had an excellent point, regardless of her motivation. True, he didn't glance toward her parked car, but that could just mean that they had orders not to make it too obvious. That's how they would be playing it if this were a TV show. Lizzie would think of that if Henderson didn't. Becca grimaced at her reflection in the window. Life had all been so much simpler a week ago.

Some of the women from Circle House started gathering in the side garden, and she recognized Sharon at the same time that the older woman spotted her and waved. No putting this off any longer then. Becca got out of the car and walked up the side path. But before she could walk over to the group, Sharon jerked her head toward the front of the building. Becca scowled in puzzlement, but directed her steps back toward the front door as if it was what she intended all along.

Lizzie Blackhawk swung the door open as she got there. "Miz Thornton." She nodded stiffly, as if Becca was a near stranger who she'd seen around town a few times, then stepped outside, letting the door close behind her. She stood on the step next to Becca, eyeing her over her mirrored shades. "Got any news for me?"

Becca ran through a quick list of responses in her head, dismissing the more confrontational ones. "Looks like Annie's back," she volunteered, settling on the thing that Shelly had almost certainly told her cousin. "And can we just switch to you calling me Becca? You know I didn't kill Leroy and I'm not hiding Erin." *Much.* She made herself smile as she swallowed that particular lie. *Fib, not an out-and-out lie.* After all, she wasn't sure where Erin was right now.

Lizzie narrowed her eyes like she could read Becca's mind. "Well now, that would mean telling me about the burglary at your place and whatever else has been going on, now wouldn't it? George Sanchez says that you chased off a burglar, but that information somehow failed to get reported. This isn't a game for me, you know. I've got a murder victim, a missing suspect, a jail with compromised security and now, a burglary. Did they take anything?"

Becca hung her head and scuffed the edge of her shoe against the step. *Stop acting like a teenager,* her inner adult demanded. "Just some old clothes, I think. I couldn't find anything else missing."

"Yours or hers?" Lizzie got more alert, all of a sudden.

Becca looked back up as the energy of their conversation shifted. A ripple of panic went through her. "Hers, I think. Why? Is this some kind of weird profiling thing? Please tell me no! I hate those shows."

Lizzie was scowling now. "It might be. I want you to come down to the station and file a report as soon as you're done here. And I want your word that you'll do it. I'm not the enemy here, Miz Thornton, and I wish you and your...friends would remember that."

She jerked her head in acknowledgement at Becca's stricken look and stood aside to let her go inside. "Ask for me at the station when you get there." With that, she turned and walked down the front path without a backward glance as the door shut behind her.

Becca watched her leave with a bundle of mixed emotions, then went and signed in. She could see Sharon down the hall waving at her when she looked up and she smiled back at her as she navigated her way through folks in chairs and using walkers as they roamed slowly through the lobby. A quick glance into the cafeteria showed the staff and volunteers packing up bingo supplies or maybe putting them out.

Now Robin had joined Sharon and they both looked pleased to see her. No, more than pleased. Relieved. Now what did they have to be anxious about today? Lizzie's visit, maybe?

Something told her she was about to find out. With a heavy sigh, she followed them into the same common space they'd met in the last time.

Robin shut the door behind them. "We've got this signed out for the next half an hour so we can talk without being interrupted." Tension rippled in her voice and movements.

For an instant, Becca thought about bolting. The weirdness just kept coming and she just didn't have any more energy for it. Their nervousness must be contagious. Between that and Erin and what Lizzie had just said about their burglar, it all felt like way too much.

But now the rest of the Circle was starting to trickle into the room and her longing for escape bumped into her desire to learn what was going on. And, somewhat to her surprise, she realized that she was worried about making a good impression. These could be her friends too, once she got to know them. She and Erin and the other current Pack members were going to need all the friends they could get, the way things were going. She drank in a deep breath and sat down at the table that they ushered her toward.

"We found out something, something you gals need to know," Sharon began once the others were either seated or had wheeled themselves up to the table. "We compared all our notes, everything that we could remember that any of the other wolves had ever told us, and when I wrote it all down, it looked like this." She laid a piece of paper down on the table. A slightly crooked timeline ran across it, with tiny notes written in a meticulous script.

Becca picked it up and squinted at the writing for a few minutes. All around her, the Circle fidgeted, then held its breath, or so it seemed. She wondered what they were all waiting for, but then she found it. Trailing her finger across the page to keep her place, she found something else. Then a few more hints, suggestions. Consequences. Change. She read them over again, this time realizing that some of the paragraphs had been highlighted very lightly in yellow.

Finally, she looked up. The other women looked back with a whole range of expressions, running from eager interest to nervous trepidation. She suspected she might look like her face was running the whole gamut right now. "Why save this for me? Why not call Shelly and give it straight to her?"

Sharon rubbed her nose. "Honestly? We wanted another opinion first. If you see it, then you can back us up when we bring it to Shelly. Not that she'd ignore us or anything, but none of us want to look…like crazy old werewolves with overactive imaginations." A corner of her wrinkled lips quirked up in an almost smile.

"So…" Becca paused, hunting for words before continuing. "You think that Wolf's Point's magic is changing over time? Is it getting weaker?"

Robin cleared her throat, after a glance at Sharon and the others. "That, we're not sure about. We were all wondering what was going on after the mess with Paula and after Margaret was killed. It shouldn't have been possible for Annie to kill her as easily as she did. Margaret was picked to be Alpha, just the way the magic had picked the others. Or so we all thought." Robin tapped the paper in Becca's hand, pointing to a note that Becca hadn't read yet. "Then we compared notes on this and had a look at an old diary of my mother's that I found."

Becca put the paper carefully down on the table and rubbed her cheeks with her hands. There were too many implications here for her to absorb at once, she was too new to all this, why was she here? The thoughts swirled around her until she wondered if the other women could see them. As if by magic, a cup of water appeared in front of her, and she reached out, grabbed it and drank it in a single gulp.

She put the cup down and drew in a shaky breath. "Alright, so maybe Margaret wasn't called, wasn't supposed to become the Alpha? Or maybe the magic isn't as dependable as we thought? It didn't do much for the Women's Club. Or against Annie and her men, not until the end anyway." It was harder for her to talk about this than she realized. She felt so "new wolf," and it wasn't as if she'd had much experience with the valley's magic. Apart from being called to begin with and helping call it up at the cave, of course. Which was more than most, she supposed, but still. What if she said the wrong thing, screwed something up somehow?

Mei Lin frowned at her. "The original magic was not intended to meet every challenge. Neither the First People or the settlers could have known what was to come. It was only intended to call protectors like us."

Robin and Sharon nodded and Sharon added, "Before the Club burned down, I used to read the archives a lot, and Mei Lin is right. There have been natural disasters, manmade disasters and even other issues with the Pack over time. Those have been pretty rare or at least, all of them didn't get written down. But the Pack keeps going, women in each generation are called, and we bring some measure of protection to Wolf's Point and the valley beyond."

Becca rubbed her fingers against her temples and frowned at the notes on the table in front of her. "So," she began again after a long pause, "does it look like this is where it starts to change? Adapting itself to new conditions, maybe?" She tapped a spot on the page in front of her.

"Ah." Robin nodded. "That's what I was wondering too. Not sure what that would mean though. Maybe different kinds of Alphas? Or the Pack itself will have to adapt in some new ways?"

Becca bit back a sigh. She wasn't a leader or even an experienced wolf. How was she supposed to bring this to Shelly and the others? And if she did, what were they supposed to do next? Things were bad enough right now with everything else going on. Did they really need to deal with this on top of it all?

Robin patted her shoulder. "Look, we don't expect you to fix this or resolve it. We just wanted an outside opinion from a current Pack member, and we can see that you're seeing what some of us thought we were seeing. We'll keep talking about it and you can take it and the notes to Shelly and the others." She waited until Becca looked up and nodded, before asking, "Now, what brought you out here today?"

"Shelly was wondering if there was a way to use the cave paintings like a camera. We surprised Annie doing some kind of ritual there and we're trying to figure out what she was up to. Make herself human again, maybe? Or something else?" She hesitated about telling them about Erin. Was it safe to let them know where she was if Lizzie was coming by to visit? Divided loyalties could be hard to juggle, and Lizzie was related to Sharon and maybe to more Circle members than she knew about yet.

There was an astonished murmur around the table as if this possibility hadn't occurred to any of them before. An ancient woman in a wheelchair whose name Becca hadn't learned yet gave a cackle. "I told you that we hadn't seen the last of that girl!" She chortled and gave the room a wrinkled grin.

"Well, looks like you were right about that, Moira." Sharon wrinkled her nose, her expression puzzled. "I can't see what kind of ritual she'd know how to perform that we wouldn't know about though. Anyone remember anything about calling the wolf-women from the past? Or changing yourself from one form to another? I already told Shelly everything I knew."

Becca pulled out a small pad and paper and started writing a list of what they'd talked about already. If anyone said anything worth recording, she was going to be ready this time. But the room devolved into cacophony as everyone began talking at once, and it took a few minutes to sort out who was saying what. As for what was relevant, who knew?

Robin ran out of patience first and thumped the table to get everyone's attention. "Let's go around the room one by one, please. If you won't have anything to contribute, just pass. We can always talk about more later. Start with your name since Becca hasn't met everyone yet."

Becca gave her a grateful look and listened as they each spoke in turn. It was a grab bag of bits and pieces, half-remembered anecdotes and rumor, but she wrote it all down in the hope that it would prove useful later. Finally, they came back around to her and Robin again and the other woman passed. Becca nodded and put her pad away. "I'll come back in a couple of days to see if anyone remembers anything more. If you need me, I think you have my phone number. Thank you so much for your ideas and your memories."

Robin and Sharon unlocked the door and guided her to the front desk as other residents wandered into the room that they'd been meeting in. "Art class next," Sharon said with a small smile and shook Becca's hand. Robin did too, as did a few of the others.

Becca noticed that a few of the other residents gave them some side eye and she couldn't help but wonder how well the Circle was received. At the very least, they had to look like a very tightly knit clique, and that always made some people antsy. She felt a little sad as she drove off to Gladys' house.

It didn't seem like a bad facility and clearly the Circle had managed to hold their community together, but here in Wolf's Point, shouldn't they be able to be open about who they were and what they had been? Maybe when the Club was rebuilt, they should have an elder's meeting space or something. She added it to the list of things to talk to Shelly about when they weren't up to their eyeballs in emergencies and resigned herself to an evening with Gladys.

# CHAPTER 20

WHEN THEY FINALLY GOT TO the warehouse, Erin was surprised to find herself feeling sick to her stomach. There was her blood trail, leading from the woods to the boarded-up window that she'd broken through. There was the musky scent of bear, hanging over the building like a cloud. She even thought that she could smell a little of Barbie's perfume, lingering like a bad aftertaste.

Carla reached out tentatively and touched her shoulder. "Are you okay?" she whispered. "Should we go to the cave now, let you rest for a bit and then come back later?"

It was a lovely offer and Erin really wanted to consider it, preferably from inside Millie's Café over a slice of pie and a cup of coffee. She wanted mundane things, her life without blood and rage and bodies in her car and kidnappings. She wanted to be home with Becca and Clyde, working on the house, doing accounting projects for her clients. Running through the woods with the Pack. Taking Becca up on the offer she'd been foolish enough to turn down and start finding out where those feelings went.

And yet here they were. Shelly had sent them on a mission and now there was nothing to do but to follow through on it. After all, the more they found out, the better the odds of proving her innocence. *Unless I'm guilty.* That thought hovered like a blood-red cloud in Erin's head, and she couldn't drive it away no matter how hard she tried. All right. If she couldn't deny her fears, she'd have to embrace them.

She drew a deep trembling breath. There were no consequences that she hadn't considered already. Now to go find out whether or not she was worried for nothing.

She gave Carla a shaky smile. "I'm okay. I think. It just hit me kind of hard. Everything smells like bear and blood and cheap perfume to me out here. For a while there, I wasn't sure that I was going to be able to get away before I changed and they got their pictures."

"Whoa. That sounds…really gross. And stressful."

"It is. And it's giving me something that feels like a flashback to being locked in that cage again." She shook herself all over, like a wolf with a wet coat. "But I gotta get over this; we don't have time for it. Let's go check things out."

Carla nodded and together they ducked back into the woods and began to circle the building. It turned out that there was a parking lot on the far side. The concrete was broken up and part of the fence was torn down. Graffiti splashed its way up the concrete walls and a couple of the lights had been broken. All of that looked like old damage as far as they could tell.

There were gashes from bear claws in the trees leading away from the building though, and those looked a lot newer. Erin pointed toward those with a small sigh of relief. They smelled fresh, so maybe they were in luck and Jim and Kari weren't using this as a hiding place any more.

Erin and Carla kept moving, coming back around in a full circle, checking for any hint of what might be inside. There was no sign of the van, but given the state of the parking lot, they might have opted to park out on the road. Apart from that, there were no lights, no noises, no new scents. But it was a big old building and it had thick walls so it was hard to be completely sure.

Erin wondered if all the camera equipment and the lights were still inside. They must have had a way to lock that stuff up, unless they'd moved them all out very quickly. There weren't any security cameras visible outside the building, but maybe there were some inside? She tilted her chin at Carla to indicate that she should keep watch and eased forward quietly to the door next to the boarded-up window. Resting her head against the wood, she listened for noises inside.

The werebear should be back to human now, so that was something. Or at least one less thing to worry about. That didn't rule out weapons of other kinds or their threat to reveal the Pack to the outside world, which was on a whole other level. But the only thing that she could hear was the hum of electricity inside. She tried the knob and found it locked, as she had expected. The boards felt pretty solidly nailed down when she tested them too. Getting back in looked like it was going to be harder than getting back out.

"What if I boosted you onto the roof?" Carla asked. She was looking up over Erin's head. Erin stepped back and followed her gaze upward. It looked possible: the roof had an overhang that came down pretty low at this end. But then what? It was metal and they didn't have any climbing gear. Plus if she fell or Carla put her back out or something, they'd be stranded and vulnerable out here.

"I think we're not quite spry or equipped enough for that. Let's look for another entrance or maybe something we can use as a ladder. If we can't find anything, we'll have to go back and come back with better equipment. At least we'll know what we're up against." Erin began walking back the way they had come and Carla followed.

Erin rounded the side of the building first, then dropped on her belly behind one of the overgrown bushes that surrounded it. She signaled wildly with one hand at her hip to let Carla know that she should stay out of sight. A quiet crackle of footsteps told her that she had been obeyed, but it wasn't quiet enough.

The creature that was trying to break into the warehouse swung a wolflike snout in their general direction, nostrils fluttering as it took in the breeze. Erin sniffed the wind wildly for a minute, waiting for her wolf to rise. Then the wind shifted. *Annie again*. What was she doing here? And more importantly, did she smell or hear them? Erin eyed the sharp claws that tipped Annie's fingers and grimaced. Her fingers dug into the soil beneath her, seizing a couple of handfuls of rocks and small concrete chunks to throw if she needed them.

Carla was hovering behind her. She could feel the other woman's uncertainty and wondered for an instant if she had even seen Annie. Then Carla stepped backward, right onto a stick. Annie stiffened and snarled. She took a step toward them and Erin started to gather her feet under her, though to fight or run, she wasn't sure yet.

But Annie just sniffed at them for a moment, then spun away and loped out of the parking lot on four feet that didn't quite work right. The remains of the shirt and pants she was wearing didn't make it any easier, but Erin guessed that she was still human enough to not want to be running around the woods bare-assed naked with big furry patches.

Without a second thought, Erin ran after her, the sour scent of unwashed wolf-human trailing behind Annie creating an unmistakable trail. *Then why couldn't I smell it before?* She dismissed the thought. If she could just find out where the other… woman, sort of, was hiding, maybe she could also figure out just what else Annie had been up to. It was a long shot, but she thought it might be worth at least a quick look.

Behind her, she heard Carla race a few steps after her, then stop. Good. Someone had to make sensible choices and check out the building. Or maybe call for help, if that was required. Annie took a trail that twisted sharply upward through the woods. If there was one disadvantage to living somewhere with so many hills and mountains, Erin thought, it was that it was only worthwhile naming the most unique ones. They could be anywhere outside town at this point. Erin ventured a quick glance at the moon and tried to figure out what direction they were running in.

After a minute, she realized they were headed north and she wondered why. Maybe there was a cave up there or an old abandoned cabin. Annie had to be hiding somewhere since she sure wasn't running around town like this.

It took her a few more minutes of panting and scrambling to recognize the view. Annie was heading back to the peak where Erin had been when she found the body in the trunk of her car. Where she'd started the ball rolling on this particular set of disasters that were currently wrecking her life. Why? What was she doing?

Annie kept moving, vanishing from sight around some boulders, and Erin slowed down. No point in walking into a trap. If Annie killed Leroy, there was nothing stopping her from doing the same to Erin. Maybe she should just go back to the warehouse and call Shelly. Or Lizzie.

The trail ahead of her dropped into the shadow of the trees and she stopped, inhaling rapidly. Her wolf was on full alert, prowling in the back of her mind, anxious and angry. Well, to be honest, her whole self was anxious and angry. What did this ex-wolf-turned-slayer-turned monster want from her or any of them? It wasn't like they knew how to turn her back. Or forward or whatever it was that she might be hoping for.

Eyes gleamed from the shadows under the trees in front of her and she caught a whiff of the other's scent. Enough of this. She stopped and cleared her throat. "What do you want? Why are you here?"

She heard a quiet woof of breath, then Annie turned and kept moving up the trail at a slow lope, looking behind her from time to time. Maybe she couldn't talk anymore? The moonlight gleamed off her fur and her bare skin, just enough that Erin wondered how she was hiding from hunters and hikers. For a brief instant, she almost felt sorry for Annie. But not for long. She'd done plenty to deserve what had happened to her.

Erin took in a deep breath. If she was going to keep following her, she needed to do it before she lost the trail. *Just a little further,* she told herself. *Then I'll go back for help.* Shelly and Becca wouldn't want her to put herself in danger, not again. There'd been plenty of that lately. Her phone buzzed in her pocket, startling her from her thoughts. She stepped off onto a ledge and took a good look around before she pulled it from her pocket. Shelly. She debated whether or not to respond or to wait.

The scramble of claws on the rock above her came almost too late to be a warning. She twisted to one side as Annie leapt, flinging her body on top of hers. They rolled on the rocks, each scrambling for purchase. Annie's snout hovered just above Erin's face, her breath rank with the scent of rotting meat. Erin gagged and twisted away, but Annie's claws sank into her shoulders just enough to hold her still.

"Ssstoppp." Her voice was a harsh rasp, her wolflike lips struggling to create speech.

It was a shock to hear it and Erin froze for an instant, looking up into dark eyes that were still more or less human. Not that she could read their expression, unfortunately. "Cave," Annie hissed. "Maagggiccc." She gestured with her snout...chin... whatever you could call what she had now and Erin bucked her hips upward, throwing Annie off her. Then she punched out, hard, driving the air from Annie's lungs.

Or tried to. Annie's stomach was a lot harder than she was expecting, more washboard than a middle-aged woman's curves, and Erin barely turned away when a sharp-clawed hand swiped at her face. Annie was growling now, her face growing longer, less human. "Shit," Erin muttered, scrambling backward to put her back against the rock.

Her phone buzzed again, the noise growing more insistent. Annie tucked her snout in, scrambling upward into a crouch. Her nostrils flared as she sniffed the wind and growled deep in her throat. Erin could hear something now too. *Cavalry's here,* she realized a moment later. Several Pack members were scrambling through the woods behind them, headed their way. After a moment, Annie turned and fled, continuing up the trail they'd been following.

Erin lurched to her feet and took a step after her, then froze. What was she hoping to find? A big sign that said: "It was me, Annie. I killed that guy"? She sighed in frustration, then looked down at the spot where Annie had been crouching a few moments before.

Something shiny caught her eye in the moonlight and she reached down to touch it, then pick it up when she realized what it was: a battered military dog tag with badly corroded letters. Had Annie left it there or had it been there before they got here? Molly, Adelía and a couple of the others clambered up onto the ledge, each holding a homemade weapon, and Erin slipped the tag into her pocket. She could look at it later. "Um… hi? Nice wrench?"

# CHAPTER 21

AN EVENING WITH GLADYS TURNED out to not be half as bad as Becca had feared. Not fun, exactly, but not too bad. Gladys was a lot less abrupt and unpleasant on her own turf. They prepared dinner together and made low-key conversation about the town and the wolf preserve, where Gladys volunteered. The regular wolves were a little jumpy around her at first, but had gotten used to her over time, or so Gladys maintained.

Becca considered Clyde's reaction to her when the moon started getting full and wondered if the wolves were just frightened out of their wits. But it would be impolite to contradict her host, so she let that speculation pass. After dinner, they sat in Gladys' country kitsch living room and watched an old movie before they got sleepy enough to go to bed.

Or at least, Gladys did and Becca went along to be polite. It was something to do and just enough to be somewhat distracting. Gladys even had a tiny guest room so Becca didn't even need to sleep on the sofa. And Becca tried to be grateful for that hospitality as she lay awake for hours staring at the ceiling.

She really was grateful, once she stopped to think about it. It was just that she missed Erin and her own bed and Clyde and… who was she kidding? She wanted to be home with her own family. Which brought up another fear: how were she and Erin ever going to rebuild what they had, after all this? Assuming they even had the opportunity? Things might never be the same. A tear ran down Becca's cheek and she wiped it away before it hit the pillow.

She gave up wiping them away after awhile and she was still crying when she fell asleep some time later.

THE NEXT MORNING SENT HER back to work at the store, so at least there was that semblance of normality. But it didn't last long. Shelly and Molly came in with a tale about Erin chasing Annie up into the mountains, or perhaps luring her up there. They weren't sure which one of the two it was, or perhaps it was both. Shelly assumed that it was about the murder charge and Erin thinking Annie had done it, Molly thought it might be that and that she might also have been hoping to find out something about Jim and Kari.

Their words washed over Becca in a wave, including the information that Erin was staying with Carla at an undisclosed location that wasn't the cave. But clearly was because her friends were terrible liars. She felt a flash of irrational jealousy, followed by a different kind of flash. Her skin burned while her emotions roiled. Why was Carla getting to spend time with Erin? That was her job, dammit. Or, at least, it was where she wanted to be the most. Didn't that amount to the same thing?

It took a few minutes to realize that Molly was telling her about Carla and Erin finding the warehouse where Erin had been held, but she wasn't paying as much attention as she could have been. And by the time that she thought she had wrapped her brain around everything that had happened, it felt like everything shifted. Molly had left for work and Shelly was working the front of the store while Kira restocked and she was out on the sidewalk, having been gently ejected from the store to go to lunch.

Looking around her gave Becca a sense of déjà vu. Had it only been a few months ago that they'd been dealing with Annie and her men on this very street? She drank in a breath of downtown air, letting her wolf sift through the various scents. Her back tensed with every new noise, every fresh scent. What was she so worried about? The werebear? Erin cruising down the street to break off their potential relationship before it really got started? Random strange werewolves?

After a moment, she twitched a little, shaking off some of her fears. All of this could happen, but they wouldn't be any easier to handle if she was half-asleep and mid-hot flash on an empty stomach. The sign for the new café caught her eye from a couple of blocks away and she started walking toward it, negotiating her way through the sidewalk displays and wandering pedestrians.

An acquaintance held the door for her at Muffins N' More while she was hesitating on the doorstep. The way he did it suggested that he thought he was doing her middle-aged self a favor, something that she found both amusing and irritating. She consolidated that into a nod and stepped inside, pushing down a small wave of concern about being disloyal to Millie of Millie's Café fame, a downtown Wolf's Point mainstay, merely by walking into this place.

The waitress and a vaguely familiar-looking man converged on her at the same time. "How many?" "Ms. Thornton, I—"

Becca glanced from the waitress to Larry Milchester. His voice was sonorous in the wave of lunchtime crowd noise. "Do you have a minute?" At her nod, he gestured at the waitress, who brought them to a corner table and seated them. Becca gave the décor a quick glance as he checked his phone, and sniffed. Store-bought antiques, some handmade kitsch, seats so new, they crackled. Millie's next time, she promised herself.

Their waitress appeared and Becca gave the menu a quick skim before picking a chicken sandwich and a side salad. The waitress disappeared and the lawyer put his phone away in an inner pocket of his jacket. "Ms. Thornton, I need to call Shelly later today, but I wanted to check in with you. I won't ask you to tell me if you know where Ms. Adams is, of course, but I am wondering if you might be able to get a message to her."

Becca stared at him with narrowed eyes. He still smelled off, not human, not wolf. *Not werebear, either.* She wrinkled her nose. After all, Shelly trusted him, so that was going to have to be enough for now. Right? "What would it mean for me if I were able to do that, hypothetically? Would I turn up as an accessory or something if things went…badly?"

Larry Milchester looked at her, his expression unreadable, at least to Becca's anxious gaze. Something not human flickered in the back of his black eyes for a moment and she braced herself for trouble. A quick glance at the rest of him, his broad shoulders with muscles bunched as if for flight or fight, suggested that he sensed what she was feeling and was having a few issues with control himself.

The waitress interrupted their standoff by putting Becca's order between them. The atmosphere eased immediately once they stopped making eye contact and Becca let out a small relieved sigh. "I should eat lunch while we talk, if you don't mind."

He gestured his assent and glanced casually around the room, almost as if he was looking for someone. Or was making sure that no one else was listening. "It's more in the nature of passing along anecdotal information. Much like you would if you were speaking to a neighbor." The corner of his thin lip tilted up in a not quite smile. "Which, in effect, you would be. The initial lab analysis came back and suggests that Mr. Callan had been dead for five or six hours before he was placed in the trunk of Ms. Adams' car." He glanced at her, eyes a normal dark brown for the moment.

Becca stopped mid-bite and put her sandwich down. It took her a second to process what he was saying, then another minute or two to review what she could remember about the day when this whole mess started. "I'd have kept a diary if I'd realize I might have to remember this kind of stuff," she murmured at last. "But I'm pretty sure she didn't leave the house until about two or three hours before she started hiking." A huge sense of relief washed over her. The likelihood that Erin had killed Leroy in a fit of rage or something was diminishing fast.

"Perhaps Ms. Adams kept an appointment book, one that you might be able to locate. It certainly couldn't hurt to verify that she had a client meeting that morning, or equivalent. Thank you for your time, Ms. Thornton. I need to go now, but I look forward to discussing this further." He stood up and nodded to her, the angle suggesting a bow. For a big man, he moved both swiftly and quietly, fading through the restaurant and out the door like a ghost. Or a big predator.

Becca grimaced, then finished her sandwich. She paid the waitress and started walking back to Peterson's, her brain whirling with the implications of what she'd just been told. Erin must have some kind of calendar either in print or on her computer. A thought struck her then and she stopped in the middle of the sidewalk, causing a woman walking behind her to walk right into her. Apologies exchanged, Becca moved into a store doorway to get out of the way. Their burglar, had that been what they were looking for?

It was a staggering realization. She hadn't checked to see if Erin had an iPad or even a little volume with a padlock on it when she'd gone looking for clues. What had she missed? She frowned across the street, not really seeing the people there, at least not until one of them looked very familiar.

She'd recognize Kari's blue eyes anywhere, not to mention that perfectly coiffed blonde hair. A bolt of fear went through her and she glanced around quickly, wondering if Jim was somewhere nearby. A cautious sniff told her nothing, except that Kari wore too much perfume and could use a shower.

The other woman was clearly looking for something or someone. She was pretending to look through a sales rack of outfits in front of Emmeline's Closet, but her gaze was directed at the hardware store. Was she contemplating home renovations? Or, more likely, spying on her?

Becca was contemplating walking across the street and confronting her when she noticed another familiar face about a block away. Deputy Lizzie Blackhawk was out of uniform and driving her own car, but she also seemed to have the hardware store staked out from where she was parked. Unless…she was watching Kari? Now why would she be doing that? Becca sent a quick text to Shelly to let her know that she was checking something out and would be a few minutes late.

When she looked back up, she couldn't see Lizzie anymore and Kari had shifted to looking in the window of the shop next door to Peterson's. Was she planning on going in? Becca suppressed a growl. What other game was this woman playing? Since Erin had gotten away, the whole exposé plan must have collapsed. Was she hoping that the hardware store staff would transform into wolves just in time for her to capture it on film?

Maybe it was time to go find out. Becca strolled down the block and across the street, before walking in the front door of the store. "Something's up," she murmured to Shelly. "Let me work the front while you stay out of sight." Shelly quirked an eyebrow but used a customer's question as an excuse to turn the counter over to Becca.

Becca fidgeted a bit, trying not to watch the front door too hard. Instinctively, she pulled a box of screws from behind the counter and started counting. Kari didn't take long. She barely gave the rest of the store a glance before barreling up to the counter and peering at Becca. "Hello." The other woman's voice was pitched low and quiet. "I was hoping to find you here."

"Were you? And why is that? Doing a bit of home repair?" Becca could hear the rage in her own voice and inhaled deeply to try and regain control. *How dare this foolish woman threaten the Pack? How dare she scare and hurt Erin?*

"Well, we want to be good neighbors, and we noticed that you and your…housemate haven't been home for the last few days. Would you like us to take in your mail, maybe take care of some plants?"

Becca tried to picture Kari in a black hoodie and jeans, with her face covered up, and leaned forward for a closer sniff. She did smell somewhat familiar, but she was too short to be their burglar. Which left her husband as the most likely suspect. Her suspicions about her new neighbor hardened. "You have got to be kidding. I think you should leave. Leave the store, leave this town, leave the valley. We already know what he is and you don't want any more trouble than you've already gotten into."

"Are you part of 'we,' then, too? Just like your pal, Erin? We suspected you were, but it's always nice to have confirmation." Kari smiled, her blandly pretty features shifting into something predatory.

Becca sucked in a breath. This confrontation was a mistake. She was letting her fury at Erin's kidnapping, as well as the break-in, get the better of her. "I don't know what you're talking about. Erin and I are part of a neighborhood watch and we've seen the company you keep. This town isn't a good match for," she paused and drew her mouth down like some of the more snobby ladies from the Women's Club, "the likes of you and your…husband. We have a very low crime rate, you know, not much violent crime. Comes from having good people live here."

"Oh, indeed. We know. It was one of the reasons that we moved here." Her plastic smile had turned stiff. "But I'm pretty sure that whatever you think you know about us is nothing compared to what we know about Erin. And I don't think you want that getting out."

Blackmail? Who did this woman think she was? A wave of pure rage coursed through Becca and she leaned forward, elbows on the counter. She let her wolf out, just a little, and rejoiced at Kari's flinch. "Even if there was something to know, I don't think anyone would believe you. Most folks around here would think you're telling lies about a nice bunch of upstanding community members. And if you were to leave town suddenly with a murder charge nipping at your heels, I'm pretty sure that your credibility would drop quite a bit." She growled the words softly, the scent of Kari's blood overpowering the scent she wore.

"Murder! Why would you think that we murd…" Her voice trailed off. They locked eyes and Becca's wolf slipped closer to the surface. She could picture her teeth in the other woman's throat.

The door chimed as it opened, making the other woman stumble back as the bright sunshine outside poured in. Lizzie Blackhawk paused in the doorway before stepping inside. "I always seem to be interrupting something around here lately. Why is that, do you suppose?" She closed the door and leaned against it. "I don't think we've met yet. I gather you and your husband bought Becca and Ed's old house?" She pushed her mirror shades up on her head and studied Kari.

Becca dug her fingers into the counter and took a deep breath, getting her body and mind back under control. She could hear Shelly and the other customers rustling around and talking in the aisles around them now. Better make sure that no one saw anything particularly odd going on. "Hi, Deputy," she managed, forcing her voice to sound calmer than she felt. "K—our new neighbor was just heading out. She just stopped by to check out the store and say hi." *Even though I never told her where I worked.*

The realization staggered her. This went much deeper than the burglary. This woman, and presumably her werebear spouse, had been *studying* them, not just Erin. But who told her about the Pack to begin with? A flood of face rose up in Becca's brain: people in Wolf's Point, the Circle, other Pack members, Annie, her men...Leroy.

She charged around the counter just in time to realize that Lizzie had let Kari out the door and was standing in front of her. Lizzie frowned as Becca's words poured out in a torrent, "They did it! Her husband's the one who broke into our house! Why did you let her go? Where did she go? We need to catch her!"

"Or we could take a few minutes and you could tell me what's really going on. I don't think she'll get that far."

Becca glared at the deputy. "Why not? Whose side are you on?"

Lizzie gave her a long look, then held up one of Peterson Hardware's longest nails. "I believe one of these found its way into her back tire."

Becca's jaw dropped and she blinked slowly as she took the nail. "You knew? Or at least you suspected that she was up to something? Do you know about Jim?" The roiling emotions in her head choked off her words for a moment. Was Erin on the run for nothing? This was getting to be too much to endure.

Lizzie nodded at the counter behind her. "Suppose we wander back up there and I pay for a few more nails so things look nice and normal?"

Becca glanced back in time to see a young couple approaching the register with a basketful of stuff, and with an exasperated sigh at Lizzie, she bustled over to wait on them. A few minutes of polite chitchat and some hardware advice and she sent them on their way. A quick glance down the aisles showed Shelly on her way to them, but no one else in the store, and she flipped the sign to "Back in Five Minutes" and locked the front door.

"Now will you tell me what you know and what you think is going on? I'll tell you everything I can, but some stuff you'll have to get from Shelly." She nodded at her boss, who was leaning up against the shelving across from the counter.

Lizzie set a box of nails on the counter. "'Suspect' is probably more accurate than saying I actually know things for certain. It's obvious that things started getting weird...weirder when that couple moved to town. Not too hard to figure out they've got some woo-woo crap of their own going on, based on your reaction to them. Now, I don't know that they killed Leroy, and I'm guessing you don't either or I'd have heard about it by now. But I do suspect that you all know something about them and that you know where Erin might be and that you've all been holding back on telling me about any of it."

A red flush crept up Becca's cheeks despite everything she could do to hide it, and quickly fanning herself to imply that it was a hot flash didn't seem to convince Lizzie. The deputy leaned against the counter and scowled at her, the nail rolling around between them like a little compass point.

"It's not like we set out to hide things from you," Becca said finally when the silence got to be too much to bear. "But you've got the sheriff to answer to and your kid to take care of and you're not…a lot of the time, I don't know what's going on either." She trailed off. It wasn't like Lizzie didn't know she wasn't a Pack member, but it felt unkind to rub that in. She knew that the other woman wanted to be a member very badly and was hoping that she would in a few years.

"I don't expect you to tell me everything, but I'm guessing that Shelly told you that I'm planning on running for sheriff next year. If I'm going to do that, I've gotta look at least somewhat impartial. I also need a big case to make my name stand out so people recognize it. Solving Leroy's murder would do that for me. Are you still with me?" Lizzie's expression suggested that she was having some trouble being this straightforward about her plans, and Becca guessed that this decision was pretty recent.

"So if we crack this case for you and give you a murderer, you drop the case against Erin? I'm not opposed to doing that exactly, but I think by now you know that Erin didn't kill Leroy and that the only thing you really have to charge her with is that damn confession." Shelly had joined them at the counter, her expression distant.

"You're Pack. The magic makes you what you are, but it makes you protectors as well. Seems to me that we've none of us got a choice but to get to the bottom of this pretty quickly. What's the deal with Blondie and her hubby?" Lizzie's gaze shifted from her cousin to Becca.

She took a deep breath, and at Shelly's nod, tried to lay it all out as succinctly as possible. "Her husband's a werebear. They were TV personalities, show hosts or something from a few years back. Now, they're trying to break back into the biz by doing a reality TV show of some kind, online, we think, about the Pack. They kidnapped Erin from the jail so they could film her changing." Becca finally ran out of breath.

"A were-what now? How did they find out about you in the first place?" Lizzie rubbed her hands on her cheeks, her expression a combination of bewilderment and weariness.

"And I'm ninety percent sure that he's our burglar. I think he was looking for something to connect Leroy and Erin so they could pressure her into cooperating. Sorry, Shelly, I just figured this part out. I was talking to..." She trailed off. Should she mention what Larry had told her in front of Lizzie? Or was that, what did they call it, "privileged information"? Why was everything so complicated all the time now?

Shelly sighed. "Out with it. Who were you talking to? Sounds like we're putting all the cards on the table."

"I ran into Larry Milchester at the new café when I went there for lunch, and he said the results had come back and that Leroy had been dead for five or six hours or so before he wound up in the trunk of Erin's car. So I thought that maybe the burglar was looking for something that would have proved Erin had an alibi for when Leroy was killed? Maybe she came out of whatever blackout or whatever was wrong with her, found him in her trunk and just assumed she'd done it?"

Shelly's gaze sharpened and her nostrils flared. "What kind of something, Becca?"

"Maybe a calendar or a diary or something? She meets with clients and auditors and so forth, and if it's something confidential, she usually doesn't tell me much about it." Becca looked at the counter for a second and frowned. "Now I'm trying to remember what I was doing. I might be her alibi, for all I know." She rubbed her face with her hand, stretching the skin down until her palms met under her chin.

Lizzie glanced at Shelly. "An alibi would help. As would some kind of medical condition that would explain a blackout. Other than turning into a werewolf."

Someone knocked on the front door and Shelly went over to check on it with a soft grumble. Lizzie eyed Becca while they waited. "Can you find her appointment book?"

"I think so. She doesn't like those online calendar things, doesn't trust them, so I think I know where she usually keeps the one she does use," Becca added, picturing Erin's basement office and desk.

"How about you and me go check that out right now? If I'm supposed to be looking for more suspects, I'd like to get a move on." Lizzie dropped her shades back down on her nose and walked over to the door, just as Shelly opened it to let in a couple of customers. "I need to borrow Becca for an hour. Can you manage?"

"Well, seeing as you're not really asking, I guess so." Shelly arched a dark eyebrow at her cousin.

Lizzie grimaced back at her and ushered Becca out the door. "I'll bring takeout tonight after work. We're all due for a family night and I know you've got that Women's Club board meeting tomorrow night."

"Oh...crap. I'd forgotten about that. Takeout sounds great. I hope Andy's coming too. See you later." Shelly turned and headed back into the store as Lizzie pulled the door shut behind her.

"So all is forgiven?" Becca asked, with a sidelong glance.

"Takeout heals all wounds. Well, takeout and some shouting and some apologizing and all that stuff." Lizzie led the way to her car with a shrug. "How are you and Gladys getting along?"

It was Becca's turn to shrug. "Could be worse. I'd rather be home with Erin and our dog, but I'm glad that Gladys was willing to put me up for a couple of nights."

"Your enthusiasm is overwhelming, but yes, I do know what you mean. Let's try and get this figured out as fast as possible so we can get things back to what passes for normal around here."

"And get your campaign jumpstarted?"

"That too.

"You can practice your acceptance speech on the way."

"I'm excited already."

"Now who's enthusiastic?" Becca rolled her eyes and followed Lizzie out to her car.

# CHAPTER 22

E RIN FORGOT ABOUT THE DOG tag for a while, what between explaining what had happened with Annie to the others the first time and discussing it in greater detail on the way back to the cave. Once they got there, they picnicked on the ledge outside around a small fire. Carli had news about the insurance policy settlement; it looked like they were going to be able to start building a new Women's Club as soon as they hired contractors. Adelía and Carla wanted to talk about that, and then speculate about what Annie would do next, and Molly looked like she just needed a nap.

Finally, Erin raised her hand for silence. "I think we've been over this enough for today and I know I'm getting really tired. Who's babysitting me tonight? And who's reporting in to Shelly?"

Carli nodded. "I'll head home and talk to Shelly on the way. I need to tell her about the insurance settlement too."

Adelía stood up and started cleaning up. "The kids will be driving Pedro nuts by now so I'll head back. Molly, you're staying tonight, right?"

Carla looked like she wanted to say something, but whatever it was, she swallowed it back down and started helping with the cleanup as Molly nodded. Erin gave her a minute to share whatever was on her mind, then went to help Molly get set up for the night when she didn't say anything. She suspected that Carla wanted to stay at the cave overnight again, but she could tell them as much in her own time.

Besides, she wanted to think about what Annie might be up to as much as any of them and she needed some quiet to do that. That way, they wouldn't get to see her desperate hope that Annie had killed Leroy and framed her and that it would be easy to prove and this would all be over with. And it was going to be hard to think her way through that much hope. Just because she wanted it to be true didn't make it so. She was still trying to come up with a motive, not to mention the details on how all that could have happened, when she finally fell asleep.

Maybe that hoping and thinking was what called the dream later that night. Certainly something did. In her sleeping mind, Erin could feel the paintings on the walls moving slowly around the cave, and she got up to follow them. Were their ancestor wolves disturbed because they were sleeping in the cave or was it something else? She could feel their agitation as she walked, fingers trailing slowly over the stone.

Part of her got lost in the memory of the ritual that she and Shelly and Becca had done to call the painted wolves to life to fight Annie and her men. What had the paintings done with Anderson and the others who had disappeared that night? Why change Annie, but not them? The paintings weren't telling.

As she walked, she could almost see something moving in the back of the cave, beyond where the Pack usually met, buried in the shadows. Because it was a dream and she was conscious of that, she walked further into the cave instead of yelling out a warning, wondering what she would discover in the darkness. The shadows enfolded her, dimming Molly's solar lamp until she was alone in the shadows.

No, wait, there was something else here. Glowing eyes waited for her back where it was darkest, and she froze, her body struggling to wake or flee. An instant later, there were more eyes, all glowing in the lantern's light. They encircled her, the only way out the way she had entered. She trembled, sensing that her body was desperately trying to wake her from this dream or vision, whatever it was. A voice rolled out of the darkness, echoing around in her head and filling the space around her. It was deep and hoarse, as if it had been unused for a long time.

She didn't understand the words. But her bewilderment must have come across to whoever was speaking, because something changed in the way the voice spoke and the words suddenly began to make sense. Not all of them, especially since some of the sounds seemed to be in wolf, rather than any human language. But that was enough to wake her wolf brain up until she was conscious of the smell of other wolves, a sense of kinship with whatever it was that waited in the darkness. After what felt like forever, her wolf brain took over, driving her human self into the back of her brain, there to be over-whelmed by sleep.

When Molly shook her shoulder to wake her up, dawn was just beginning to light the mountaintops outside. "Hey, Erin, you okay? Sounds like you're having a nightmare."

Erin rolled over, her mouth full of sand and her eyes full of sleep. Her first glance fell not on Molly, but on the back of the cave, searching for glowing eyes and creatures she hadn't been able to see clearly. She scrubbed one hand across her face and swallowed to clear her throat. Her shoulders ached a little from sleeping on the stone floor and she could feel other aches and pains making their presence felt as she stretched. Not that it mattered too much. They'd be gone once she was up and about, a long-term benefit of the valley's magic riding her once a month, but waking up could still be a bear. So to speak.

She wrinkled her nose at the thought. What had happened to Jim and Kari while they were all running around after Annie or guarding Becca? "Hmmm...did you have any weird dreams last night? Oh, hey, is that coffee?" She knew it was, of course, but she wasn't quite ready to unpack her dream, not yet. It felt like she'd gotten some marching orders and she wanted to process that feeling a bit before she brought it out into the daylight.

"Weird dreams? I think you were having enough for both of us! You kept making these tiny howls and growls, like your wolf was scared or something. What's going on? No, wait, tell me after coffee and breakfast. I remember what you're like in the mornings." Molly gave her an amused grin and went back to the camp stove on the ledge outside the cave entrance.

Erin wrinkled her nose and got up slowly, making her first stops to the latrine and then the water bucket for washing up. She wanted a hot shower and a chance to wash her clothes so badly, she could almost taste it. But it was a bit too cold to go skinny-dipping in the nearest stream, even if it had been safe in daylight, so she washed as much of herself as she could before dumping the water out and heading back to the ledge.

Molly handed her a cup of coffee and a plate of eggs and veggies, fresh from the frying pan. "Remember anything about those dreams you were having?"

Erin gave the back of the cave a quick glance, almost expecting to see glowing eyes looking back at her. But this morning there was nothing there except paintings and dark-ness. She sighed and took a gulp of coffee, then nearly spat it back out. Molly made engine fuel; she'd forgotten a lot since their brief fling a few years back. Erin sighed and sipped more cautiously before putting her mug down.

She ate a forkful of eggs before she responded, "It was weird. I thought something was watching me from the back of the cave, then a lot of somethings, all with glowing eyes." She shivered a little at the memory. "They started talking to me but it wasn't in English, from what I can remember, at least not at first. Or even all in human."

"You had a vision in the cave? Whoa, Erin, that's a big deal! We need to tell Shelly, send you over to talk to the Circle. Gotta get our elders in on this one. But..." Molly's excitement trailed off, along with her voice, as she clearly realized what Erin already knew: that talking about the dream would mean telling everyone where Erin was.

"Don't think that's an option right now. But yeah, I do think I should run it past Shelly when she stops by tonight. But I want to think about it a little bit more, try and figure out what they were saying to me, if I can." Erin ran her fingers through her short gray hair. "This fugitive thing sucks. I want a shower and clean clothes and a good night's sleep in my own bed."

"Don't you mean 'our' own bed?" Molly gave her an amused grin.

"No. We're not there yet. Or maybe we were, almost, but we aren't now. I'm not sure she trusts me anymore. Dammit. How did I make such a mess of things?"

"Oh, I think Becca is on her way to head over heels, but admittedly, all this isn't helping move things along very quickly. As for what you did, want the full list or the short one? I still don't understand why you confessed if you weren't really sure that you killed Leroy to begin with, let alone stuffed him into your car. I mean, I know you and I get it, sort of, but even for your out-of-control sense of responsibility and guilt and all, this seems kinda excessive." Molly leaned back against the rocks and gave Erin a narrow-eyed stare.

A bunch of responses went through Erin's head for a few minutes, ranging from telling Molly to piss off to telling her the absolute truth. She banged her head lightly back against the rock; what was the point of lying now? "I thought I fell off the wagon, got wasted, got into a fight and killed the guy. He was in the trunk of my car. I couldn't remember how he got there and..." She paused for a minute and closed her eyes. "There was blood on my clothes and near the car. Add that to the no memory of just how that happened and you see how I came to the conclusion I did. After that, I was so damned embarrassed, I just didn't want to talk about it."

"Shit," Molly murmured. "Okay, that is some compelling evidence. I see your point."

"I didn't start to doubt my version of events until I got kidnapped by the reality TV werebear and his partner in life and crime. Once I got to hang out with them for a bit, I realized that they probably had something to do with Leroy's death and may have been palling around with Annie too, at some point. Now all I need is some evidence to convince the sheriff and Lizzie of that, not to mention explaining the whole jailbreak thing. And explain all of it to Becca. 'All,'" she put the word in air quotes, "being a pretty big thing."

"Not to mention your remaining accounting customers. You know the news about all this turned up in the *Wolf's Point Gazette*, albeit in kinda vague terms? Lizzie and Shelly tried to keep it as hushed up as possible, but we just don't get that many murders around here. Or at least ones that end up on the Sheriff's Department's radar." Molly wrinkled her nose. "Eat your breakfast and we'll make a chart or something and see if anything shakes loose."

An hour or so later, they were both scowling at some notebook pages with lists on them. Erin thought it was still pretty confusing, but at least they were getting all the variables out where they could look at them. The possible connection between Annie and Leroy and their new neighbors was almost entirely speculation. Maybe Jim and Kari had just heard about the werewolf hunters from their site and never worked with them before. Maybe they were working together, somehow, all along, despite Annie's condition, and had a falling out.

But someone had told them about the Pack and that wasn't a huge list of suspects, or at least not ones who traveled outside the area much. It was clear that they'd come to the valley already knowing about the wolves and possibly Erin in particular. What had Leroy been up to since they'd defeated Annie and her men at the cave? Erin rubbed her temples, feeling a bad headache coming on.

Molly took the hint and left for work just as Carla clambered up. Erin went back into the cave for a nap, hoping for a less haunted sleep this time around. She dozed off as Carla walked around the cave, studying each of the paintings in turn.

What woke her later was the sound of voices. She rolled over to see Carla, Lizzie, Shelly and Becca huddled in the cave mouth, looking at something. They all jumped when she stood up, like they'd forgotten she was there. Erin grimaced at the thought and took a long drink from her water bottle. She scowled into the afternoon sunshine glowing from the entrance and growled her words as she walked past her friends on her way out, "Talking about me again?"

It was all bravado and she could see Shelly, at least, recognized it as such. Why had they brought Lizzie? Had they found something new that confirmed that she was guilty? Erin's stomach sank down to the vicinity of her toes and she couldn't bring herself to look at Becca.

"Well, yes. Of course we are." Shelly rolled her eyes, looking just like Kira for a moment. "Go pee, then come back and we'll tell you what's going on."

# CHAPTER 23

B ECCA WAS PRETTY WORRIED ABOUT how Erin was going to react when they showed up with Lizzie in tow. One look at Erin's groggy face when she saw them told her all she needed to know. They had taken her by surprise and she was afraid, feeling betrayed and isolated. It made Becca's heart ache to see it.

But when she reached out to touch Erin's arm, Erin didn't seem to notice, and she dropped her hand. Was this whole mess going to destroy what they had or could have had? On the other hand, she paused, trying to still the whirlwind in her brain, Erin going to jail for murder wasn't going to do them any favors either. She gave Lizzie a sidelong glance. She'd only be sitting here, all casual and hanging out, if she thought Erin was innocent, right?

"We'll wait for Erin to get back before we discuss things." Shelly's tone didn't leave room for much of an argument and Becca closed her mouth and clenched her jaw to hold the questions in.

Instead, they made small talk about contractors and architects and what they would like to see in a new Wolf's Point Women's Club. Not that Becca was paying much attention. Her brain swirled with memories of her years at the club before she changed, duking it out for precedence with her memory of changing for the first time there and how painful and scary it was at first. It seemed like an eternity before Erin walked back up the trail, accepted a sandwich from Shelly and sat down in their little circle.

They waited in silence while Erin ate the sandwich and finished off her water bottle. She put it down gently, like the noise might draw more attention to her. "Okay," she said, "now what?"

She still wasn't looking at Becca, but it didn't feel as deliberate as it had earlier. It was s still a barrier though and Becca knew that she had to break through it. "We read your appointment book and some of the papers in your desk!" she blurted out, then clapped her hands over her mouth. Her face flamed red and hot as embarrassment shifted into a hot flash and she forced her hands down to her sides. "And I wanted to apologize for that, but I was trying to make sure that Lizzie was convinced..." she trailed off.

"Wait," Erin glanced from her to Lizzie, then back again, "has anyone *not* read my appointment book?" She scowled at each of them and Becca buried her face in her hands. Carla raised a tentative hand and got an abrupt nod. "Fine, now you know about all my dentist appointments, my meetings, my clients…"

"We didn't read all of it!" Becca covered her face again and wailed behind her fingers. "Just the last couple of weeks of entries!"

"If I may." Lizzie interjected, "Erin, you are still a suspect in a murder investigation and you did confess to the murder. Your appointment book is potential evidence in our investigation. But no, before you ask, I didn't turn it over to the sheriff. And that's something I'd like all of you to keep under your hats."

"Our lawyer said that Leroy had been dead for five or six hours before he ended up in your trunk, see? So we had to know where you'd been and what you were doing because I wasn't sure that I remembered everything from that day. We only looked at it so Lizzie had somewhere to start to confirm that you couldn't have done it." Becca tried not to sound pleading, but she still winced at the look on Erin's face.

Shelly pulled a wrapped package from her backpack and handed it to Erin. She shook her head at Erin's unspoken question. "While I understand a little of how you feel about this, Erin, I did encourage them to check once I remembered that you used to keep a journal as well as a date book. You can blame me, if that helps any."

Erin swore under her breath and gestured at Carla. "You're now my best friend, right after Molly. The rest of you need to do some very fast talking about what you found out. I'm pretty sure that I didn't black out for six solid hours." Her knuckles were white as she clasped her hand together around her knee and Becca dropped her own hand down over Erin's and squeezed lightly. Erin's fingers trembled, but she didn't pull back.

Lizzie took a sip of her own water bottle and cleared her throat. "Right. So based on where you said you'd been and what you said you were up to that day and right before the incident, I followed a trail of receipts to stores in town, interviewed a couple of your neighbors and did some verification of security footage at the bank and the gas station. My conclusion: no, you didn't black out for a day. In fact, right up until two hours before you called me, I couldn't find any evidence that you'd had a drop to drink."

Erin shuddered and Shelly patted her shoulder. "But...I still might have once I got up on the trail. I mean, if I brought it with me." She gave Lizzie a faraway stare that suggested that her mind was somewhere else.

"You passed the labs that we gave you when we took you in. We found an interesting drug cocktail in your system, but no booze."

"Wait, drugs? I've never been on..." Erin's voice trailed off and she gave Lizzie a wide-eyed look. "Are you saying someone drugged me and planted a dead body in my car so I'd think that I killed him?"

"It's looking like a good possibility."

"But who...how?"

"And so we come around to why we're all here and Molly and the others are on their way. In the meantime, Molly told me that you had a vision in your dream last night, Erin. I'd really like to hear more about that. What do you remember?" Shelly's voice cut like a knife through the confusion and pain of the last few minutes, refocusing them all as if this was just another problem that they had to solve. Becca sighed with relief, but just a little. The mess was still there and she wasn't sure if Erin was completely in the clear yet.

They all listened quietly while Erin recounted what she remembered of her dream, right up until she got to the part about the voice that spoke directly to her wolf. "Wait, can you remember any of the sounds?" Shelly leaned forward, her gaze sharp and intent. Becca belatedly remembered her new role as archivist and pulled out her phone. She set it to record while Erin stumbled through a few yips and growls before trailing off.

"We need a hypnotist," Carla volunteered, breaking the silence. "Someone who can figure out how to put Erin under so she can translate from wolf to human for us. Or, you know, you." She blushed bright red and looked at her hands when Lizzie looked at her incredulously.

Erin frowned and cocked her head to one side. "That might be a great idea, but I'm not sure where we'd find one around here. They'd have to be Pack-friendly too."

"We do have a version of that. I think my cousin has experimented with hypnotherapy on some of his patients," Shelly put in thoughtfully.

Becca thought back to her time at Dr. Green's clinic, remembered waking up wounded with her leg cuffed to a gurney, and her stomach turned. For a cowardly moment, she hoped that someone else was going to volunteer to take Erin to the clinic. Or bring Dr. Green here, if Erin wanted to give this hypnosis thing a try. Or...maybe she should stop and consider that this wasn't about her. She cleared her throat and interjected, "That sounds like an interesting idea, if you're open to it, Erin." She gave Erin a tentative sidelong glance, trying to gauge her reaction.

Erin rubbed her face with her hands, then held them out over the cook stove to warm them. After a moment of silence, she gave Becca a weary smile. "I am open to anything and everything that makes Leroy's corpse someone else's problem and gets me back home for a hot bath."

Lizzie laughed quietly. "That may be the best list of priorities that I've heard all day. I want to figure out what the werebear and his mate are up to, but I think checking in on Annie, if you can, isn't a bad idea either. I'm liking the scenario in which the reality TV couple found out about the Pack and the valley from Leroy, and maybe Annie, then had a falling out with one or both of them. But we need some proof. We also need to show some evidence that you were kidnapped, Erin, not just involved in a jail break."

"I know you said there was nothing on the jail cameras, but did anyone check the parking lot one? Or the one at the bank across the street? Maybe it caught them taking Erin out," Carla said. She was looking into space, clearly cataloguing every camera she could remember from downtown.

Lizzie raised one dark eyebrow and shook her head at Shelly's startled glare. "We thought she broke out, so no one saw any need to check all that other stuff. And since I'm getting the family death glare, I'm sorry for the assumptions I made at the time. I should have given you more benefit of the doubt instead of assuming that you were trying to pull one over on me." She sighed contritely.

"And you're not just saying this because you'll be running for sheriff, right?" Becca couldn't hold the words back. Much as she liked Lizzie, she couldn't help but feel that all of this could have been handled better or at least, differently. *She should have just known that Erin wouldn't kill someone in cold blood.* Except she hadn't been sure about that herself.

Erin and Carla both flipped around to stare at Lizzie. "Wait! You are? Cool! You'd be the first woman! The first Native woman!" The flood of words poured out in a wave. Apparently Deputy Blackhawk wasn't going to lack for campaign support, at least amongst Pack members.

Shelly wrinkled her nose, held up her hand and looked at her watch. "Sorry to interrupt the love fest, but I have to get back to town. We'll assume that this isn't a ploy to gain our votes, unless something else happens. I think under the circumstances, Erin, you better look for Annie tonight, with Carla's help. You got closer than anyone else did, which might not mean anything, but then again, it might. Please try not to get that close again. Carla, you put me on speed dial and text or call the minute you see her. There's a satellite phone in the emergency pack if you can't get a signal." Carla nodded, her expression serious.

"Can I be on the team that goes to look for Jim and Kari?" Becca's lip curled involuntarily. Her wolf gave a quiet growl from the depths of her brain. They had scared her, threatened her, kidnapped a woman she cared deeply about and were a danger to her Pack. She wanted to taste their blood, but *figuratively*, her human brain insisted.

Shelly scowled at her. "No bloodshed. Unless there's no other option."

"It's like you don't trust me." Becca grimaced at her boss. At the same time, she was trying not to catalogue all of the recent events that would have caused Shelly not to trust her. She had to admit that there were quite a few.

Some of that must have shown in her face because Shelly reached out and rested her hand on her shoulder. "But they are dangerous and I want you to pick up Lin, Adelía and Gladys before you go anywhere. They should all be at Gladys' by the time you get to town. Start by going to the warehouse where they were holding Erin. I suspect they're either using it as a hideout or they've left a trail from there. I take it you haven't seen any new signs of them at your old place?"

Becca wondered when there would have been time, but then Gladys kept a close watch on the street. She'd have mentioned it if she'd seen anything new. She went with a shrug and a head-shake. "Alright. I'll get going now." She stood up, glancing at Erin to see she could catch her eye, at least wish her luck. For a moment, it seemed like that wasn't going to happen but at the last minute, Erin gave her a thumbs-up. "Good luck," Becca walked past and squeezed her shoulder.

An instant later, Lizzie got up too. "Hang on, Becca, I'm coming with you." They walked down the trail in silence, but Becca's head was buzzing with thoughts about how she should have given Erin a hug or a kiss or a ring or a declaration or... something rustled in the bushes nearby and she yanked herself out of her thoughts in a hurry. Her nostrils flared as she looked around, trying to figure out what it was.

Lizzie stopped when she did and looked around, her head cocked to one side as she tried to listen for whatever she thought Becca was listening to. The sky had clouded over, tinting the mountain gray and shading the trees and bushes a light shade of silvery green. Striking as it was, it made hard to see, at least for human eyes. Becca closed hers and reached out with her wolf senses to taste the woods around them.

At first, there was nothing, at least nothing out of the ordi-nary. The wind whistled, the clouds hovered, distant birds chirped, the Pack members on the ledge outside the cave mur-mured amongst themselves. Then, a flash of predator and a dash of perfume, followed by the crash of branches as whatever it was fled into the woods. Becca lunged forward to follow, only to be stopped by the deputy's hand on her shoulder. "No. Let's not go for a repeat of the stuff we went through last time. Rally the troops, then pursue."

"But..." Becca could feel herself tremble with conflicting urges. She drew in a shaky breath, trying to swallow down a boiling rage, a flash of desperation and a bunch of things she wasn't ready to analyze too quickly.

"Hey there, come on back. You can't take on a bear or even Annie, not as a nice middle-aged lady all on her lonesome. And I ain't going into those woods on a wild bear chase." Lizzie had her hands on both of her shoulders now, turning Becca so she had to face her.

After a minute, the fight drained out of Becca and she shuddered, pushing Lizzie's hands away. "C'mon then. Let's go get them before we lose the trail."

# CHAPTER 24

CARLA HAD BROUGHT MAPS IN her pack, real old paper maps with geological lines on them and everything, and once the others left, she started laying them out on the cave floor. "So I found these in one of the boxes of old survey stuff at work and I thought they might come in handy." She crouched down, peering at them in the fading afternoon sun.

Erin wondered why they weren't taking them outside where the light was a little better, but then she saw Carla's gaze flicker up to the cave paintings. She glanced up herself, wondering with a slight chill if they were doing anything out of the ordinary. All things considered, she preferred them to just look interesting. Then she wondered why Carla thought they might be.

She didn't have long to wait. "Can you..." Carla's voice trailed off for a minute, like she wasn't sure about what she was going to ask. She gave Erin a sidelong glance before continuing, "Molly said that you and Shelly and Becca did a thing and got them to move. I was wondering if maybe you could do it again, only this time get them to maybe find Annie on these maps." She looked Erin full in the face now, dark eyes full of hope.

Erin almost rolled her eyes. When had she become the big mystical magical wolf of the local werewolf pack? Erin started to laugh it off, but a memory of glowing eyes in the cave's depths and a voice speaking to her in its weird blend of human speech and wolf tongue rose in her mind. *Oh. That's why me.* If the cave gave her visions of one kind, why not another?

Why indeed? She hadn't even figured out that last dream or vision or whatever it was that the cave's magic wanted her to see. So just how was she supposed to call something up, like the location of a monster who used to be one of their own? Or try and figure out what she'd been doing here to begin with, since that was also on the table? Erin closed her eyes for a moment and longed for the quiet, boring comfort of reviewing people's tax records.

Carla cleared her throat nervously. "So, you know that whole hypnosis thing you were talking about? I've done a little bit of it. I mean, I totally understand not wanting to do it at all or have an amateur do it or whatever, I'm just thinking out loud. I'm just not sure how we can find Annie or even the werebear in all that." She made a sweeping gesture at the mountains and landscape outside the cave before she went on, "But of course, with your sense of smell, it should be a lot easier. It's just, well, she's managed to hide out for a couple of months, right? And we're all getting pulled in a couple of different directions, so it seems like finding her fast and learning what your dream was all about would be helpful."

"We weren't looking for her very hard." Erin grimaced. Honestly, she suspected that they were all not so secretly hoping she'd get eaten by a bear or something. After all the damage that she'd done, it had been hard to be concerned about Annie's wellbeing. Frankly, it was still hard, especially if she'd told these TV people about the Pack or had something to do with killing Leroy and putting him in her car or…well, really, just about anything bad at this point.

"It looked like…I dunno…like she was trying to tell you something or give you a clue when you met up with her before." Carla frowned, dark brows drawn together over deep-set eyes.

"Oh." Admittedly, that hadn't occurred to her, probably because of their previous history. Erin stuck her hand in her pocket and pulled out the dog tag. She got up and walked over to the entrance to look at it in what remained of the daylight. It was worn down in spots, with some of the lettering and numbers nearly obliterated. But the name 'Leroy' was readable. Why did Annie want Erin to find Leroy's dog tag? Wasn't finding his body enough? She turned it over a few times, but it wasn't spilling any more secrets. A grumble of frustration forced its way up through her and out of her mouth.

She closed her eyes for a minute and racked her brain for other options. Then she walked back in and sat down in front of Carla. "I'm damned if I know why she either gave me or lost Leroy's dog tag, and I still don't understand my dream. How good are you at this hypnosis stuff? I'm out of brilliant ideas."

"I'm not sure how good I am, exactly. I've been through it myself a couple of times, and I tried it on Molly once because she wanted to see what it was like, and Jonas a couple of times. At the moment, the main thing is that I'm here and Dr. Green isn't. If I can put you under, what do you want me to ask? And

not ask, because I don't want to get up in your business about
stuff you don't want to share."

Good questions. Erin gestured for a moment to think and
mulled it over. Finally, she looked up. "I think as long as we
stick to questions about the cave and what the voice said to me,
we should be fine. Not that there's much about me that you don't
already know, mind you. I just want to try and focus on this
without so many distractions."

At Carla's urging, she lay down on top of her sleeping bag
with a light blanket over her. Carla turned off one solar lamp
and dimmed the other, then put Erin's water bottle near her
hand so she could reach it easily. "Okay, here goes. This is the
sequence that I've done before. Let's see if it works on you."

WHEN ERIN WOKE UP SOME time later, the sun had set and Carla
was napping on a nearby sleeping bag. She stretched and drank
a few gulps of water before standing up and stretching. Her back
and shoulders popped and cracked, the sound echoing through
the cave. Instinctively, Erin looked into the shadows at the back
of the cave and was relieved when nothing looked back. A brief
check showed her that the wall paintings weren't moving either.
So, what, if anything, had Carla learned?

She decided to finish waking up first before she asked.
That took a few minutes, and Carla was awake by the time
she came back to the cave. Erin could hear that without even
coming inside. But Carla hadn't been terrified when she left, so
that was new. She drank in the air, parsing the strange human-
wolf scent that only belonged to one creature in this valley, as
far as Erin knew.

Should she call the others? Something told her there wasn't time. Carla wouldn't be this edgy if this was a casual encounter, so Annie must have done something threatening already. That made her the rescue squad, figuratively speaking. Moving sideways to keep her throat and stomach as protected as possible, Erin grabbed a fist-sized rock before stepping into the cave.

Annie crouched near Carla, her expression made more menacing by her long white teeth and the lengthy claws resting on her knees. Carla was wide-eyed and sitting very still, which struck Erin as a good idea. She wondered if playing dead herself would help, before dismissing that as wishful thinking. Instead, she walked carefully into the middle of the cave, keeping the rock in her hand out of sight. She paused right where they had created a labyrinth of sand when they needed to call the paintings up the last time. Maybe it would activate the cave's magic by itself. "Hello, Annie. I'd appreciate it if you moved away from my friend."

Erin surprised herself by sounding weirdly calm. Her wolf was waking up, slowly, but felt more curious than hostile. She didn't really want to attack Annie, the way she had wanted to this morning. Not without knowing what she wanted, anyway. There was also something about standing here in the middle of the cave, surrounded by the paintings, that...made this encounter different and activated a different part of her mind. Then something opened her mouth to emit a series of growls and barks.

Okay, so maybe she wasn't so calm, after all.

*What the hell?* Erin had no idea what she'd just said or what it meant. But she could feel her lip curl over one of her front incisors in a distinctly wolfy expression, so presumably that would add some emphasis. Maybe the magic could make her change right now so she could fight Annie? She surreptitiously took stock of the rest of her body: nope, still middle-aged lesbian, not werewolf. But middle-aged lesbian feeling very in touch with rage and magic and inner wolf, so that was something a bit different.

Annie must have felt it too, since she greeted the sounds Erin made with a whimper of her own. Since that also came with the other woman backing away from Carla, Erin breathed a sigh of relief, mixed with confusion and a bunch of other roiling emotions. That had been the dream language of the wolves and she'd remembered it, somehow, and spoken it. But what had she said?

Annie said something back in the language of lilts and snarls and short barks and they stared at each other for a long couple of minutes. Erin's wolf grumbled softly inside her head, and just like that, she understood what they were talking about. It was all about the cave and magic and some sort of trip? A journey? Real or metaphorical? Her wolf gave her scent and visual pictures, but abstract concepts like this were hard to translate into human. She was pretty sure that she didn't want to go on a trip with Annie.

She studied the other woman (here her human brain helpfully supplied a different term). Annie looked even more like an escapee from a Lon Chaney movie than she had the last time that Erin had seen her: all hair and gangly limbs and warped jaw. Her eyes were the same, though, and they still had some of the same angry look, though she also looked exhausted and haunted.

Annie grimaced and made another sound, this one clearly a question. Erin heard herself respond, but this time her wolf didn't supply a helpful picture that she could understand. Instead, she tried to read Annie's body language to see if it was a good thing or a bad one. This proved to be an exercise that would have been a lot easier if Annie was a tad more human.

Carla must have begun to slowly ease her way toward the entrance without her noticing. One of her shoes squeaked on the stone floor and Annie whipped around and growled. Erin growled back, the sound reverberating against the stone walls. Annie and Carla both froze and stared at her with wide eyes.

*Now what?* This couldn't go on for much longer. She was no match for Annie's claws and teeth, magic or no magic, and neither was Carla. "Just tell me what you want. Use telepathy or wolf pictures or something, but leave Carla the hell alone," Erin finally barked in purest human. "You weren't too keen on this place or being a wolf, last time I checked, so let's get this over with so you can go back to being a happy monster in the woods."

Annie snarled at that, her front fangs each longer than one of Erin's fingers. She lunged forward as if to attack Erin and Erin sidestepped. Her wolf was screaming to get out, but she had no way to make that happen, so she held up her hand with the rock in it, making the threat clear. Then, when Annie froze, she bent down and grabbed the cast iron frying pan that was drying nearby with her other hand. It wasn't much, but this bitch wasn't going to get her easy.

They circled each other, each snarling at the other, until a loud bang startled both of them into looking around. Carla held the pistol that she'd just fired into the air on Annie. Erin could smell the acrid air tracing the bullet's path. "Enough of this," Carla's voice broke into her thoughts and rang out against the walls of the cave. "What do you want?"

Annie wrinkled her muzzle, giving her face the look of a very weird dog that had somehow lost part of the fur on its face. She dropped down into a crouch and held her hands up in what looked to Erin like a gesture of surrender. Erin nodded cautiously and stepped back, but she didn't put the frying pan or the rock down.

Carla didn't lower her pistol either, but they both watched Annie and waited for her to communicate whatever it was that she was now clearly trying to say. She moved her mouth again for a few more minutes and made odd sounds, frustration clear in the small barks and growls that began to emerge from her mouth instead of words.

Finally, after a few moments of obvious frustration, she gave up and lurched slowly up on to her feet. She held her hands outstretched, claws curled in, and when neither of them made a move, she walked toward the paintings on the walls. Well, limped was more accurate. In the dim light, Erin could see that her feet didn't look like they were made to be walked on, at least not by anything balancing on two legs. And now she was back in the same place where she got cursed…warped… whatever you wanted to call what the magic had done to her for attacking their Pack. Erin found a twisted respect for her nerve, coupled with a likely vain hope that after today, they'd never see her again.

Annie made straight for one specific painting, back in the dimness of the cave's shadows. Erin couldn't see what it was without moving closer, and that was something she found herself reluctant to do. Carla had lowered her gun, but she didn't seem to be in much of hurry to get closer to Annie either. Finally, Erin pulled a flashlight from a nearby pack and pointed it into the shadows around Annie. The latter threw up a clawed hand to cover her eyes, but at least now they could see what she was looking at. The painting in question showed what might have been a human woman emerging from a dead or sleeping wolf. Was it symbolic or something? Erin couldn't tell, but she studied it for a minute before turning the flashlight off.

There was a long moment of silence and none of them moved. Finally, Carla cleared her throat. "Ummm…Erin? I think she thinks that you can change her back."

Erin threw up her hands in frustration. "I am not the were-wolf whisperer! I don't have weird magical powers or, in fact, any magical powers! If I did, I wouldn't be hanging around this damn cave like this, having vis—" Erin stopped abruptly. Her dream was coming back to her now, building in her bones, wolf and human, translating itself in a way that she finally understood. "Oh, crap. Maybe I am the werewolf whisperer." She stared from Carla to Annie in bemusement. "I might know how to fix you."

# CHAPTER 25

B ECCA WONDERED WHAT ERIN WAS up to and whether or
not she should try and call. Not that this was the most
opportune time for that or much of anything, really. She had
just parked in front of Gladys' place and she had Lizzie in the
car and explicit instructions from Shelly on what to do next.
None of those things included calling her hopefully once-and-
future-girlfriend in the middle of the action. Especially not if
said maybe girlfriend was sneaking around the woods looking
for a monster.

"Hey, you going to sit here all night?" Lizzie had gotten out
of the car, but poked her head back to stare at Becca. Reluctantly,
she pulled her keys out of the car and got out. She took a deep
breath and followed Lizzie up the walk, struggling to put her
game face on. Lizzie eyed her. "So what's the deal here? I've
never seen you look so much like my kid when I tell him to do
his homework."

"I just don't want to do it this way, that's all. I feel like we're wasting time and...," Becca trailed off with a sigh. She really didn't have a good reason for acting like this, or at least not one she could articulate. Lizzie had a point, and she might as well make the best of it. Also, she was hungry and moody and her hormones felt like they were running amok, now that she thought about it. "A snack would probably help." She grimaced an apology at Lizzie.

Lizzie reached into her bag and pulled out a piece of buffalo jerky in a package. She handed it to Becca before pressing the bell. "Always keep these on me just in case."

Gladys opened the door just as Becca bit into the jerky. "Good. Shelly said you were on your way. Do you need to change, Becca? There's a sandwich and some fruit on the table for you. We already ate."

Becca swallowed hard. Gladys was being perfectly nice. Had Gladys always been this nice and she'd just never noticed it or given her credit for it? A small wave of shame washed over her, at least until Molly winked from a kitchen chair and Becca felt less guilty. Or more transparent, which was not the same thing at all. She wolfed down the rest of the jerky as she walked into the kitchen.

Molly, Gladys and Lin all joined them to pull on their shoes and jackets while Becca inhaled her sandwich and refilled her water. "So, werebear hunting? What a great way to spend a Thursday night!" Molly grinned impishly at all of them in an obvious attempt to lighten the mood.

Lin suddenly grabbed at her vibrating pocket and pulled her phone out. She stepped away to talk to someone for a few minutes, then hung up and gestured with her phone. "I have to go and meet with Larry Milchester and Carli about the Women's Club tonight. There's some paperwork we have to review and sign. I forgot to tell Shelly about that when she asked me to do this. Will you be all right? You can call me if you need me and we can come up to the cave right afterwards."

*It was all so mundane,* Becca thought. *Like having a weird business meeting instead of hunting for werebear.* "Before you go, do you know what Larry Milchester is? I've been wondering since we had that first meeting."

"Larry?" Lin raised an eyebrow. "Well, as Shelly said, we're going to let him tell us when he wants to, but personally, I think he's a werejaguar. They have different patterns than we do, so he's not always moon called." Becca nodded slowly and Lin gave her an approving nod. Then she bid her adieus before slipping out to her car.

"Of course our lawyer is a werejaguar. Why wouldn't he be?" Becca muttered quietly to herself.

Molly threw a companionable arm around her shoulders. "Stick with us, kid. It just gets weirder. Now, shall we?"

"Shall we start at the warehouse again? Or at your old house, Becca?" Gladys sounded noncommittal, but this was the first time that anyone had suggested the latter. They all eyed each other, then looked to Lizzie.

"No breaking and entering," the deputy growled. "But I suppose some reconnaissance might be called for, and seeing as it's the nearest point, we might as well start there."

Dusk was falling as they moved down the street, looking as nonchalant as they could. For a minute, Becca found herself remembering the first time she had seen the Pack in town and how she had stood watching them from her window, thinking they were dogs. Instinctively, she glanced up at the window from across the street, but it looked as if her neighbors weren't in residence.

"Check for a car first. I'll go around back to the garage," Lizzie murmured. "Gladys, how about you come with me?"

"We'll take a look around the front." Molly jerked her head at Becca and they strolled slowly past the front of the nondescript ranch house that Becca used to call home. Looking at it in the twilight made the porch with its peeling paint and the slightly unkempt yard look more magically appealing than they did during the day.

Wait, the very unkempt yard. Becca caught Molly's sleeve. "The Yard Police will have been all over this. They can tell us anything we want to know about when they've been here and what they've been up to. Come on."

"You have 'Yard Police'?"

"In a manner of speaking. Ellen and Edward are retired and have very strong…opinions about how the rest of us should be taking care of the houses on this block. If anything happens before nine at night, they probably know about it."

"And after that?"

"They go to bed early. Before moonrise, as a rule. Which is pretty lucky, considering the neighbors." Becca led the way up a concrete path that crossed an immaculate lawn to an otherwise nondescript, but well-maintained, single-story home. She rang the doorbell gently while Molly looked around. "Hi, Edward."

The elderly man who answered the door eyed them suspiciously. He and the white-haired woman who appeared in the doorway behind him reminded Becca of voles and her wolf smacked her lips ominously in the back of her head. *Stop* she thought firmly.

"Why, Becca Thornton, what are you doing out so late? With our mailman?" Ellen was squinting at Molly like she wasn't allowed out on the streets after her delivery run.

"Hi, Mr. and Mrs. Echols. Nice to see you this evening." Molly favored them with a big charming smile.

"Sorry to disturb you so late," Becca cut in, "but we were out for a walk and I couldn't help but notice that our new neighbors don't seem to be around much. In fact, I haven't seen them in a few days, and was just wondering if you had noticed whether or not they've been around. I wanted to ask them about something that I think I left in the garage."

Edward stepped out of the house and glared at Becca's old house as if he could get the yard to mow itself. "I haven't seen them lift a finger around that house since they moved in. She came home in a big hurry two days ago, ran into the house, came out with a bag and screeched that oversized truck-car thing they drive out of here like she was racing. We haven't seen him all week." He drew himself up, wrinkled face flushing with anger. "They are not the kind of people we want living around here. What were you thinking, selling your house to them?"

Becca held up her hands in surrender. "Talk to Ed. He and his realtor found them and sold the house to them. First I heard about it was when it had already sold. I'm sorry about their behavior. Did you happen to notice whether or not she looked like she was going on a trip or camping anything?"

He glared past them at Becca's old house like it was going to answer the question on its own, but it was Ellen who spoke up, "Camping. I'm pretty sure. She had a sleeping bag and a tent in the car. She drove up thatta way." She gestured up toward the mountains to the west of town.

"Ah. Probably just gone camping for the weekend, then. I'll try and find out what's going on as soon as I track them down. Thank you very much for your help!" She herded Molly down the path, being careful not to step on the immaculate grass or the nearly perfect flowerbeds.

"So where do you think she went?" Molly murmured softly as they reached the sidewalk. "Back to the warehouse? Out of town?"

"Camping with her werebear. As you do." Becca frowned at the western slopes gleaming white under the moonlight. "They know that we know about the warehouse, so I don't think they'd go back there. There might be some clues to where they did go next, I suppose, but I think they're up there in the mountains." She pointed with her chin and Molly gave her a speculative look, then nodded.

Becca stared off to the west of town, realizing an instant later what else was out there: the Pack's cave, where Erin and Carla were probably preparing to hole up for the night. If Leroy had told them about the Pack, what were the odds that he had also told them whatever else he knew, like the location of the Pack's mountain sanctuary? Jim and Kari probably couldn't wait to get that on film and they could do plenty of other harm while they were at it. "Oh, no! We need to get back up there."

Molly caught her eye and nodded briskly. "I'll rally the troops. You call Carla and Erin." Molly turned and crossed the street, her back rigid with the effort it took to look like she was just out taking a stroll. Becca pulled her phone out, only to find a text from Carla that made her blink at the screen. She shoved her phone in the pocket and ran after Molly, not bothering to look casual.

# CHAPTER 26

ERIN SCOWLED DOWN AT THE floor, trying to remember what they had done the last time. Of course, maybe they had just gotten lucky. Shelly had found a labyrinth drawing somewhere and together, the three of them used it and a couple of half-remembered rituals that they'd gotten from Circle House and from the internet to summon the wolf paintings off the cave walls to fight their enemies.

Including the not-quite-woman who crouched before her, wolflike head tilted at an angle as she studied the lines of sand on the stone floor. For a minute, Erin wondered if Annie knew more about how to construct the ritual than she did. She'd been a Pack member longer, after all. Margaret had presumably taught her things. Until she killed Margaret and came back with a bunch of guys and a chemical cure for lycanthropy, of course, which might have dented her memory of those original lessons just a bit.

The loss of the archives and their history hit Erin like a punch to the solar plexus. If this angry woman hadn't rejected the valley's magic and the wolves themselves, they would never have ended up in this mess. Her anger and desire for retaliation had gotten them into this fix. A white-hot rage burned through her, and just as quickly, burned itself out. What could she do to Annie that the other woman would think was worse than how she had spent the last couple of months? A woman who had no desire to be a wolf, stuck halfway between human and wolf, thinking there was no way out, had already been punished to some extent.

Erin glanced away and looked over to see what Carla was doing. She was sitting against the wall, alternately bent over her phone and looking up to watch them. While Erin had been distracted, Carla had gathered a pile of candles from their stores and found the sand for Erin to make the labyrinth and placed them in a pile.

Erin walked over and knelt down, letting the sand in the open box run through her fingers. She wished that Becca and Shelly were here; she'd gotten shot when they were walking the maze and her memories were pretty sketchy. But the sooner she got started, the sooner she'd find out whether or not she could do this without help. With a sigh, she sat down cross-legged and closed her eyes, trying to remember.

The moon was starting to call her and she shivered a little, overwhelmed with memories of inhabiting her other form. As usual, everything seemed heightened, and she could hear distant sounds and smells from what seemed like miles away. Her mouth watered at the sound and smell of prey in the underbrush, her wolf snarled inside her head at Annie's scent, so overpowering and so wrong, a part of her heard other Pack members moving around the mountains outside. In short, she could access almost everything going on around them except for the information that she wanted.

She had reached out to Carla earlier, but she seemed reluctant to help Erin try to create the pattern. From what little she said, Erin gathered that she thought it was a "wolf thing." The impulse to tell her that she was part of "wolf things" now died on Erin's lips. What did that even mean, anyway? She didn't control the magic, after all. And she was only a second in command. Shelly could decide what and whom to share Pack secrets with, but there were some things Erin thought were a gray zone. Maybe this was one of them, maybe it wasn't. She sighed in frustration and ran her free hand through her hair as she stared down at the sand circle that she was trying to create.

Maybe it was time to call Shelly. Or Becca. Or anybody, really. But Shelly might remember what her inspiration was, maybe even some of the details. If following it all exactly even mattered. Maybe it was all about magic and intent, or even timing. Erin looked up and grimaced at the paintings. She thought about yelling, "A little clue would be nice!" and seeing what came back. But then, based on the last time, whatever that might be could be kind of scary.

She sighed and closed her eyes, took a deep breath and tried once again to let her memory do whatever it was going to do.

After a few minutes, she reached into the box of sand and took out a handful. She started a small inner circle, with an opening that broke out into to a second, wider circle. Annie made a snuffling noise and moved back, which she could interpret as approval. Or allergies or something. She went over to crouch next to the cave entrance, inhaling the wind with a snuffle that sounded intrigued to Erin. But whatever she was smelling wasn't a threat, at least as far as Erin could tell; the wolf-woman seemed pretty calm. She shrugged and went back to making crude open circles with a broad path between them until she ran out of sand.

She stepped back and frowned, aware that Carla had gotten up and was standing next to her. "Is that it? It kind of glows in the lights." Her voice had an awestruck quality to it that made Erin smile a little.

"I can't believe I'm going to say this, but you make me feel like I take turning into a werewolf once a month for granted. And you're right: it is pretty damn magical. It also hurts the first few times and it's hella weird. Even after a couple of years." Erin grinned at her, then glanced over at Annie. "I think we better wait until moonrise. I think I or we can tap into the cave's magic better then."

"Do you need the rest of the Pack?"

"I have no idea. Probably. You feel like bringing everyone else up here to see what happens?" Erin directed this last question to Annie, who had turned away from the entrance and was watching them. Annie tilted her head to the side, dark lips twisting over an incisor with a small snarl. Erin's wolf snarled back from the back of her brain and she found herself sinking into a crouch to make herself a smaller target.

"Whoa, whoa! Everybody calm down a minute here! I realize that there's a lot of history here and maybe I don't even know all of it, but I'm pretty sure that the magic won't work if you two kill each other." Carla was standing between them, her hands shaking as she held them up.

"What if we just wound each other a little bit?" Erin muttered, not very softly.

Annie inhaled sharply, then slowly lowered herself to the cave floor, throat outstretched. She placed her clawed hands on the floor at either side of her muzzle, closed her eyes and appeared to be waiting for something. For a minute, Erin had no idea what she was supposed to do. Go over and nuzzle her? Nip her shoulder? Give her a reassuring pat on the head? None of those were very appealing.

Carla's phone buzzed sharply and she scrambled for it, dropping it to the floor with a loud bang in the process. While she was able to answer it, Erin made herself edge a bit closer to the still prostrate Annie. "Alright. I get that you're trying to suggest that you're not a threat. But you sure have been up until now, so why should I take you seriously?"

Annie sat up slowly. Her face, elongated as it was into a muzzle, twisted sharply as she tried to use what still must be human vocal chords to speak. "Cure." It sounded like a cough when she said it and the word hung there between them like a cloud that wouldn't disperse.

Erin stuck her hand into her pocket, her fingers encountering a metal object. She pulled the dog tag out and held it out by its chain. "'Cure' the way Leroy tried to do it? Or cure the way you think the wolves can do it? Do you want to be human or wolf or both?" She left unspoken her other question: *and why do you think I can do anything about it?* Save that one for later.

Annie grimaced at her again and gestured toward the dog tag and shook her head. Well, as long as they were playing Twenty Questions, Erin asked the next question on her list, "Did you kill Leroy?"

The other woman responded with a series of growls and yelps that didn't even make sense to Erin's wolf, sitting watchfully at the back of her brain. *This was going well.* "Can you write?"

Carla's voice cut across whatever Annie had been about to growl or signal. "They're on their way. The werebear and his mate have left town and they think they are camping out near here. Molly and Becca think that they plan on trapping us here tonight and seeing if they can get something on film that will expose the Pack. They said we should assume that they're armed and dangerous."

"Of course they are. Dammit!" Erin smacked one hand on her forehead and muttered a few choice comments under her breath. She looked at the labyrinth she'd made and wondered if she should blot it out or try to use it to call something up right now in hopes of heading off trouble at the pass.

The scrambling noise behind her made her whip around just in time to see Annie disappearing into the twilight. "I think she might have the right idea," Carla added softly.

Erin looked around, imagining what would happen next. Even if the cave was deserted, Jim and Kari would know they had been there, could film the paintings and broadcast those. All they needed was for this to become a local tourist attraction and someone to send in investigators to figure out what it was. "We can't just let them have free run of the place. Look what happened to the Women's Club. We can't lose this place too. This is our spiritual home."

Carla looked like she wanted to argue, but she bit her lip and looked around before nodding. "Okay. So either we have to decoy them somewhere else or we have to try and hide this place, somehow."

"Decoy...hmm." Erin tapped one long finger on her lips. She ran through some ideas while Carla turned off or hid the remaining lamps. There was a pile of fabric in one of the far corners of the cave, back where Erin had heard the voices, and whatever it was suddenly seemed to have captured all of Carla's attention. "Maybe both. What's that?"

Carla tugged the biggest piece of cloth free. "That would be some really dusty dirt-colored cloth. Maybe someone was expecting something like this to happen or they needed to hide the cave before?" She turned aside to cough as Erin walked over and helped her unfold it. By the dim light of the remaining lanterns, they could see that the heavy canvas had been painted to look much like the hillside outside.

"But he'll still be able to smell us. We'll need something more than this. I think I may still need to be a decoy after all. But I need to know where to lure them and you need to tell the others where they can find us." Erin started tugging the canvas over toward the entrance.

"Well..." Carla hesitated, like she wasn't sure about what she was going to say next, then she continued, unrolling the canvas as she spoke. "There are other caves. There's a couple down by the river that might work. But once you were inside it, I'm not sure about exit routes. We used to use some of them for training when I was in the National Guard."

"Ah, those caves. I know the one by Painted Rock, at least. That one is big enough to have a bunch of nooks and crannies in it. I might be able to hide from them long enough for the Pack to get there, maybe with Lizzie and some serious backup." Erin reached up, feeling along the top of the cave entrance for something to hang the canvas from.

Her fingertips found a rough ledge, chiseled into the rock, then a couple of square heavy objects. "You're right. Someone planned for this or something like it. There's what feels like weights up here. Give me that end and I'll try and get it secured."

Carla was a few inches shorter than she was, though much broader and more muscular, but that wasn't going to help with this. Erin stood on her toes, wondering how an earlier generation of wolf-women could have fastened this curtain across the entrance without a spare ex-basketball player in their midst. She glanced around for something to stand on, then dropped the canvas and raced over to drag a nearby small boulder that they used for an extra seat during meetings.

Teetering on the rock, with Carla supporting her and dragging the canvas along, they got the entrance covered. Erin hopped down and wiped her hands on her jeans. "Okay, so what do you remember about the cave by Painted Rock? And yes, it has to be me. I'm the one they'll be looking for. You'll have to stay here and guard things as best you can."

Carla grimaced, but nodded. A few minutes later, Erin was on her way up the mountainside, looking for a trail that would take her down away from their cave and away from the path that the Pack generally used. She paused to take a swig from her water bottle, then spat some of it out, marking the beginning of a trail that even a werebear couldn't miss.

# CHAPTER 27

B ECCA DROVE HER LITTLE COMPACT car out of Wolf's Point as
fast as she dared. Carla had sent her a text back before they
got into her car, saying something about Erin going off to lead
a false trail away from the cave and them hiding the entrance,
all of which was great but not exactly reassuring. Where was
Annie? What did Erin think she was doing and why couldn't
she just wait for them to get to her? And what were they going
to need to do to get either Jim and Kari or Annie to confess to
killing Leroy so things could go back to, well, what they were
before? Kind of.

   She couldn't resist a small snort at that thought. Before
things were always Not Normal, she thought her life after the
divorce was boring and had hoped for some more excitement.
Well, she had it now and then some. At least this time around,
there would be backup.

"Penny for your thoughts?" Gladys gave her a wary frown from the passenger's seat as she turned the car to go up the dirt road to their usual parking place. The moon was just coming up to light their way and the light thrummed into Becca's blood, just enough to make her feel wolfy inside.

"You ever think about what your life would be like if all this hadn't happened?" She gestured toward the mountain, the moon, the other Pack members clambering out of the now parked car.

"Wasn't that much to it," Gladys snorted as she got out of the car. "My husband died, I got laid off from my job and couldn't find anything else, so I moved back to where I was from. I got a part-time job, joined the Women's Club and a Scrabble league, and found a church to volunteer at. Then I started turning into a wolf and frankly, I was pretty excited about it after the initial shock wore off. I mean, I'd heard some rumors around the Club and I knew Margaret Anderson to chat with, so I had some idea of what might happen."

"Wait, you knew Margaret?" All this time, she'd had access to someone who could tell her more about Margaret and she never thought to ask! Becca nearly walloped her forehead with her hand as they followed Molly and Lizzie up the trail.

"Most of us knew Margaret to one degree or another. If you were that curious about her, why didn't you just ask? I mean, not Shelly, because she doesn't like to talk about her. Or Erin since she didn't know her, but me and Carli and Adelía and Lin and all the older wolves knew her." Gladys gave her a puzzled frown, like it was the most obvious thing in the world.

Becca sighed. She suspected it would be impolite to suggest that Erin's version of Gladys' first transformation sounded a lot more intense than their neighbor made it seem. "If Annie killed Margaret, how come she's not in charge? Do the Alphas always get killed?" A blood-soaked vision out of a nature documentary filled her brain for a moment and she shook her head to clear it.

"That version of wolf pack behavior has been discredited," Gladys responded with a sniff. "Shelly is our leader, but she won't be fighting anyone to the death if they challenge her or whatever other nonsense is still out there. I don't think Margaret intended to fight Annie at all, let alone what happened before that."

They climbed upward in silence for a few minutes, Becca torn between asking more questions and catching her breath. Curiosity won out eventually. "What did happen? Why do you all think that Annie killed Margaret?"

Molly waved one hand behind her, shushing them. She and Lizzie split off to opposite sides of the trail, each one behind a different boulder. Great. What were they supposed to do now? Becca looked frantically around for a big rock of her own, then hit the ground, just as Gladys did the same above her. They were all wearing earth-tone colors and the moon wasn't very high yet, so maybe they could hide? Becca wondered what they were hiding from but didn't dare raise her head to look around.

Something ran up the mountain ahead of them, and the faint scent that trailed after them was a familiar one. What the hell was Annie up to? Carla had said that she was in the cave with them, so why was she out skittering around on the mountainside now?

A few moments later, rocks and pebbles on a nearby ledge shifted. Jim was keeping watch, Becca's nose told her as much, but was he looking for Erin or Annie or them? She longed to climb up and hit him with a rock until he told them what he was up to. And confessed to killing Leroy and trying to frame Erin. That would make a perfect ending to this evening. She had a brief fantasy of the couple in cuffs being hauled away to jail by Lizzie.

She couldn't help but wonder if Lizzie had the same fantasy. A series of small noises told her that the deputy was cautiously drawing her gun. She must have seen either Annie or the werebear, maybe both. So what were they supposed to do? Distract Jim for her? Run away? It was hard to decide.

Everything exploded into motion with that thought. Molly darted out from behind her boulder, Lizzie on her heels, as a rock sailed through the air. The werebear roared, presumably because he'd been hit, and then Becca was scrambling to her feet and running after the others. She wondered what they were going to do once they caught up with him or, well anyone else, but she was still hoping that Lizzie, at least, had a plan of some sort. Or maybe she'd come up with one, once they got there. Grimly, she hauled herself up over the rocks and tried not to slide back down the mountainside.

Jim the bear took off, scrambling up a trail that Becca could barely see from where she was. Kari had to be somewhere nearby; they seemed to function as a unit. She tried to look around for the other woman while she was running and almost inevitably, fell flat on her face. Cursing softly, she sat up, making sure that nothing more than her dignity had been bruised.

That position gave her a bird's-eye view of Annie, loping down the mountainside, toward the bear. He shot off on a nearby trail and a shot rang out. All the wolves and Lizzie hit the deck once again and Annie vanished. Becca kept her head down for a long couple of minutes, waiting for a signal or something to tell her that it was time to move.

In the end, it was Lizzie and Molly who got up, crouched low, and headed up toward the ledge that Jim had been standing on.

Becca got up and gave Gladys an assist in standing up. She sniffed cautiously and frowned. "What?" Gladys eyed her askance.

"I think Annie went after the bear. And maybe Erin? She's up ahead of them, I think? I can smell bits of all of them up that way." She gestured up the hill and west of the ledge that their companions had just reached. What was Erin doing? Didn't she know the entire mountainside was crawling with wolves and deputies and a werebear and a monster? Why was she running up the mountain away from her own friends instead of toward them? Unless she couldn't smell them or see them. Or she thought she was leading the bad guys away from the cave.

The wind shifted and her nostrils flared. Her wolf sang itself awake. *Erin.* Becca made an abrupt turn and started clambering up the trail to the right of the one everyone else was on, running as fast as she could. She could hear Gladys call something after her, but she was too focused on keeping her footing to pay attention. Scents old and new filled her brain, each warring for attention as she tried to sort them out. If Kari had fired that shot, what was to keep her from firing one at Erin? Did Erin even know they were up here?

A moment's pause to catch her breath and she remembered that Erin did know they were coming, that Erin must be trying to lead their enemies away from the cave. But what was Annie doing? Hadn't she been in the cave with them? It was all horribly confusing, and Becca dismissed all of it in favor of climbing faster. Time enough to figure out what everyone was up to when she caught up to them. Besides, from the sound of things, Molly and the others were on the trail below her, so there would be reinforcements for...whatever was coming next.

# CHAPTER 28

E RIN STOPPED TO GLANCE AROUND, making sure that she was at least partially covered by a nearby boulder. She crouched down in its shadow, hoping the moonlight wouldn't make her exposed face glow to supernatural eyes. At that thought, she dug her fingers into the dirt and rubbed some of it across her forehead and over her cheeks and nose. Some camouflage had to be better than none at all.

She tried to tap into her wolf-senses as she looked around. A deep breath told her that there were wolves and humans not too far away. Molly and Becca and some of the others must have come out here after getting her message. A gunshot rang out and Erin hit the ground, heart pounding. Where had that come from? She swiveled her head carefully, trying to pinpoint it.

A moment later, the thought that it might have hit someone struck her, and she wondered if she should go back, run down the mountain toward the Pack members somewhere below. But what then? If she could draw off the werebear and his mate, then they'd be in less danger. Annie too, for however much that mattered. She shivered a bit at the memory of the brief hint of the other's rage that she had seen earlier, but gave a mental shrug. Whatever Annie wanted was for Annie, not for the rest of them.

Of course, if she could figure out how to summon the cave's magic and turn the other woman back to a human, maybe she'd leave again, this time for good. *But what if she doesn't? Or what if she comes back with more werewolf hunters? What then?* Erin puffed out her cheeks and blew a breath out.

She suspected that Shelly wasn't going to be happy that she'd shown the former Pack member as much as she had of what they'd attempted. It wasn't like Annie wasn't smart enough to figure out how to set up her own labyrinth, if she could get her wolfy fingers to work that way. But then what? She still needed Erin or Shelly or Becca or another wolf in the magic's good graces to tap into whatever the cave could do. Erin grimaced. What if Annie went after the other two again? Time for her to get moving, lead them all to...

Her mind went blank. Where was she going? The cave near Painted Rock, like they'd discussed? The warehouse? Maybe that would be better. She knew her way in and out now and there were big rooms in the interior. Maybe she could lure them inside and lock them in. Or bump them off one by one, like an Agatha Christie story.

She rolled her eyes at the direction her thoughts were taking and dashed out from behind the boulder, her brain already mapping out the best and least obvious route to the warehouse. She started running down a nearby deer trail, a distant crash behind her telling her that something large was on her trail.

# CHAPTER 29

B ECCA RAN AND CLIMBED AS fast as she could toward the spot that she thought Erin was heading toward. She slipped once and clobbered her knee on a rock, then scraped her palm on another. There had to be an easier way to do...whatever she thought she was doing. Once she found Erin, what was she going to do, apart from apologize for doubting her? Or not doubting her exactly, but leaving things open to the possibility that maybe she murdered a bad dude and stuffed him in the trunk of her car? Or...

She almost stopped running so her thoughts could catch up, but there were noises behind her and the ghost of scent before her and she couldn't bring herself to turn back or stop. At least she'd be with Erin while they confronted Kari and Jim or Annie. Or all of them. She shouldn't have to do that alone.

*Wolf, wolf, wolf,* her brain helpfully howled, throwing itself, in spirit at least, toward the moon that was slowly rising above her. She sucked in a deep breath, then another, crouching on all fours to climb faster, willing her hands to change into claws for easier climbing. Erin was somewhere up ahead of her, their enemies were behind her, or so she hoped, along with the rest of the Pack, and now it was all about the catching up.

It no longer mattered why she needed to catch up. Protect Erin, confront Annie, fight off Jim and Kari once and for all, it all roiled up inside her, weaving itself through the anxiety and terror and frustration for the last few weeks. Becca's heart raced faster and faster, her body shifting just a little, then a little more.

She barreled up the cliffside, dimly aware that someone behind had fired a shot at her. The bullet ricocheted off a nearby rock and she outran it, nearly at full werewolf speed now. She charged up and over the next ridge and onto a long ledge. And into a semi-familiar figure. She and Annie rolled dangerously close to the ledge before the other woman twisted free. Becca faced her in her half-changed state and Annie snarled, fangs gleaming in the moonlight. They circled each other, oblivious for the moment to everything around them.

A second shot echoed against the rocks and Annie growled, eyes narrowing to slits as she looked past Becca. *The enemy of my enemy is probably not my friend, not this time.* The thought flashed across Becca's brain as she scrambled behind the shelter of a nearby rock. Or, at least, what she hoped was shelter.

Annie backed up, then charged forward, leaping over the cliff. Becca yelped in surprise, torn between risking the bullets and satisfying her curiosity. Was it a sheer drop below the ledge?

She couldn't remember. She hadn't heard a body land, but then, she wasn't hearing anything else either.

Becca drew in a slow, deep breath and felt her body shift slowly back to human. *Wait, what was happening? Don't I control this?* Her body stretched and twisted, the fur disappearing. Becca looked down at the tattered remains of the clothes she'd been wearing and swore softly. This night just kept getting better and better. What the hell was she supposed to do now?

A sound nearby caught her attention and she glanced around, trying to see what or who it was. If it was Jim and Kari… or even Annie, then a middle-aged nearly-naked lady werewolf with no protection didn't stand much of a chance. Her pulse raced as she tried to locate a hiding place or an escape route. She crouched further back into the shadow of the boulder, hoping that whatever it was would pass by.

The rabbit that bolted past her hiding place would have been pretty surprised to find out just how much emotional turmoil it had caused. Becca slumped back against the bolder, heart pounding, eyes closed and hand clutched to her chest. Why had she run after Annie all by herself like that? Oh yes, Erin. Who was probably somewhere else by now. Her heartbeat slowed as she sent out a prayer to whatever might be listening that Erin was safe and that what she had smelled on the trail was an old scent, maybe left over from Erin and Carla patrolling around the cave.

Something big crunched its way through the bushes downslope, and she was instantly alert again. For a moment, she wondered about his scent, a mix of human and bear. Did he have some way of controlling his changes? Unbidden, Leroy's face popped into her mind. Had they been working together? It made sense. That had to be the connection: they must have met

Leroy after he fled the valley, or maybe they knew him before then and reconnected with him. He must have told them about the Pack or let enough details slip that they figured it out.

Maybe they got fired from their jobs, or maybe the whole reality TV werewolves thing was just a weird get rich scheme. Had they killed Leroy in some argument over money or something else? They must have done, right? Because it couldn't have been Erin. But then, how did they get his body in Erin's car? And what had they done to Erin to make her forget?

It took a moment to realize that she was being watched. She looked up to find Kari standing on the lip of the ledge and smirking at her over the barrel of a gun. "I thought you gals would wear more clothes for hiking. Oh, but you shifted and went back, didn't you? Aren't you the clever one, managing that? Clearly, we picked the wrong one before, didn't we?" This last comment was directed to the gigantic bear that clambered up to stand at her side.

Becca bit back a groan of horror. There was nowhere to run and no way she could fight anything that size. Her wolf snarled in the back of her head, its rage futile. At Kari's gesture, she stood up slowly, hunched over to hold what was left of her shirt and pants together. Then she slowly followed the bear up the mountain, hoping that the Pack was able to follow them, while Kari walked behind her, gun in hand.

# CHAPTER 30

Erin glanced behind her, listening for pursuit. She'd certainly heard it a few minutes ago: the rattle of rocks, the occasional sound of a feminine voice cursing softly, the slight scent of perfume on the air. She had run as fast as she could up the nearest hill and was heading down the other side when those sounds were replaced by the noises of the forest, cars on the distant highway, a small plane far overhead.

Where the hell had they gone? She'd been leading them away from the cave, just like she had planned. The Pack had to be back there somewhere, chasing after them, right? Where was everyone? She was counting on some reinforcements, or at least hoping for them. Of course, she thought as she slipped behind an outcrop, it might have helped if she had actually told someone that.

She listened very carefully for something above and beyond the wind and the birds and small animals in the woods in the valley below her. Then she thumped her head gently backward against the rock behind her. They were supposed to be following her, dammit. So where were they? She wondered if it would be worthwhile to backtrack, to stand around on a high ledge waving her arms around and screaming, "Here I am! Come get me!" and see what happened.

Some pebbles rolled down the hill, a long way below the ledge she was crouching on, and she was immediately alert. Something was attempting to move stealthily upward, and Erin grinned at the rock face in front of her. Now that was more like it. She erupted from her crouch in a tangle of limbs and scrambled upwards, moving as fast as she dared in the pale moonlight.

The moon wound its tendrils through her brain, making her feel both more wolfy and more tired. If this went on for much longer, she was either going to go hunt rabbits or go to sleep somewhere, so if they were going to follow her, they'd better get on it. The rock she was grabbing at broke off in her hand just then. *Shit*.

There was a strange hiss of air from behind her as she fell, then a guttural shout that sounded choked off followed by a sharp pain, almost as if...something had hit her hard from behind and they had fallen back down to the ledge where she'd been hiding seconds before. She sprawled down on the rocks face first, cursing and scrambling to get back on her feet. Something solid squirmed out from under her and knocked her back down again, this time sending the air shooting out of her lungs and leaving her limp and gasping.

"Quietttt." Hot breath hissed against her ear and she tried not to flinch as a fang grazed her skin.

Erin took a cautious sniff. Why was Annie sitting on her back, about to drool in her ear? Let alone grabbing her for an exciting fast trip downward? She dug her fingers into the grit beneath her and heaved upward, banging her head backward into the space where she thought Annie's snout would be.

The other woman yelped, then snarled, but pulled back enough for Erin to twist around and yank all but one leg out from under her. They stared at each other from inches away, silver eyes burning into gold ones, until finally, Erin broke the standoff with a hiss of her own. "Get off my damn leg." She pulled hard and Annie leapt sideways on all fours.

"Now what do you want? And what's the big idea of hitting me and making me fall down a rock face?" Erin rubbed a sore spot on her back and spat some grit out, but didn't stop watching her assailant. She was getting more unpredictable, as far as Erin could tell.

Annie moved her snout, struggling either to form words or change back or something, Erin suspected. After a few minutes, she shook her head and brushed a circle of dirt clean of rocks and debris between them, then flattened it with a few swipes of her claws. She started to write something slowly in the dirt, but Erin resisted tilting her head or moving closer. No telling how that would go over.

After a few minutes, Annie stopped writing in the dirt and sat back, gesturing at Erin to take a look. Erin eyed her for a moment, then stood up to look cautiously over at the scrawled letters. She cursed softly as they gradually became readable. "Dammit, Annie, they have Becca? If you know where they're hiding, take me there! Let's go!" *Timmy's fallen down a well, you say, Lassie?* popped into her head and she bit back a hysterical giggle.

Annie held up a paw and crouched, looking at Erin expectantly. Since she wasn't moving, Erin realized that there was more that she intended to say and tried to swallow the giant lump of frustration, fear and urgency in her throat with a gulp. "Do it fast," she snarled.

There followed some rapid scratching in the dirt, Annie's snout scrunched in concentration while Erin watched. She wondered if their former, or maybe not so former, foe, had murdered Leroy and stuffed him in her trunk without any help from their neighbors. Of course, Lizzie told her that her fingerprints were on the body, so maybe she did that herself herself. But why? She was pretty sure that she hadn't killed him, so was she planning on driving the corpse to town or something?

She wondered if Annie would just tell her if she asked, scratching her confession with her claw into the dirt, leaving her to take a picture of it for the Sheriff's Department. Erin stretched her arms behind her head and wished that she trusted her present company enough to just close her eyes and meditate for a few minutes. All she wanted right now was to curl up at home with Becca and Clyde and a nice cool glass of lemonade and rest. But for that to happen, she needed to rescue Becca. *And clear my name.*

Annie made a weird noise and Erin made herself focus again. She squinted down in the moonlight, trying to read the irregular shapes of the letters in the dirt. The message this time was longer and there were no breaks between some of the words so it took a while to read. "What? What do you think they'll do to Becca in the meantime?" She looked up with a glare, biting back the urge to scream and yell.

She didn't ask the next question: "What if I can't change you back in time to save Becca? If I can't do it at all?" Those questions hung unspoken in the moonlit silence between them. Part of her wondered why Annie hadn't just tried to corral Shelly into this little adventure, but then their Pack Alpha hadn't gotten herself involved in a murder case, gotten kidnapped and gone on the run. She was much harder to find and rope into something like this.

Erin's brain whirled. Becca was in danger but she herself would have to go all the way back to the cave with Annie before she could even find out what was going on? Let alone run to the rescue? Her brain scrambled through a bunch of desperate plans to try and change that outcome before coming up empty.

"Please…" She hesitated before letting her guard down. There were no other options, as far as she should tell. If Annie didn't have enough basic humanity to respond to her plea, there was probably nothing more that she could do. "Can we go after Becca first? I swear to you, on anything you want, that I will go back to the cave with you and do whatever I can to help you turn back." She closed her eyes for a moment and hoped as hard as she could.

Annie made a noise and Erin's eyes shot open, instantly alert. Her wolf brain yelled at her to be ready for whatever came next, whatever she need to do to protect this ridiculous human skin she was wearing in front of this monster. The two halves of herself warred with each other, the human side demanding that she wait, the wolf that she change and fight.

The wolf-woman stared longingly down the slope in the direction of the cave, her face settling into an expression that let Erin see how exhausted and alone she was. It was almost, but not quite, enough to make Erin feel a little sorry for her. But there was a lot of water under that bridge and Annie had done some things that were absolutely unforgiveable. She wondered if Margaret had ever felt sorry for her, had let her guard down just before the end, in hopes of reaching her.

Annie turned and looked at her, the longing and the tired fading back into the expression she'd worn since she first came back. After a long minute, she scrambled up and began loping up the trail that led away from the Pack's cave and up the steep hillside. Erin pulled herself together and jogged after her as well as she could, hoping that she was getting her wish.

It wasn't long before she also wished that she'd packed along more than a water bottle and a piece of jerky, but she pulled that out of her pocket and gnawed on it as well as she could, in hopes of silencing the growling in her stomach. This was beginning to feel like a very long night and for the first time, she wondered if Annie was sure that they had Becca or was maybe taking her somewhere else for her own ends.

She had just started to wonder if she could signal the other Pack members when Annie stopped abruptly at the edge of an old lumber road. It hadn't been used in years, judging by the overgrown vegetation and the big stony lumps that defined where equipment wheels had left their mark. Erin realized that they were now headed down the slope and closer to the woods.

Now she just had to figure out why Annie had stopped. She squinted into the trees, then down the road, letting her acute hearing and sense of smell help her vision out. Woods, the scent of distant cars and people, a wood fire some distance away and then there it was: Becca and the bear and his mate. Her upper lip twisted back with a growl and she nearly charged down the slope without thinking about it.

Annie sidled over and blocked her path with a soft noise that could have meant anything. Erin interpreted it as her reluctance to be eaten by a bear, were or otherwise, and she had to bow to the wisdom in that, at least for the moment. The wolf-woman stepped forward slowly on four legs, following a faint trail that Erin could barely see. It was plain that she was hoping to come up on their site from downwind.

Erin picked up a fist-sized rock, then shoved another one into her pocket. There wouldn't be many of those once they got down into the trees and she had a bloodthirsty desire to use one or both of them on Jim and Kari. Not as satisfying as tearing out their throats with her wolf fangs, perhaps, but it would have to do for the moment. Maybe she could do both. Becca had better be unharmed or this would be more than a fantasy. A white-hot rage gave her an extra burst of energy, and she was on Annie's heels when they reach the overhang above the campfire.

Becca was sitting against a tree, her hands tied in front of her. Her eyes were closed, but Erin could see her nostrils flare. She had probably caught their scent, but she didn't given any other sign that she wasn't just trying to sleep. Kari was on guard, a rifle balanced against her shoulder, as she walked in a circle around the fire. The werebear was nowhere in sight.

Annie went low, sinking into the ground, and Erin followed her lead. Where the hell was he? And what form was he in? She sniffed anxiously, hoping that Annie's sense of smell was better than hers right now. The two of them might be able to handle him for a bit, but not if they were up against the rifle too. They had to split them up somehow. Erin sent up a silent prayer that the other Pack members weren't far behind. They were going to need some help very soon.

A not very distant growl shook her to the bone and she whipped around, body strung tight, on red alert. From the corner of her eye, she saw Annie slink down and vanish into a crevice.

Great, now she was being left alone to deal with what was coming. Now where the hell was he? A whiff of bear preceded a cloud of oily, heavy scent, too close, too close. Erin gave a snarl of her own, the larger of the stones in her pocket now in her hand. She'd make sure to do some damage this time, at least.

Jim emerged from around a boulder, wearing his outer bear form uncomfortably to Erin's eye. Not that it would make her any less dead if he got ahold of her, of course, but he didn't look right. His eyes were unfocused, his fur patchy, and he looked as if he was about to shift back into human form at any moment. He might be sick or wounded or…the memory of Becca when they found her in the ditch after Annie and her men dosed her with their cure popped into her head. Leroy's cure.

Her grip tightened on the rock as his massive head swung in her direction and his nostrils flared. His eyes got more bearish, and Erin threw her rock right at his face with as much force as she could muster. The stone hit true and the bear yelped, the noise echoing off the stones around them.

A shot rang out and Erin ducked instinctively as Kari's bullet hit the rock over her head with a loud ping. *Dammit.* A loud shriek made her jump and Jim whipped around and began galloping down the hillside toward the fire. Erin looked down, incredulously, to see Annie and Kari rolling on the ground near the fire, struggling for control of the rifle.

Becca was off to one side sawing her wrists frantically against something that Erin couldn't see at this angle. She hurtled down the slope using the same route that the bear had used, hoping she wasn't going to be too late. Becca yelled something at Annie, alerting her to Jim charging ever closer, and the wolf-woman snarled and yanked her arms free of

Kari's grip. She struck the woman hard up against the side of her head and she went limp.

Jim roared and galloped across the clearing toward Annie and his wife. Annie stood in a half crouch, eyes wild as she watched him come, muscles tensed for a leap to take her out of his path. Becca rubbed her bound wrists faster, her motions frantic. There wasn't enough time, not enough time for any of it. He was going to kill them all and Erin couldn't do anything about it.

In despair, she hurled her second rock at him, but this time, it went wide and she missed. He reared up and over Annie, giant clawed paws in a blinding swipe at her head. She leapt sideways, then darted in for a swipe of her own. He howled and kicked her away, then Erin slipped and slid the last few yards down the slope into the clearing, not seeing what happened next. There were more howls and snarls and she tried to ignore them as she struggled to get to her feet. She had to free Becca, get the rifle, stop all of this if she could.

Kari was moving again, rubbing her head and starting to look around. Erin scrambled for the rifle, lunging forward to grab it before the other woman could. Annie screamed in pain and crashed into her, blood spraying both of them. Then, just as suddenly, Becca was there, cut ropes dangling from bleeding wrists. She kicked out at Kari, the motion stiff and awkward, but threatening enough that the other woman flinched and Becca grabbed the gun.

She pointed it at Kari and said in a voice that Erin had never heard from her before, "Stop it right now or so help me, I will shoot her." Her eyes were locked on Kari's, but the werebear paused midlunge, shaking his giant furry head like he was being buzzed by gnats or something. He swung around to stare at Becca and roared, the sound driving Erin to cover her ears as it echoed against the rocks above them.

"I…" Becca said, very slowly and loudly, "have had about all I'm going to put up with of your nonsense. You move, she gets shot. Back away from Annie and change back if you can."

Kari held up a hand and Erin wondered if she was waiting to be called on or something. She couldn't see her face from this angle, so it was hard to figure out what was going on. She started to stand up but kept her movements slow and cautious as she tried to make sure that she wasn't blocking Becca's line of sight to the bear.

She missed the first part of what Kari was saying, but did manage to catch, "—can't make him change back. I'm not even sure that he can do it at all now." Her voice trembled and Erin saw Becca's eyes narrow. She walked up to stand at her side, still keeping an eye on the bear and Annie, who was now lying on the ground with her eyes closed and her arms crossed over some vicious slices across her ribs.

"What do you mean he can't change back? What did the two of you do?" Becca frowned, her voice sounding tight and tired.

The cure, it had to be. "Did you kill Leroy because it didn't work? Or because it did and then you realized that you couldn't control it? And what did you do to me to make me forget? How the hell did his corpse end up in my car?" Erin could feel her features twist into a human imitation of her wolf's grimace and her entire body shiver with rage. They had made her think that she murdered someone, betrayed her friends, betrayed herself and…

She threw herself at Kari, her fury almost enough to make her ignore the roar of rage from the bear, Becca's cursing and the sound of a gunshot. She found herself hurtling through the air and instinctively tried to curl up in a ball to protect her head. The air was full of noise and she hit the ground hard, lying still and stunned for what felt like a lot longer than it probably was as she tried to make herself move. *Becca.*

She managed to roll over and utter a small scream as her ribs touched the hard ground. It could barely be heard in the cacophony. Becca and Kari were struggling for the gun and Annie was fighting the bear again. It hardly made sense to think of him as Jim or whatever his real name was anymore; there was nothing human looking out of those eyes.

Annie, at least, appeared to have gotten her second wind. Her fangs and claws ran red with blood and Erin could see several deep wounds in the bear's back and shoulders. She twisted awkwardly and painfully, the motion enough to make her bite back several more screams, as she managed to rise into a bent-over crouch. She reached for a fallen branch and using it as a cane, she limped back toward the fray.

A yell from behind her made her turn, breath hissing through her teeth. The backup team had arrived at last. Molly and Carla and Shelly were charging down the slope, yelling, with Lizzie and Gladys right behind them. Becca managed to knock Kari over just as they appeared and it looked for a moment like she might be able to recapture the gun at the same time. Erin gritted her teeth, trying to move faster. There were too many things that could go wrong, too much danger. She had to help.

The clearing swirled around her and she went down on one knee, bracing her hands against the ground as she tried to stay conscious and keep moving. Inside her head, her wolf was trying to wake up, trying to take over and change this stupid human meat shell that was so vulnerable and defenseless.

A loud thud and a howl made her stop and look up to see what had happened. Molly and Carla were taking on the bear, hitting it with branches while Annie kept up her attack with claws and teeth. There was a swirl of limbs and fur and Kari screamed something. The bear shook its head, reared up as if about to strike, then dropped back down and began galloping his way downslope.

With a screeching howl, Annie ran after him, a trail of blood in her wake. Shelly caught Erin just before she fell over and eased her down to sit on a rock near the fire. Becca handed the gun to Carla and raced over. "Are you okay, hon? No, that's a stupid question. I can see that you aren't. Let us see how bad your ribs are." She kissed Erin lightly on the forehead and Shelly braced Erin's shoulders while Becca slid her shirt up.

The hiss of breath through Becca's teeth told her how bad it was, then things spun slowly around once more and she faded into a pain-free darkness.

# CHAPTER 31

"**O**UCH," SHELLY MURMURED AND WINCED at the sight of Erin's purple and black skin. "That's going to take a bunch of arnica and at least one change to clear up."

Becca scowled at her. "Could you take this more seriously, please? I mean, she just got hurt. Her shoulder is still a mess. Who knows how long this will take to heal on top of that?"

Shelly nodded a brief apology, and together they lowered Erin gently down onto a smoother patch of dirt. Becca poured some water from the bottle that Shelly handed her onto a bandana and gently patted Erin's face. While she did that, Shelly got up and went over to join Molly.

The sound of something scrambling in the brush up the hill had them all on high alert, but it was only Carla, descending the slope somewhat faster than was safe. But she managed it and jumped the last few feet to land in front of Shelly and Molly.

"Lost him," she said by way of greeting, not looking any of them in the eye.

Molly reached out her free arm and pulled her in close, gently kissing her forehead. "It's okay, sweetie. Sometimes, you need a wolf's nose to find what's out there." She handed the gun to Carla, then cocked her head at Shelly.

Shelly nodded to her, then jerked her chin up the hill. In a moment, Shelly, Gladys and Molly had started climbing up the bear's trail. Becca thought she could just see the shadow of a tail on Molly's butt. She wondered where Annie had got to, but Erin was coming around now and Barbie, no, Kari—she was done not taking them seriously—looked like she might make a grab for the gun, so she focused on that instead of the wolf-woman. Once she had Erin settled and lying quietly across her lap and Carla keeping a very close eye on their captured foe, she relaxed a little, but not for long.

The roar of a nearby truck engine made them all jump. A bunch of possibilities, each worse than the last, danced through Becca's brain: a new pack of would-be slayers, reality TV show fans, the entire Sheriff's Department. She eased Erin off her lap and rested her head on a rolled up bag that one of the others had dropped. From the way she was breathing, she had dropped off into a restless sleep.

But just as Becca was standing up, the wind shifted and she breathed a sigh of relief. "Reinforcements," she told Carla over her shoulder. Adelía, Carli, Lin and the others were as welcome a sight as Becca could recall seeing in days. She filled them in quickly and Lin crouched down by Erin while the others took off up the trail. Becca came over and sat on the ground next to Erin's head just in time to hear Erin sigh and turn slightly to let the older woman tug her shirt up to look at her ribs.

Becca watched in fascination as Lin pulled a small kit from her bag. Her fingers danced carefully over Erin's bruises, her touch gentle, but it was still enough to make her patient flinch. Finally, she grunted deep in her throat and pulled out a small bottle from the kit she was holding. Whatever it was looked like a gel of some kind, and when she cracked the bag open, the sharp scent of alcohol and herbs hit Becca's nose.

She bit back her questions in favor of watching Lin rub the liquid carefully over the bruises on Erin's side and back. Erin gave a sigh of relief that made Becca raise her eyebrows. "Ginseng, myrrh, some other things that grow near here, steeped in vodka. It is similar to the dit da jow that is given to injured martial artists." Lin spoke as if Becca had asked her questions aloud.

Before Becca could say anything, a roar so loud that it made her cover her ears for a second echoed through the clearing, followed by a huge crash. The women all looked at each other and Kari sat up, eyes wide, as she stared around at the mountains. The silence stretched out taught as a wire as they looked in the direction that Shelly and the others had gone. Becca could feel all of them straining their ears and noses as far as they could, trying to figure out what had happened. Kari scrambled to her feet, her face so pale it nearly glowed, and said in a shaky voice, "Dammit, you're not going to shoot me and we all know it. Come with me if you want. I have to know what happened."

Lizzie suddenly appeared on the trail, scrambling down faster than Becca thought was safe. She landed in a crouch and gestured toward Kari. "Carla, we gotta go and take her with us. Let's get this stuff settled. Yes, you're coming with us and I don't want to hear any arguments. I've got a deadline to meet." She nodded at Kari who exploded into angry commentary about how she wasn't leaving.

Carla looked from her to the rifle, then back again. "We can just shoot you in the leg and carry you down, you know. Leave your man to the wolves, unless you want to join him."

Kari stared at Carla wild-eyed, then glanced around, as if noticing for the first time that she was surrounded by were-wolves. Becca could feel her wolf looking out of her eyes and she wasn't the only one. She curled one corner of her lip. "Go with them or try and outrun us."

The other woman stiffened like she was going to try it, then collapsed crying instead, the fight running out of her as swiftly as it had risen up. Carla grabbed one arm and Lizzie the other and they hauled her to her feet. Without a backward glance, they dragged her swiftly down the trail away from the Pack.

Erin groaned. "Aren't we ever going to find out if they killed Leroy? And how he ended up in my trunk?"

Lin patted her uninjured shoulder. "That mystery will still be with us tomorrow. Right now, I think we have other things to deal with."

"Is...Jim dead? Did we win?" Erin's eyes were getting glassy, and Becca reached out to catch her as she slid back down onto the blanket that they had put down under her.

"Just rest for a few minutes, hon." Becca murmured the words softly. She stroked Erin's hair as her eyes shut.

Lin rummaged around in her bag for a minute and produced a couple of small white pills. "Chamomile," she said to Becca's unanswered question. With a bit of coaxing, she got Erin to swallow them and after a few moments, she went limp as she fell asleep. Together, they rolled Erin up in the blanket and moved her closer to the fire before sitting down to wait for the others.

# CHAPTER 32

B ECCA WOKE WITH THE DAWN, thinking for a moment that
this was like every other morning waking up with the
Pack…except for the dead werebear at the bottom of the cliffs,
the overwhelming scent of blood and the commotion amongst
the other Pack members. Becca got up slowly but when she came
back from peeing, she caught Shelly's eye as she started to walk
up to the ledge above them to look down at what the others had
already seen. Shelly shook her head and began herding them all
back down the slope.

The morning was brisk and they had a chilly cleanup of the
clearing ahead, getting rid of some of the evidence of the battle
they had fought. Becca had slipped into a walking daydream by
the time she'd checked on Erin and they were done. It took her a
few more moments to notice their somewhat unexpected guest
hidden behind some boulders.

Annie was looking considerably worse for the wear. She was covered in blood and one of her eyes was swollen shut. Her right back leg was twisted at an awkward angle and she didn't respond when Shelly called her name.

Adelía gave Shelly a cautious glance, then knelt near Annie's head with a water bottle. The wolf-woman looked unconscious from what Becca could see of her face, but she gave a slight cough when Adelía ran a wet bandanna over her face. Lin grabbed her medical bag and crouched down next to the two of them.

The rest of them drank what water they had and ate the last of the supply of jerky and energy bars they all carried with them now. Becca woke Erin up and got some jerky into her. When Erin had drunk heavily from her water bottle and was looking more alert, Becca gave her a tremulous smile. "How are you doing?"

Erin gave her a wry grin. "Could be better. Feels like a couple of busted ribs, maybe. At least it doesn't hurt as much as it did yesterday." She looked like she was going to say something more, but Shelly cleared her throat just then to get their attention.

"We've got to get Annie down the mountain. I'd prefer the clinic, but she's telling us that she'll only go to the cave. Not like she can stop us, but I'm not sure that Dr. Green can save her either. But either way, we'll have to carry her and we don't have any way to build a stretcher."

This far above the tree line, there weren't any handy big sticks for it anyway, even if they could piece together enough cloth to make one. Becca took a quick look around just to be sure. Adelía followed the direction of her gaze and shook her head. "Nothing we can use for poles up here. We'll have to improvise."

Molly groaned. "Jackets?" Adelía nodded, taking off her own. She and Molly knelt down and started knotting the assembled pile together while the Pack members who weren't tending to Annie or helping tie jackets together stomped around and rubbed their arms.

When Becca looked back up from getting dressed, Lin was cleaning Annie's arms and exposed skin with a wet bandanna and the coat sling looked just about ready. Molly and Adelía stood up and stretched it, testing the knots in each direction until they were sure it was secure. They brought it over and laid it down at Annie's side, and very slowly, they eased her onto it. Molly, Adelía, Becca and Shelly each slung a sleeve over their shoulders and lifted Annie before beginning a slow walk back down the mountain.

It was hard going, between the loose rocks, the cloudy morning's dim light and Annie's nearly dead weight suspended off their shoulders. By the time they reached the ledge up the mountain from the cave, Becca could see stars and was having an active fantasy about seeing both a chiropractor and a massage therapist in the very near future.

"Break time," Shelly announced and they lowered Annie very carefully to the ground. Lin came over and applied more herbs and ointments while the Pack members who'd been carrying the stretcher sat or lay down and pulled out their water bottles.

Erin came over and sat down next to Becca. "How are you holding up?"

Becca snorted, "I think I should be asking you that. She's not getting any lighter, that's for sure." She collapsed on the ground, crossing her arms behind her head for a cushion, and studied Erin for a minute. "When we get back and we get all this...fixed, I want a do-over. Every conversation, everything for the last couple of weeks, rewound to when I first moved into your place. I've missed so many things going through life half asleep. And I don't want this to be one of them." She could feel her ears turn red as she blushed, but she'd been rehearsing this speech in her head for days now.

"I think Lizzie and the sheriff might have some thoughts about that, but otherwise, I really like where you're going with this." Erin gave her a wry, sideways grin.

Shelly got up and they all stood up with her. "Let's get this done. Lin, could you please reach out to the Circle and see if a few of them would be willing to meet us at the cave? I think we'll need all the help we can get." She glanced around and Becca and the others moved over to stand by Annie's makeshift stretcher.

At least she was asleep now. Becca still didn't pity her, but she couldn't find it in her heart to wish that much pain on anyone else, even an enemy. They picked her up as gently as they could, the other Pack members going on ahead to make calls, to organize and to set up the cave for whatever they were going to do next. Becca made herself focus on that, and not the pain in her shoulders or the cold that was nipping at her exposed skin. You could never summon a hot flash when you needed one.

Adelía began to sing softly and Becca let herself drift a bit with the tune. Her Spanish was pretty rusty, but it sounded like a song about lost love and winning your beloved back. Adelía had a sweet, quiet voice and it made the hike go a bit faster than the first half, even though portions of the trail were harder to navigate.

All four of them collapsed after they lowered Annie gently to the ground on the ledge outside the cave. Becca squinted over at Erin from where she lay, noting that at least she looked better than she had. She was glad someone did. A chorus of quiet groans seemed to echo her thoughts.

Lin walked quickly over to Annie's side, medical supplies in hand, and Becca struggled to sit up, hoping to be helpful. Annie opened her good eye a slit and reached out one clawed hand with a speed that almost made it blur. She grabbed Lin's hand and growled, "The cave."

Lin growled back, her face twisting up like she smelled something bad. Becca was closest and grabbed Annie's arm. "We're there and we'll get you inside soon. But right now, you need to let go of her."

Annie didn't look as if she heard her for a long second and Lin bared her teeth. Becca wondered if she was going to have to bite Annie's hand; those claws were sharp and she could see a few drops of blood on the older wolf's arm. But then Annie let out a breath like a sigh and loosened her grip.

Lin yanked herself free and inspected her arm for damage. She took a few minutes to apply ointment to the cuts and cautiously flex her fingers. She glanced up and nodded to Becca. "Thank you. Can you keep her calm while I check her?"

Becca sighed, but made herself sit up and get closer to Annie's side. "I can try?"

Lin nodded and pulled a couple of packets from her bag. She applied something to the wounds on Annie's face. The latter jerked convulsively and Becca grabbed her arms before she could reach for Lin. Adelía reached over and grabbed her shoulders, murmuring soothingly in Spanish as Lin swiftly bandaged her eye. She checked her over and added some more ointment and another bandage to her stomach wounds before sitting back. "That's the best I can do. I think we can move her again."

Becca sighed quietly and rolled her shoulders. She and the others each stood up and grabbed a sleeve. Erin stepped up next to Becca, who looked at her and said, "Not a chance. You can keep me company, though."

Erin nodded. "What happened with Kari?"

"Shelly had Carla and Lizzie take her to town. She's under arrest, I assume."

Becca got Erin caught up with what had happened since the fight. Everyone else chimed in occasionally. The look of relief on Erin's face when she heard that Kari had been arrested, even without all the answers that they were all hoping for, was worth every stumble and every shoulder ache of the trip down, as far as Becca was concerned.

When she finally got a chance to look around, she could see that someone had pulled back a painted cloth that had been hanging over the cave entrance. There was a cheery fire going just inside, with a kettle hanging over it. A couple of lanterns lit up the interior and a pallet of blankets was laid out in the middle of the cave, presumably for Annie.

The wolf-woman looked unconscious now and her breathing was labored. They picked her up carefully and set her down on the pallet before gathering in a loose semicircle near the entrance. Shelly arched an eyebrow back at Annie. "Why does she think that Erin can fix her?"

Becca shrugged and murmured, "Because she thinks we made her this way to begin with, possibly on purpose? And Erin was around for her transformation when we did the first ritual and convenient this time?"

Erin sighed and asked the question they were all thinking, "Even if we or I can, do we want to?"

Shelly wrinkled her nose. "Valid question. Well, she is my cousin so I feel some responsibility there. It should get her out of the Pack's hair, if we can pull it off. Once she changes back, I'm pretty sure I can get her to swear on things that she cares about that she won't come back. I suspect this is why she went up against Jim. It's meant to be an exchange, a redemption of sorts, I think, from what I know of her personality. The question is: do we agree with that? I think we all need to weigh in. There isn't time to bring everyone up here, so it will have to be those of us who are here." She gestured at the group around her.

Becca murmured, "I feel like we're at the end of an Agatha Christie story and you're about to tell us who the murderer is."

Shelly snorted. "Except we already know that part, absent a few details. For that matter, we already have a pretty lengthy list of sins that we know Annie to be guilty of. The question is what we want to do about her. Thoughts?"

Adelía spoke up, her voice soft, "I think we should try to heal her, if we can." Lin wrinkled her nose, but after a long moment, nodded her assent. Gladys looked even more reluctant, but in the end, she nodded as well.

Molly frowned. "After everything she's done? Even if we are able to cure her and make her human or the magic takes her back and makes her part of the Pack, how do we know that she won't just make more trouble? It's not like we can trust her."

Shelly glanced over at Erin. "You've spent the most time with her in her current state. What do you think?"

Erin blew out a breath and frowned at the ground for a minute before looking back up. "I can see both sides. When she came here with those guys, it was like she was on some sort of religious crusade to make us convert or die. She took that very, very seriously and I truly believe that she still wants to stop changing forever. She hated being a werewolf before this happened, I can only imagine that she hates it even more now. I suspect, though I can't say for certain, that if we could heal her, she'd leave town and not look back. But I'm not sure how we could enforce it, without, you know, going all wolfy and letting nature takes its course. That said, I'm equally sure that there's no danger of the magic changing her back into one of us. I think our foremothers want her gone almost as badly as we do."

Becca gave her a little smile, then turned back to Shelly with a much more solemn expression. "Is there some place for her to go if we can change her back?"

"Looks like we got here just in time for the fun part." Becca spun around, startled, to find Robin standing behind her with a couple of the other women from Circle House. Carla and Lizzie were with them too, and they all stepped forward into the circle as she and the other Pack members made room.

Robin smiled at Becca, then focused on Shelly and the others. "She was family and she could be so again, even in a distant place. If the issue is punishment and you feel that she hasn't experienced enough of that, what would be sufficient to pay for her crimes? Shelly, what do you think?"

Shelly glanced sidelong at the still form in the middle of the cave floor. "Exile," she said at last. "We can never trust her again and while Margaret made mistakes, she didn't deserve to die for them." All of them nodded in agreement.

"Do you think we can cure...turn her back into a human?" Adelía asked. "She seems to hate what she is so very much. And being all alone in the mountains after always being in a group..." She shook her head as she trailed off.

One of the other women from Circle House, one whose name Becca hadn't caught yet, tilted her head like a wolf. "So you would make her human, then exile her?" After a moment, Adelía nodded. "Any objections or other thoughts? No? Looks like you have your recommendation, Shelly."

Shelly nodded in turn. "But how do we do it? I mean I think we can reconstruct the ritual we made that called the paintings, but what if they don't want to change her back?"

Lin glanced around at the walls and answered, "I'm not sure we ever have that much control over what the magic chooses and how it does so. Look at all of us, or her, for that matter. It finds something within each of us, something it values for reasons of its own. I think we can only channel it and call it up, then let it decide."

Becca blinked at her, processing her words. It occurred to her that this was the longest speech she had ever heard the other woman give and wondered if she needed to be listening more or they all needed to be more encouraging. It was definitely the best explanation she'd heard for how they'd all gotten into this particular situation.

Shelly nodded. "Excellent point, Lin. Do we have a plan for how to tap into the magic, one that works for sure instead of trial and error?" She glanced at Robin and the other women from Circle House, and they looked at each other.

Finally, Robin reached into her backpack and pulled out a crumpled and stained notebook. "I found this in the wreckage that was left after the Women's Club burned. You remember, Shelly, you asked me to poke around a little after the ashes cooled? This was in the box of stuff I brought back for us to sort through. From the dates, it's about fifty years old and it's got some records about how the Pack used to organize things back then."

Shelly held her hand out and Robin carefully handed it to her, with a small wince as a bit of paper flaked off and landed on the stone floor of the cave. Shelly opened the book slowly and carefully, holding it up so she could see the pages in the dim light. A quiet silence followed, then Lizzie stepped forward and handed her a small flashlight. "Thanks, cos."

Becca tried to keep herself from standing on tiptoe to see what was on the pages. Some of it was fueled by curiosity, some by the excitement of discovering that they hadn't lost everything in the fire after all. There was Pack history to study and learn from! The intensity of her reaction took her aback for a few moments; she'd never been this excited about studying before, but then, maybe werewolf lore would be different.

Shelly began reading excerpts out loud, pausing when the writing was hard to read. After a few minutes of paging through the crumbling pages, she found what they were all hoping would be there. "Here it is. An old ritual for calling the paintings." She drew in a deep breath and let it out. "Well, let's see if it works." She began calling out directions.

Erin nudged Becca. "Penny for your thoughts, assuming anyone has one of those anymore? Shelly wants us to try and stabilize the labyrinth that I started."

Becca shook her head a bit to clear it. "Candles too?"

"Yep, we'll need four, one for each direction."

"How are you feeling? Do you want to rest while I finish the circles?"

Erin rubbed her head a little. "Might not be the worst idea. How about I'll follow you around and make witty conversation while you finish up?"

Becca grinned. "Sounds like a fine Saturday night to me. Except it's Sunday morning now, I think. Make that early afternoon. I wonder if we have to wait until nightfall to do all this stuff."

"Maybe. Shelly sent a delegation off to get some more food and cook us dinner. Lin and Adelía think they have Annie stabilized for now, so I think the plan is to do setup and eat first, then tackle the magic making afterwards." Erin made a jazz hands gesture at the walls and wrinkled her nose. "I don't know whether to hope this works or that we'll get to see them carry her off to Wolfy Valhalla."

"I don't think she's earned Valhalla, not even with taking on Kari and Jim. I do think making her completely human again might be the best way to make her mostly harmless though. Man, this would have been the weirdest conversation in the world a few months ago!" They shared a quiet laugh as Becca finished trailing sand on the floor to finish the pattern. It sparkled a little in the sunlight from the entrance, making it look like magic already.

"Human or weird hybrid or wolf, she's gotta leave the valley," Erin added somberly. "I don't know what she had to do with Leroy and our weird neighbors, but I'm guessing that they're all connected somehow."

Becca nodded as Shelly walked over to hand her a couple of candles and give them both some more directions. They went to work, and after a few minutes, had something set up that almost any TV watcher would recognize as a ritual space. Erin murmured, "Now we just need some flaming torches and those long monks' robes." Becca smirked and finished setting up the last of the four candles.

"Chow time!" Molly called from the entrance, summoning them all to the fire she and the others had been tending outside. Whatever they were cooking made the wolf in the back of Becca's brain salivate, and she shook her head to clear that particular image. Breakfast seemed like days ago now. She resisted the temptation to go over and take a look at Annie; what if the other woman died while they were getting all this set up? Would she haunt them forever then?

From the corner of her eye, she saw Adelía take a couple of bowls of stew over to Lin and sighed a bit with relief. The Pack was doing as well as it could by their fallen foe and erstwhile member. There wasn't anything much that she could add.

She and Erin got in line at the campfire and Molly quickly served up bowls of stew from the big pot. Soon, all of them were sitting on the ground or on the rocks on the ledge outside the cave, enjoying the venison stew that had been filling the air with luscious scents. "When did anyone have time to hunt a deer?" she murmured at Erin.

"A couple of days ago. Jonas and Carla went hunting and I made stew and a bunch of extra stuff and froze it because I knew we'd need it. Which reminds me: you two are on meal duty next month." Molly smiled cheerfully at them over her spoon.

"Wait, there's meal duty? I didn't realize..." Becca trailed off, feeling silly.

"We share it around. It'll be easier when we have the Women's Club building back again since then we can cook there or have stuff brought in and so forth. But that'll be a while yet."

"Which reminds me—" Becca started to ask about the Club and the non-Pack members and a bunch of other things that were suddenly crowding her brain, wanting to get out, when Shelly stood up and motioned for silence.

"Once we finish and clean up, please form a circle in the cave. Stand just inside the outer ring that Becca and Erin made on the floor." She looked a little apprehensive, at least to Becca, but otherwise medium-sized and in charge. Whether they succeeded or not today, they were going to give it their best shot.

# CHAPTER 33

E RIN WISHED SHE'D GOTTEN A chance to see the notebook for herself. It would have been nice to know whether or not there was something special she needed to do. The last time had been such a haze of pain and peril after she got shot that it was hard to remember much of anything. Yet she still felt that Annie and probably some of the others expected her to be better prepared because she'd "done this before."

She followed Becca up to the washing station that they'd set up near the campfire and helped her wash their dishes and cups as well as some of the cookware. Once everything was set out to dry, though, there were no more delays. Some of what she was thinking must have shown on her face because Becca squeezed her arm reassuringly. "It'll be okay. We'll do the best we can. It's not like we can control it, so there's always going to be some random stuff happening."

Becca smiled up at her and Erin's stomach did a leisurely flip. She hoped that she'd have a chance to tell her that she was gorgeous and kind and sexy and had the most kissable lips some time very soon. If Kari confessed and she was no longer on the run. She bit back a quiet groan.

"Shoulder still hurt?" Shelly asked from her other side.

"Yep. I've been getting hammered on a lot lately." Erin gave her a mournful grin.

"You have! Let's lay off the werebears and the shootings for a while, shall we?" Shelly gave her a twisted smirk of her own and they exchanged fist taps. *Once Howling High Girls Basketball, always Howling High Girls Basketball,* Erin thought as she turned to face into the circle. Annie was in the middle, her breathing strained, but audible, as Lin and Adelía both got up and joined the others.

Carla and Lizzie glanced at each other, then at Shelly. Lizzie nodded and Carla trailed Lizzie outside to go sit around the campfire. Erin watched them go and hoped that the magic was planning on calling Lizzie. She'd be a terrific Pack member. So would Carla if…well…here her thoughts trailed off. It had picked Annie after all, so maybe better choices going forward were the best any of them could hope for. She turned her attention to Shelly.

Shelly looked at the battered book in her hand for another moment, then handed it back to Robin. "There's a chant and we need some volunteers to drum." One of the Circle House women, who looked as if she might be Shelly's aunt or cousin, stepped out of the Pack circle and grabbed her pack. She pulled out two small hand drums and gave one to Lin, but kept the other. Once she was back in the circle, Shelly continued, "Thank you, Sarah. You and Lin can drum while we walk the circle and use the chant to rouse the magic. Erin, I think you know what to do"

Sarah nodded and walked to the entrance to the crude labyrinth, Lin and Erin at her heels. The other women grabbed some of the blankets that weren't being used to keep Annie warm and the two sat on those. Sarah flipped her long black braids back over her shoulders, picked up her drum and began to pound a steady rhythm. After a moment, Lin began to follow her while Erin walked nervously over to stand at the entrance.

Shelly started chanting in a language that she didn't recognize, not at first, but as they all began to move forward to the drumbeat, she thought she recognized some of the words. They went to her head, along with the candlelight and the sound, until she felt as if she was drifting above them, watching her body follow the Pack around the cave. She stepped forward and began following the curved lines on the floor, moving like her feet knew what they were doing.

Some of the others had begun to do small dances as they walked around the circle in time to the drums and Erin enjoyed watching them from her new aerial perch, hovering above her body. Becca murmured softly, "You okay? Still with us?"

"Barely, but yeah. Checked out for a minute there." Erin spoke softly. Her vision was still hazy, her mind elsewhere, as the drumbeat sank into her bones and blood. She had closed her eyes when Becca's gasp made her open them again. The paintings were starting to move. It called to the wolf in her blood and made her skin ripple like it was growing fur. Glancing at the others, she could see it having the same impact on them. The whole atmosphere was charged and heated now and they were all responding to it.

She took five more steps and found herself in the center of the labyrinth, standing next to Annie's pallet. Her eyes closed and something took over her body. She could feel her lips part and sounds in the language that she had heard in her dream began to pour from her mouth.

Annie opened her eyes, lifted her head and gave a weak howl, and the sound sent chills through her. A moment later, Robin tilted back her head and howled back. Then, one by one, they all did it, the sound ricocheting off the stone walls and filling all of the cave's nooks and crannies. Erin could feel chills run down her arms, right under the fur that she could almost feel.

Whatever was controlling her mouth said something in very stern tones to Annie, who lowered her head submissively. Then, without fanfare, it departed, leaving Erin with a dry throat and slightly itchy eyes. Shelly stepped inside the Pack's circle and held her hand up while the others danced around behind her. She yelled a phrase that felt like a wave of sound flooded the cave, above and beyond the howls and the drums. The paintings on the walls began to spin, called fully into life by the magic they were making.

Becca stared wide-eyed as the painted circle spun off the wall, each wolf-woman following the one in front of her, and drifted over their heads to create an inner circle. Molly nudged Becca and they kept moving, dancing a little as they went and trying not to look at the paintings too hard. Erin walked out from the center, following her path inward to join the Pack's circle. It felt like her starring role in this was over for the time being.

She still didn't look directly at the paintings. Their motion made her queasy for one thing. For another, it felt like something their brains weren't ready to really grasp. The painted circle spun tighter around Annie and Erin couldn't see her any more. She wondered what final form they would turn the other woman into, but there was no way she was going to interfere. On the heels of that thought came a brilliant flash of light that made her close her eyes as she danced. The drummers kept on, somehow, but the Pack's dancing circle got more chaotic, then stopped.

Erin cautiously squinted one eye open and looked around. Everyone was either looking at Annie or at the walls. The light had returned to normal so she glanced first at the walls, just in time to see the paintings step back up to their original places. Then she looked at Annie.

Adelía and Lin were helping her sit up; she looked a lot less battered than she had earlier so apparently the ancestor wolves thought she was worth some healing. She also looked older than she had before and more at peace than Erin had seen her before. Shelly walked over and squatted in front of her so that their eyes met. They looked at each other for a long time without saying anything until finally, Annie dropped her gaze, her shoulders rigid.

Shelly nodded and asked her a question that Erin didn't hear. Becca poked her gently in the arm. "I think they changed her back to the way she was before she started changing. Look at her eyes," she murmured softly to Erin.

Erin could see what she meant. They were still the same dark rich color when she looked back up and let Adelía help her stand, but there was nothing extra there, no hidden wolf looking out of them. She still didn't look exactly normal. Annie always looked a bit unbalanced to her and the new hundred-yard stare she had going on right now reminded Erin of some of the former junkies she'd met at meetings.

She could feel the shock ripple around the room. None of them had ever really considered losing their wolves, even after they joined Circle House. Once a Pack member, always a Pack member. But here it was, and they'd all seen some portion of it happen. Erin felt a weird sense of loss that had nothing to do with Annie herself.

Adelía and Shelly took Annie outside and Lin followed them while the rest of them began to slowly clean up the cave. It took a few minutes for Erin to realize that Lin had come back in and she wasn't alone. Carla trailed along behind her, looking nervous and puzzled.

Shelly met them near the entrance, her head tilted to one side the way it did when she was baffled. They talked quietly for a while and she was tempted to sneak closer to listen in. It wasn't like Shelly would object, but she wasn't sure how the other two would feel. They were looking pretty serious.

Finally, though, Shelly reached out and took their hands in hers. She smiled, though she looked a bit nervous, at least to Erin. "Well," she said loud enough for everyone else to hear, "are you ready for me to tell everyone? Or would you like to do it?"

Carla looked like she was about to flee outside and back to town. Molly stepped forward and put a hand on her shoulder. She looked from Carla to Lin to Shelly and her eyes got really wide. Her free hand went up to her mouth like she was trying not to blurt something out.

Lin smiled, her face nearly glowing. "I'm ready. How about you, dear?"

Carla closed her eyes and Erin could see her shudder a little. She walked over to join them, Becca at her heels. Finally, Carla nodded, her eyes still closed tight.

Shelly gestured to bring them all over. "As most of you have realized, the cave's magic has changed Annie. She's human now and Lizzie will be taking her to town to get her statement about

Kari and everything else that's happened. Or at least the parts that Sheriff Henderson is ready to hear. Then she'll be leaving Wolf's Point permanently. But that's not all that's happened." She paused to take a deep breath before continuing, "We've just gotten some news. Lin is going to begin her transition to Circle House over the coming months. And we're getting a new member. I'd like you all to meet Carla. She's been called and she'll be joining us as Lin moves into her new roles, both at Circle House and as one of the co-directors at the Women's Club."

There was a torrent of questions and comments and in the midst of it, Erin leaned over to Carla. "You okay?"

Carla looked up at her with tear-filled eyes, but she nodded and smiled. And after a moment's hesitation, Erin grinned back and hugged her.

# CHAPTER 34

THE HIKE DOWN TO THE cars was a pretty leisurely one. They packed out a fair amount of the food and supplies that they'd been stashing in the cave, but even with the extra loads, Becca felt more relaxed than she had in weeks. "I wonder if Kari has confessed yet," she said dreamily.

Erin made a face. "I hope so or I'm likely to be headed back to a cell. Clyde still at Shelly and Pete's? We should make sure I'm not headed out of town on the run first, then go pick him up."

"Sounds delightful," Becca murmured. They reached the cars right about then and loaded up everything they had hauled down the hills into the trunks and the back of various trucks and so forth, then loaded themselves in on top of all that. Without any discussion whatsoever, they all followed Shelly's truck back to town and down to the county jail.

"Why…" Erin had dozed off in the back of Becca's car and had clearly just woken up.

Gladys gave her a toothy grin over her shoulder. "Gotta clear your name. We're done with this being on the run stuff." She and Becca exchanged a cheerful fistbump.

Erin rubbed her eyes and looked startled. Becca winked at her and got out of the car. After a minute, Erin did too. She took a quick swig of water from her water bottle and gave the building's door an apprehensive glance.

"Lizzie says you can come inside and will get to leave of your own accord," Shelly remarked as she walked by. "Let's go get the rest of the story."

They all trailed up the steps after her and walked inside. Lizzie was coming out of a room down the hall just as they all walked in. "Anyone carrying any weapons? Put them in here and get them on your way out." She held out a plastic tub that rattled with the sound of a couple of hunting knives when she turned it over to one of the other deputies. "We've got her in here, but the room's too small for everyone, so Shelly, Erin and Becca come with me. Everyone else gets to watch behind the glass." A tilt of her head sent the rest of the Pack to trail down the hallway to a door labeled "Witnesses."

Becca reached out and grasped Erin's cold fingers in her own. "It's going to be okay."

Erin squeezed her fingers back and they followed Shelly and Lizzie into another room.

Kari lifted one lip in a snarl when she saw them, but she was handcuffed to a metal loop on the table, so she couldn't do much more than that. Lizzie sat down across from her and gestured the others into chairs behind her. "Want to tell them what you told me?"

Kari's shoulders tightened, then sagged. "Jim isn't...wasn't always like he was when you saw him," she said softly. "He'd gotten turned before I met him, but he had a big cage in the basement of his house, and I'd just lock him up before the full moon and release him in the morning. We managed just fine. Until we lost our jobs and the house. Then we met Leroy. After that was when things started getting pretty nuts." She rubbed her cheek on her shoulder and sighed. Lizzie slid a cup of water across the table.

She drank noisily and awkwardly for a few minutes. Becca stiffened at the mention of Leroy's name. So they had all been working together. Having that confirmed made her wonder if Annie had been in on it too, at least at the beginning. She forced a tremor of rage from her voice as she asked, "Then what happened?"

Shelly caught her eye with a quick glance, but nodded. They all looked at Kari and she glared back at them, defiantly and silently. Lizzie looked at her watch. "Going to need this room soon, so I suggest that you tell us what you plan to tell us, Ms. Johnson. You've already confessed that you and your husband were responsible for Leroy Callan's death. We just want to fill in the remaining blanks and get enough information to drop the charges against Ms. Adams."

Kari looked from one to the other of them, blue eyes narrowed in a ferocious glare. Shelly caught her eye, and from where Becca was standing, she could see her boss's lip curl up over one long incisor. It made her glad that she wasn't looking at Shelly's wolf right now.

After a long moment of dueling stares, Kari drew herself up convulsively. Then the words started to pour out of her in a flood. She and Jim had met Leroy by chance in a group for people with what she kept calling Jim's "problem." He told them that he had a cure, but that it needed a bit more testing.

They were desperate by then and were hoping to get Jim turned back into a full-time human so they could start over again without needing all the extra equipment that it took to keep him under control when he shifted. The more stressed he got, the more bearish he became. So Leroy's offer sounded a lot more promising than it might have under other circumstances.

She paused and Lizzie handed her another cup of water. Kari took it and drained it in a few gulps. She wiped her mouth on the back of her hand and looked around at all of them. "Alright, so to make a long story short, Leroy tested his concoctions on Jim and they worked for a little while. Then they stopped and he tried new ones. There were side effects, like him turning under the new moon as well as the full moon. Once that fucker, Leroy, realized what was happening, he bailed, no address, no phone number, nothing. We tracked him here. He had already told us about this town and your setup, so we knew some of what to expect. We figured one more human changing around here wouldn't be so noticeable so we originally just planned to fit in and lay low."

"Sounds very cozy," Shelly said, her voice tightly controlled. "So how does Erin figure into all this?"

"And where did you get the cash for my old house?" Becca added. She clapped her hand over her mouth when the words popped out. Finding out about Erin was much more important, but she couldn't help but wonder how some destitute former TV personalities had come up with the kind of cash they had paid her and Ed. She wondered if it was stolen and they'd have to pay it back.

Kari sighed dramatically and Erin began to fidget. She leaned back as far from the table as the cuffs would let her. But she kept talking, which made Becca's wolf want to eat her just a little less. "Fine, fine. We got suspicious when we couldn't find Leroy and broke into his place to see if we could figure out where he'd gone. He had some papers about this town and a lot of cash, so we took that. We also took some other stuff, the drugs that he used to make the stuff he was giving Jim, and we sold those too. That money had been ours to begin with, after all. Wasn't even stealing. Then we came here." She drew a deep, shuddering breath and closed her eyes.

It felt like an hour before she started talking again, but Becca's surreptitious glance at her watch told her it was only a minute or two. Kari's voice trembled a little now as she said, "We found him out at the warehouse, and he said he was looking for some cave and a wolf-woman he had to find. He kept insisting that she had something he needed, didn't say what. We argued about what was happening with Jim and what he'd been doing. Jim…got savage. By the time I got him to stop, it was too late. So we needed a new plan."

She glanced around at all of them, her glance contemptuous and calculating now. "Between Leroy and his notes, we learned a lot more about you. What's-her-name, Annie, told him about this place back when they first started working together, told him about everything she could remember about you and how her changing worked. So we know your dirty little secrets and I'm still going to get rich telling the world about them." She laughed, the sound harsh and echoing against the rocks.

Becca stepped forward. Whatever happened next, she wanted to be as ready for it as she could be. Kari was breathing hard, like she was nearing a breaking point of some kind. Whatever she was seeing in their faces now was scaring her, at least a little. "How did you find Erin? And what did you do to her? Why doesn't she remember you or Leroy?" Becca could feel her wolf flare with the words, scrambling inside her to get at this interloper, this outsider who presented a clear and present danger to her Pack. To her beloved, too, if she was being honest.

Kari shivered and the mirth drained out of her face. Erin's expression was cold and furious. "Yes, Kari. What did you do? You nearly destroyed my life...our lives, and for what? You had money. You could have left after you killed Leroy and no one would have ever connected you to it. Why buy Becca's old house and kidnap me? Why frame me for a murder that your husband committed?"

Shelly dropped her hand onto Erin's shoulder lightly, anchoring her to the room and the company they were in. Becca could sense the power in that motion from two feet away; it even soothed her a bit. Not enough though. She still wanted to shake Kari until she gave up all of her secrets. And perhaps some more after that, just for the fun of it.

A furious, feral expression twisted Kari's features. "Why should we have to settle for crumbs? We were sitting on the biggest story of the decade! We could have gotten rich showing everyone that werewolves were real! We could have gotten our old life back, gotten Jim treatment and gotten him cured. I saw you hiking in the woods and I thought you might be one of the wolves. And Jim could smell the wolf on you, so then we were sure. You put your pack down and went to go pee and I swapped out water bottles with you. Mine had something...extra in it. We thought we could frame you for the murder, but then I had a better idea and we went and got you out of the jail."

"And the break-in?" Becca asked, keeping her hands below the table. Her fingers kept clenching into fists.

Kari laughed a little, then broke down into a little gasping sob. "Oh, that was Jim's idea! He thought that Erin might have something that would prove that she had an alibi and if we found it, she'd be easier to control."

Lizzie tilted her head. "Wow. Kidnapping and drugging your victim, breaking and entering, not to mention being an accessory to murder. You've got quite the growing rap sheet. Anything else you want to share?"

Kari blinked at her as if she didn't understand what she had just said. Then blurted out, "I want to call a lawyer."

"I'll bet you do. I think we're done here." Her expression clear that she wasn't going to hear any objections, she herded them out into the hall and beckoned to another deputy. The Pack gathered in the lobby while she gave him instructions, then walked over to Shelly. "I'll get everything squared away about Erin, but she'll have to come in and make a statement tomorrow."

"I'm right here," Erin murmured plaintively. "I can hear you." Becca slipped a careful arm around her waist and gave her a tiny hug. Erin found herself being moved gently toward the door and away from the deputies, Becca on one side, Molly on the other, Carla and the others following up close behind.

"But maybe I should…" Erin began.

"Pie," said Becca firmly. "A hot lunch and Millie's pie and then we're going home. In the morning, we'll come back when Lizzie is ready and you'll fill out whatever she wants you to fill out, unless we need to talk to the lawyer first, and then we'll go get Clyde. After that, we have some unfinished business as soon as you're all healed up."

"Oh? Oh." Erin grinned. "And pie would be nice right now too."

# CHAPTER 35

I T TURNED OUT TO TAKE more than a day for Lizzie to be ready for Erin, so the next morning, they met Shelly and the rest of the Pack for an impromptu gathering at Circle House. Everyone was crowded into the meeting room and Erin was soon surrounded by well-wishers, hugging her, patting her shoulders and smiling.

Becca moved over to one of the side chairs to let Erin be the center of attention for a bit. It was lovely to see her smiling and relaxed again and almost as nice to see the Pack and the Circle House women all together and looking happier than anyone had in ages. She could feel herself relax and grinned up at Robin as the other woman handed her a cup of juice from the big bowl at the main table.

"They only give us the healthy stuff, mind. It's not very sweet," Robin warned.

Becca took a cautious sip, then gave Robin a thumb's up. "Not bad. I like it better without all the extra sugar." She looked around and spotted Molly and Carla coming through the door. Becca waved and they came over. She couldn't help but notice that Carla looked completely freaked out.

Shelly said something Becca couldn't hear and gestured to everyone to start hauling chairs into a circle. She got up and obliged, pausing to give Carla a reassuring smile as she did so. Sure, this was going to take some adjustment, but really, in Wolf's Point, what didn't? Lin entered a moment later and Becca smiled at her, a little more uncertainly. She wondered how anyone transitioned from the Pack to Circle House. Was it obligatory? Could you stay at home?

After a moment, she wandered out of her thoughts to find that everyone was silent and looking expectantly at Shelly. Their Alpha made a sweeping welcoming gesture with her hands that took them all in and smiled. "It is good to have us all together again. We should make this a regular gathering. Today is special because we have news and things to celebrate. First, I want to welcome Erin back to us. The murderers have been found and her name is cleared." Erin stood up and waved awkwardly as everyone clapped, then sat back down.

"We have found an architect and a construction company to begin work on the Women's Club. Lin will be working with Carli to oversee this as she begins her transition to the Circle House community. She will be telling us more about that after I finish." Lin bowed slightly, then moved to a chair behind Shelly.

"Many of us participated in a ritual this weekend, one in which we called upon our ancestors and the powers that they imbued this valley with to heal a former member of our Pack. Annie Sara Hunter left the Pack long ago in spirit, and now she has left Wolf's Point to live as a human for the rest of her life. When she invaded our valley several months ago and was defeated, the power here changed her into a half woman, half wolf, left to roam the hills Packless and alone. But she risked her life to stop another evil from attacking us and our ancestors judged her worthy of a second chance."

Shelly glanced around as if gauging their reactions. No one looked too torn up about the news so she added, "Lizzie sent her out of town with some of our cousins. She'll be living with some relatives on the West Coast. They have an idea of what they've let themselves in for and will let me know if she shows any signs of wanting to come back here. She seemed pretty happy to be leaving, so I'm sure this is permanent, but please know that we're keeping an eye on her."

Becca let out a breath she hadn't intended to hold. Annie had been a big part of her transition; not a good part, mind you, but a central figure in everything that had happened to her this year. It felt odd to realize that it was over, the threats, the menace, the obsession. She wondered for a brief moment just what you went on to do as a second act, after having been a werewolf, a werewolf hunter and then a monster. Plus whatever she had done before she started to shift.

"The last thing I wanted to announce," Shelly continued, and Becca could feel Carla and Molly stiffen, "is that most of us already know that the valley's magic has always made its own choices about who will change and who will not. Sometimes, those choices seem arbitrary or even bad, as with Annie. Sometimes, they are simply unexpected. Someone new is being called to join us, someone you have known as a past self. She has been a staunch ally for several years now and supported us against Annie and her men, risking her life and physical wellbeing to do so. I, for one, am honored to be able to announce this. Carla Mendoza, please step forward."

There was an audible gasp from several Pack members and Becca saw Molly frown anxiously. She got a little anxious herself and wondered if she should get ready to say something on Carla's behalf. What happened if the Pack didn't accept her? From the way Shelly was talking, it sounded like this had never happened before.

For a moment, she wondered how she would have responded, back before she got to know Carla a little better. *Or, you know, started turning into a wolf once a month myself.* Then she noticed that Erin was looking at her and that Erin was now standing next to Shelly and Carla. Evidently, things were moving along without her again.

She glanced around quickly, looking for clues as to what she was supposed to do next. Robin was walking forward from the back of the room to step up to Carla and Becca scrambled out of her seat to follow her, Molly at her heels. Erin stood at Carla's shoulder as Pack member after Pack member shook her hand or hugged her, depending on their personalities.

Gladys was one of the last to get up and Becca caught her eye, wondering what the problem was. Her neighbor looked puzzled and a little angry, and Becca left the group around Carla to go and stand next to her. "What's up, Gladys?"

"I don't understand this at all. I mean, we're special. The magic chooses us because of where we are in our lives, what our bodies are doing, what we bring to protecting the valley. Only older women are ever chosen, not men, not the cute young things down at the mall or the high school cheerleading squad. Just us. That's the way it's always been, as far as I know. But now there's this situation and I don't understand it at all." She gestured around the room with a fierce sweep of her hand.

"Well, we know that this process isn't exactly scientific. It picked Annie, after all, and her mother before her, and neither of them were exactly 'protectors of the valley' material. So either it makes mistakes or it operates outside any logic we can comprehend. Or maybe it's learning and changing and growing along with us. Right after it picked me, I kept thinking that it should have picked Lizzie. Then I met Annie and I couldn't figure how it picked anybody."

"So why not pick someone who's already proved their dedication to the Pack, regardless of who they are or what kind of body they have?" Gladys scowled at her fiercely.

Becca gave her a measuring look. "Something Erin said to me not too long ago really resonated for me today: bodies change. We are proof positive of that and between menopause and becoming wolves, we all know how much they can change. Since we've already embraced that, why not someone experiencing a different change along the way?"

Gladys made a face. "What you're carefully not saying is that I'm being rude and obnoxious and second-guessing the magic and Shelly and rejecting a new wolf for no good reason. And, much as I hate to say it, maybe you're right. I'll do this now, then go home and think on it. You all set back with Erin now?"

Becca nodded. "Thank you for everything you've done to help me and everything you've done to get us to this point. If you need to talk or…just hang out, please let me know. I know we'd both like to have you over for dinner soon. Maybe a Scrabble game, so you can kick our butts."

Gladys stood up with a wry smile and nodded. She walked over and awkwardly shook hands with Carla. Becca saw Shelly pat her shoulder gently, then she walked over to talk to Lin. "Nice job," murmured a familiar voice at her side.

"Well, I'm learning from the best. How about we go pick up some takeout, then go home and puppy-proof the house again?"

"You come up with the best plans." Erin grinned back down at her.

Molly wandered over and rolled her eyes at them. "Get a room, you two. Seriously, thank you for supporting Carla. I know how nervous she is about all this. Speaking of which, would you like to come over for dinner later on this week? You know us, any excuse to barbecue with friends."

They both grinned at her and nodded. Erin said, "I'll call you tomorrow and we'll pick a night." She leaned over and gave Molly a hug. After a minute, Becca stepped up, and when she and Erin moved apart, she reached out for Molly too. The other woman gave her a pleased and surprised grin before scooping her up in a strong hug.

They exchanged a few more hugs and farewells on the way out, then emerged into the autumn sunshine to find Lizzie sitting on a bench outside. She looked tired and she was out of uniform. She also hadn't seen them yet because she was bent over her phone, frowning at the screen. Becca had a wild impulse to run and hide before she noticed Erin was back.

But Lizzie looked up before she could do anything about it. "Let's get this part over with too," Erin muttered to her. Becca reached out and grabbed her free hand in her own and together they walked over to the bench.

Lizzie nodded as they walked up, then said, " So, Carla. Huh. How's everyone taking that?"

Erin shrugged and Becca answered cautiously, "Not too badly, from what we've seen, but it will take some of us a while to adjust." She paused, then burst out, "I hope you get called...I mean, when you're ready." She flushed when the words were out of her mouth; she hadn't meant to say that, at least not until everything was resolved for Erin. Glancing sidelong at Erin's expression, she wondered how long that might take.

"Thank you." Lizzie's expression didn't reveal anything, but she stood up slowly. "Look, I know we're not in a good space right now—"

Erin held up her hand. "Hang on. I called you and confessed to a murder and practically begged you to take me in. I'm not sure how you could have said no, under the circumstances."

Lizzie nodded. "It's not that part. I was kind of an asshole to Becca because I thought she was hiding you after Kari and Jim took you out of the jail."

Becca nodded in her turn. "Yep, you were that. But I would have hid her, if I could have, so you weren't too far off on that."

"And I nearly missed out on resolving a kidnapping because I was busy being angry and thinking that you and Shelly were lying to me." Lizzie ran a hand over her hair and scowled. "Not my finest moment and one I need to look at as I get my campaign started."

"So definitely running for sheriff?"

"Yep. It's time for a change for the better, I think. I'm not comfortable with the kinds of decisions I see Henderson making and I'm worried about some of the new deputies. I think I can do a better job and build a better relationship with all of our community." Lizzie looked from Becca to Erin. "Are we square?"

Erin gave Lizzie a long considering glance before saying, "I think so."

Becca gave a long look of her own, then nodded. "We'll get a campaign sign and put it up, when you're ready. Maybe even put in some volunteer time."

Lizzie gave them both a rare smile and they all shook hands, then she went inside. "Are we really all good?" Erin murmured to Becca.

"Iffy. But I think I'll get over it. As long as nothing else like it happens again. Back to the original plan for the evening?"

"I can't imagine anything I'd like better." Erin took in a deep breath and let it out with a contented sigh as she followed Becca to her car.

# CHAPTER 36

A FEW DAYS LATER, BECCA LET Clyde out into the newly fenced off dog run that she and Erin and Molly, Jonas and Carla had just finished that morning. He ran out into the sunshine and circled the length of the enclosure, clearly looking for Pete and Shelly's dogs. He spun around, fur gleaming gold, and gave her a short, hopeful bark.

She smiled at him and took a deep breath, letting the scents of Wolf's Point roll into her, then through her. She could see their neighbors taking their dogs out for walks or working in their yards or heading out somewhere, all the yards and houses full of life except for the house across the street. Over there, a realtor pounded a "For Sale" into the front yard and the house itself stayed dark and still.

For the first time that she could remember, the sight made her smile. A noise behind her told her that Erin had come back downstairs and she turned, her smile deepening just a bit. "Ooh, dimples! Haven't seen those in forever!" Erin grinned at her. She still looked tired and bruised and worn down, but much better than she had a few days before. By next full moon, she could finish healing.

Becca reached out and put a careful arm around her. "What did you think about when you were up in the cave all those nights?" she asked, her tone suddenly wistful. Was it wrong to hope that Erin would say that she had thought of her, had dreamt of her? At least once in a while?

Erin gave her a wry sidelong look and she started laughing at herself as much as for the pure joy of it. "About what you'd expect. Rocks, cave paintings, whether or not I'd bumped off Leroy, why I'd bumped off Leroy, if I was going to get arrested again, everyone who was checking on me sticking around to snore all night, werebears, what Annie was up to, all that fun stuff." Erin laughed softly as she leaned into Becca. "I do seem to remember thinking about something that got interrupted the last time we were standing here, kind of like this."

Becca turned and looked up her, brushing a lock of gray hair away from her face. She hesitated, then reached out to put her arms around Erin's neck. "You mean this?" And she pulled Erin down for a long, slow kiss.

It wasn't like their previous kisses, all rushed and awkward like they were college kids. No, this one felt like they both finally knew what they wanted. Becca could feel her whole body shiver with a desire that she had thought she was never going to feel again. "I...I would like to go inside and rip all your clothes off, please. Very carefully. Are we ready for that stage yet?" She murmured the words into Erin's lips, part of her wondering if there was a more grownup and appropriate way to say that.

Erin pulled her in tighter by way of answering and Becca could feel the tension in her arms and legs, the tremble of her breath. No, this was going to be just fine. "I think we might be," Erin murmured back, sliding her lips over to Becca's ear and nibbling gently on it. "I have no idea what you like and don't like. But I'm looking forward to finding out."

Becca gave a happy little moan. "Me too." Clyde chose that moment to interrupt them with a loud bark. When they looked down, he was sitting at the end of the run and gazing up at them with his fuzzy yellow head tilted to one side. Becca smiled at him. "You want to stay outside for a little longer, fella? I think you'd like that."

"I think I'd like that, too," Erin murmured into her hair. Clyde bounced off to go explore the yard, then drink noisily from his water bowl. "We'll hear him if he starts barking or something."

"Why do I feel like we adopted a kid?"

"Because we kind of did. Now, where were we?" They exchanged another kiss, then another, before making their way upstairs to Becca's room. The next couple of hours were spent in a slow, leisurely exploration of each other's bodies. Becca found out that Erin was very ticklish around the knees and Erin found out that Becca had an adorable throaty little gasp when her neck got nibbled on. There was kissing and licking and stroking and tasting and awkwardness and silliness, too, and everything that a good beginning should be.

By the time they had dropped their drowsy heads on their pillows, Clyde had started barking outside. Erin ran a long finger down Becca's nose. "I'll bring him in and feed him if you start dinner?"

"This is that domestic bliss I've heard so much about, isn't it?" Becca chuckled. "I want a redo and then maybe find out if we both fit in the tub later."

"I do like the way you think. But you remember that it's movie night over at Gladys' tonight, right?"

"Oh."

"We'll have time tomorrow. And the day after and the day after that and any other time you like when neither of us is otherwise engaged with necessary things. I promise you that." Erin kissed her again, her lips conveying a joyous urgency that made Becca tingle all over.

There would be a "later" and that alone was the best word Becca had ever heard. She took a quick shower and finished getting dressed before going downstairs. Then she threw the window open to let in some fresh air while she started prepping dinner. The breeze brought in a wave of tantalizing and familiar scents along with the tangy scents of autumn and she took a deep breath, letting her wolf brain analyze and savor them for few moments.

Then she closed her eyes to lose herself in her thoughts, imagining their future and what might come next. There would be friends and a Pack and runs in the moonlight and learning at Circle House. And there would be Erin and her. Maybe that was part of what Wolf's Point's magic was all about, at its best. She smiled as she chopped the vegetables.

# BIOGRAPHY

CATHERINE LUNDOFF IS A TRANSPLANTED Brooklynite who lives in scenic Minnesota with her wife, a fabulously talented bookbinder and artist, and the two cats that own them. In former lives, she was an archaeologist and a bookstore owner, though not at the same time. These days, she does arcane things with computer software at large companies and hangs out at science fiction conventions.

She is the author of over 100 published short stories and essays which have appeared in such venues as *Fireside Magazine*, *Nightmare Magazine*, the *SFWA Blog*, *Respectable Horror*, *Sherlock Holmes and the Occult Detectives*, *The Book of Extraordinary New Sherlock Holmes Adventures*, *American Monsters Part 2*, the LHMPodcast, *Haunting Shadows (Wraith the Oblivion 20th Anniversary Anthology)* and *The Cainite Conspiracies (Vampire the Masquerade 20th Anniversary Anthology)*. Her books include the novels *Silver Moon* and *Blood Moon* and the single author short story collections *Out of This World: Queer Speculative Fiction Stories* and *Unfinished Business: Tales of the Dark Fantastic*. She is also the editor of *Scourge of the Seas of Time (and Space)*, as well as two other anthologies. She teaches writing, editing and publishing classes at the Rambo Academy and elsewhere and is the publisher at Queen of Swords Press.

# ABOUT
# QUEEN of SWORDS PRESS

Queen of Swords is an independent small press, specializing in swashbuckling tales of derring-do, bold new adventures in time and space, mysterious stories of the occult and arcane and fantastical tales of people and lands far and near. Visit us online at www. queenofswordspress.com and sign up for our mailing list to get notified about upcoming releases and offers. Or follow us on Facebook at the Queen of Swords Press page so you don't miss any press news.

If you have a moment, the author would appreciate you taking the time to leave a review for this book at Goodreads, your blog or on the site you purchased it from.

Thank you for your assistance and your support of our authors.

# More Queen of Swords Press
## Titles You May Like

### Catherine Lundoff
*Silver Moon*
*Blood Moon*
*Out of This World: Queer Speculative Fiction Stories*
*Unfinished Business: Tales of the Dark Fantastic*

### Multi-Author Anthology
*Scourge of the Seas of Time (and Space)*

### Emily Byrne
*Medusa's Touch*
*Knife's Edge*
*Desire*

### Alex Acks
*Murder on the Titania*
*Wireless and Other Steam-Powered Adventures*

### A.J. Fitzwater
*The Voyages of Cinrak the Dapper*

CPSIA information can be obtained
at www.ICGtesting.com
Printed in the USA
FSHW021609230321
79687FS